To Steal a Bride

Terri Mackenzie

Book Cover by Getcovers

First edition 2025

Contents

Chapter One

Oliver Beaumont, youngest son of the Earl of Shrewsbury, stared at his infuriatingly perfect older brother. Henry, as always, was immaculately presented, encapsulating everything a viscount ought to be. In contrast, Oliver slouched in his chair, his cravat rumpled and his coat stained after a long night. Exhaustion tugged at him, not helped by the pounding in his head. He had hoped to retire straight to bed, but Henry had summoned him to his study, no doubt ready to launch into a lecture.

Henry laced his fingers together. A poor start. When he did that, he was invariably planning some sort of horrific punishment, usually at Oliver's expense.

"You," Henry said, the words deliberate, "cannot continue in this way."

"In what way?"

"Drunken. Foolish. Frittering away your allowance."

Oliver scowled. This again. Ever since he had graduated from Oxford—just—two years ago, Henry had been on his case to find an occupation. Never mind that most young gentlemen who entered the law or took a living had certain attributes that Oliver would never have.

"Are you threatening to cut me off?" he demanded.

Henry held his gaze. The Beaumont blue eyes had never looked as severe on his brother as they did now. "I ought to. Louisa says you are still learning how to be a man, but when I was your age—"

"You needn't remind me. When you were my age, you were serving in the army, commanding men and seeing horrors that my privileged mind cannot comprehend." Oliver rolled his eyes. "I am perfectly aware that I am a disappointment in every regard. But I simply do not see the need for you to force me into an occupation I am wholly unsuited for. All for the crime of being born the younger son."

Henry gestured at the letters on his desk. "Did you think an older son has no obligations? Every man has, though those responsibilities differ according to one's position in the world. Your misfortune, as you put it, has allowed you to live out of my pocket for two full years now. It's time for that to change."

"Ah, so you *are* cutting me off." Oliver folded his arms, knowing he sounded like a petulant child but unable to see a way around it. If he addressed the real reason he disliked the prospect of finding an occupation, he would have to admit to a secret Henry would find shameful and that would make him even more of a disappointment.

At least when he acted the idiot, that was a choice. He would always rather be perceived as a wastrel than incapable.

"And," Oliver added, "when I marry, I will have a property of my own, so what is the pressing need for an occupation?"

Henry's brows slashed down over his eyes. He always appeared so *stern.* If Oliver had not known his true father was a drunken buffoon of a man who lurched through the clubs of London with an embarrassing lack of dignity, he might have presumed it to be the man before him. Only a decade separated them, but it felt like far more.

"You are three-and-twenty," Henry said. "And in order for you to support a wife adequately, you ought to have some concept of responsibility—which you currently lack. Louisa promised you a property out of her own fortune when you come to marry, but she made such a promise in the understanding that you would not be marrying immediately."

Oliver's head ached. He had indulged rather too freely the night before, ignorant of what conversation would follow. "And if I marry now, I would be ineligible to receive the estate?"

A muscle ticked in Henry's jaw. "No," he said at last. "Louisa merely trusted that you would have more sense."

"More sense than not to claim my inheritance at the earliest available possibility?" Oliver spread his hands. "Why this insistence on an occupation under these conditions? After all, an older son may do as he chooses, safe in the knowledge that he will inherit. Thanks to Louisa"—although he spoke mockingly, he had a great soft spot for his sister-in-law—"I will be granted an inheritance. Thus, I may behave as an older son might."

"That was not the purpose of the inheritance."

"Surely it was to provide security?" Oliver tilted his head. "The same security our father cannot provide for either of us."

Their father was a man so consumed by vice that he had almost forgotten he had a family; he had gambled away his fortune, his daughters' dowries, and would have gambled away the house had Henry and Nathanial, Oliver's brother-in-law, not secured his properties between them.

Henry heaved a sigh. "What is the purpose of an inheritance when one does not have the responsibility to deal with it?"

Oliver dragged a hand through his hair, slouching further in his chair in an attempt to irritate Henry further. All he wanted was to retire to bed and wake up in a new world where nothing of this nature was expected of him. Oxford had been bad enough, staying up all night to parse the contents of a document he was obliged to study—only to emerge with an indifferent understanding of the text itself. He had tried his hardest to write essays and dissertations, only for his tutors to rip apart his lack of understanding of spelling and grammar.

Everyone in the world thought he didn't try, but all he had learnt was that trying got one nowhere; his inheritance, thanks to Louisa, was the only hope for his future. Otherwise, a man like him *had* no future. And he refused to play a game rigged against him.

"If you do not choose a path for yourself, I will have no choice but to cut you off from my financial support," Henry said, an inflexible note entering his voice. "You may appeal to our father, of course, but he will have little enough to spare you."

"You might have spared me the lecture and reached this point sooner. Am I to live on the streets, then?"

"I offered you my living," Henry said, exasperated. A living that Oliver both did not want and could not take. What parson could not read or write with any degree of fluency? "And failing that, I know a solicitor you could clerk for. There could be a career in the law for you."

"And then you would be proud of me?" Oliver sat up straighter, finally, spurred into anger by the rejection he had always known was coming. Every man's worth was dictated by his position in life—without position, and without ability, he had nothing. "Or is such a thing an impossibility I should not wish for?"

Henry pinched his nose. Another bad sign—it meant he had reached the end of his limited patience. Oliver had seen that expression more than once over the course of his years. "I want you to do as every man must. Why is that so difficult?"

"Perhaps I will marry," Oliver said, offering his brother a lazy smile he knew would infuriate. "Then this entire problem would cease to exist. Louisa will offer me a modest estate in the event of my marriage; thus, all I need do is bring her a wife."

Henry pushed up from his chair, hands braced against the desk. "And who do you propose to marry? You have been to no *ton* events, and very few mothers would be eager for their daughters to marry the wastrel younger son of an earl."

This was true; Oliver was an excellent flirt, well-practised in the art, but he had never been a serious target for anything more meaningful. When it came to marriage, all the pretty, spoilt brats of the *ton* wanted a man of means or a title. Preferably both.

Still, this was an obstacle he could overcome easily enough with some forethought. There were endless women in England—surely *one* would be amenable to marrying him.

"Fear not, brother," he said, sweeping into a bow that made his head pound still further. "I shall contrive easily enough."

"What will you do?"

Oliver gave a grin he didn't feel. "Simple. I will marry the first lady who will have me."

The village of Dalston held few charms, or so Oliver had assumed when he travelled north. That, however, was before he spied the buxom beauty strolling along the road, a basket over her arm. With her blonde hair, pert nose and pretty blue eyes, she was the very picture of country grace, and Oliver slowed his horse to a walk to better observe her.

He had been in the country for two days, having fled to Cumbria where his friend, Victor Prescott, was rusticating. Two days of exquisite boredom and nothing to do.

Until now.

The girl glanced up, sensing his attention. Her brow raised, and a calculating expression entered her eyes as she assessed him. He knew, instinctively, that this was precisely the girl he had thought of when he'd said to Henry he would marry the first girl that would have him.

He dismounted his borrowed horse and touched the brim of his hat. "Forgive the intrusion, but I couldn't help noticing you were burdened by your basket. Allow me."

She surrendered her basket, filled with muddy potatoes and the dusty leaves of cabbage. "You are too kind, sir. Are you new to the village? I usually recognise every face, but I confess to not recognising yours."

"I arrived just two days ago."

"From where?"

"London."

A wistful look crossed her face. "I always wished I could go to London. I've lived in Dalston all my life, and it is so very far from the capital."

"It was a damned long journey," he agreed.

"Do you intend to stay long?"

"It rather depends." Judging her receptive, he leant closer, lowering his voice. "I cannot return until I find a wife."

"Oh!" The next look she offered him was both coy and assessing. "And do you have a lady in mind?"

"I hadn't." He let the words hang in the air, and she caught them with a sly, calculating smile. Her dress was not pretty or fashionable, but she had a good figure, and she was startlingly beautiful. A lady he could have on his arm proudly, but who would not be too prideful to wish for something more than the small estate he would inherit. Or so he hoped.

In short, provided she was amenable to his intentions—and he rather suspected she would be—she was perfect. He extended his hand. "Mr Beaumont, at your service."

"Miss Isabella Brunton." She placed her fingers delicately in his. "I hope we shall get to know each other better, sir."

He brought her fingers to his lips. "I am quite certain we will."

Chapter Two

Emily Brunton wiped her forehead with the back of her hand. It was quite incredible the way how, at this temperature, one could be both freezing cold and sweating. Her knees ached as she knelt before the fire, the logs she had hauled in smoking futilely. Her temper, never the most reliable at the best of times, threatened to boil over.

Isabella was once again late. She had left quite some time ago to take the eggs to market, and as had become routine over the past two weeks, had yet to arrive back home.

Emily sat back on her heels and sighed, brushing the soot off her dress. The time had finally come when she would have to speak with her sister about the desires of men and how dangerous they could be—and how someone as pretty as her would be a target.

Isabella would not like it. But it had to be done.

The fire refused to light, the smoke growing thicker the more Emily attempted to coax flame from the embers. The problem was the damp wood—but she simply could not cut it fast enough, and sourcing the wood was difficult enough at this time of year.

Her bones ached with the cold as she rose, abandoning the fire to its own devices and wrapping the blanket back over her shoulders as she started on what would be a very miserable cold dinner.

Finally, as she had quite given up on her sister, Isabella burst through the back door, a scarf around her neck and her cheeks flushed red from the cold. Her eyes sparkled, and she looked like a girl in love.

Emily's heart contracted.

She had long known that Isabella chafed at the natural restrictions placed on them by their straitened circumstances, but at this sight of her sister's joy—caused by something outside of Emily's control—she felt it like a punch to her gut.

"Shut the door," she said, attempting to keep her voice normal. "You're letting the heat out."

"What heat?" The brightness on Isabella's face dimmed at the sight of the smoking fire. Still, she shut the door.

"Where have you been?"

"I told you. I went to sell the eggs."

"Mm."

"Mr Pickett says it's going to snow." Isabella scraped the mud from her boots. "He says he can smell it in the air."

"Well, Mr Pickett is usually right about such things." Emily peered out of the window at the sky. "And the clouds do look heavy. Thank goodness you got back before any bad weather struck." Something that would not have been a consideration if she had been back when Emily expected. "Did you get everything?"

"Flour, butter and mutton." Isabella hoisted her basket onto the table. "Mrs Landstone says the price of coal has gone up again."

Just in time for snowfall. No doubt Emily would have to open new blisters on her hands chopping more wood so it could fail to light in her hearths. "Never mind," she said. "At least you got mutton. Any more news from the village?" Emily watched Isabella's face for any sign of a blush. But Isabella's face merely lit up again.

"There's a ball next week at the *Rose & Crown*. Sixpence entry fee." She looked at Emily expectantly, as though Emily could conjure money from nothing.

If she could, she would not have spent the past fifteen minutes battling with damp wood and unwilling flame.

"We can't afford it, dearest," she said.

Once again, Isabella's face fell. "You went dancing at my age," she muttered.

"That was before." Before their mother had died and their father had fallen into the greatest depression of his life. Before they had struggled to afford food and coal and shoes. "But speaking of before," she said, taking a deep breath to prepare herself, "I have something I want to tell you."

Isabella slumped into one of the chairs by the table. "Are you trying to explain why I shouldn't want to go dancing?"

"No. It's natural for you to want to go dancing—and if I could make it happen, I would. This is about something else, although it is connected." She hesitated, resting her hip against the kitchen side. Her bones ached with exhaustion, but Isabella had been so caught up in her own world, she hadn't noticed.

Young love. Emily hoped it wasn't.

"*Please* do not attempt to give me advice on romance," Isabella said, petulance in her voice.

"Why should I not?"

Isabella rolled her large, expressive eyes. "Because you have no experience in the matter. You might be seven years my senior, but that does not make you an expert."

Emily nearly laughed. "What would you know about my experience?"

"Do you mean to say you have a beau?" Isabella sat up, instantly interested. "Is it the butcher's son? He has been making eyes at you for the past six months or more."

"No," Emily said with as much patience as she could summon. "I have no intention of marrying him—or anyone."

"But why?" Isabella looked utterly nonplussed. "Is this all you want for the rest of your life?"

"Of course I would prefer for things to be better, but—" She sighed. "That's not the point. Have I ever told you about Lord Marlbury?"

"*Marlbury?*" Isabella looked even more confused. "From Bidlington Hall?"

"Yes."

"What about him?"

"When I was seventeen, he and I began . . ." Emily hesitated, searching for the right words. "Well, we formed an attachment," she decided on. "He told me he loved me and would marry me, and I foolishly believed him."

Isabella's jaw dropped. Emily could hardly blame her—after their mother died, when Isabella was just ten years of age, Emily had done her best to shoulder the burdens of the family—and that left her no space for entertaining romance. Not that she ever would have done: Lord Marlbury had been more than enough experience for one lifetime.

She had vowed then and there she would never fall in love again. No man would ever again have power over her.

"You and *Lord Marlbury*?" Isabella said in a near-whisper. "Surely you can't be serious."

"I am. Of course, I did not know then what sort of man he was. We were both young and—oh, very foolish. I thought for certain we would marry and I would be with him for the rest of my life."

Isabella fluffed her curls, glancing in the window at her reflection. "But you weren't."

"No. He left me, and then Mother died, and the rest of my life happened." Emily didn't mention how terrible those ensuing few weeks and months had been—in the midst of her family's grief, she had to endure her broken heart and shattered dreams. For a time, she had wished she would go to sleep and never wake.

All the years since providing for Isabella could not eradicate her guilt that she had ever thought such a thing.

Isabella tilted her head. "Did you lie with him?"

"I—" Familiar shame tightened her throat. "Yes. And there has not been a day since then I have not regretted it."

"Well, of course. You failed to convince him to marry you." Isabella's mouth tightened into a moue as she thought. "Of course, it is tragic that he used you in such a way, and I'm sorry for it."

"Gentlemen often use ladies in such ways, especially gentlemen who think they will never have to bear the consequences—and many don't." Emily leant across the table, holding out a hand. "I know you are seeing someone, Bella."

"And so you think to warn me away from him with the story of your tragic love?" Isabella asked, shaking her head. "Do you think I would be so foolish, Em?"

Yes. Emily didn't say it. "I want you to be careful."

"Then I shall be careful." A smile burst across Isabella's face, rendering her radiant. "And I vow to never fall in love. Such a promise is easy done. How is that?"

"Bella—"

"Don't be so serious!" Isabella rose and dropped a kiss on the crown of Emily's head as she passed, as though she were the older, wiser sister. "I know what I am doing, never fear. And I have a plan."

"A plan for what?"

"You'll see." Isabella smiled mysteriously, and Emily's heart gave another anxious lurch. "I doubt it shall be long now." She blew Emily a kiss as she left the room, and Emily stared at her fingers on the table, knuckles cracked from scrubbing at their clothes in the cold. Once, she'd had ladies' hands; she was, technically, a gentleman's daughter. Only the gentleman in question was dead, and he had left his daughters with next to nothing to survive on.

If she could have saved Isabella from the fate of being penniless in a small village in the middle of nowhere, she would have, but not by having her sister ruined by a gentleman.

There were no lengths she would not go to in order to prevent that from happening.

"Tell me you're not serious," Marlbury said.

Oliver reclined across the sofa, the wineglass tipping dangerously in his lax fingers. "Why not?"

"Marriage." Marlbury clucked his tongue. "And to the Brunton girl?"

"She's the prettiest face I've seen since retiring from London, and more to the point, she's amenable to the match. She wants an escape, and I will have property to bring her back to once my sister-in-law releases my inheritance." Oliver loosed a long sigh. "She is the ideal candidate."

"She is penniless."

"It's not as though I need an heiress," Oliver pointed out, draining the last of his wine. "And I rather doubt an heiress would have me. My brother was right about one thing—there is rather a dearth of rich ladies lining up to wed me. I am not the eldest son of a marquess." He looked pointedly at his friend. Lord Marlbury was the son of the Marquess of Rotherham, and when he came to marry, he would have his pick of the *ton*. "*I* do not have dowagers thrusting their daughters upon me."

Marlbury poured himself another glass of brandy. "All I'm saying is why marry a country bumpkin?"

"Because I refuse to return to my brother without a wife. This *country bumpkin* is prepared to marry me. Moreover, she *wants* to marry me."

"Don't tell me she's in love with you."

"Of course not," Oliver said scornfully. "She barely knows me—what she wants is escape from her dreary life here, and I am the most convenient means for her to do so."

Marlbury grunted, looking displeased by the prospect. "But settling down? *Marriage*?"

"Very little will change, save I won't be beholden to my brother." Oliver held out his glass for a refill, this time with brandy. "She is hardly expecting me to be a devoted husband—and I suspect she has little desire for me to be. She knows what she is about. You and I can kick up as many larks in London as we like."

"You make it sound easy, but I'll tell you something that won't be." Marlbury held up a hand, pointer finger directed at the ceiling.

"God?"

"Her sister."

"Ah." Oliver hesitated only a second. He'd been in the area for a little over two weeks, and that was long enough to learn about Miss Emily Brunton. According to gossip, she was a shrew of the worst kind. A veritable dragon. Isabella had defended her in lukewarm terms, but hadn't informed her of their plans, which suggested the sister would not approve.

"Once we're married, she won't be a problem," Oliver said.

"Isn't the Brunton girl under the age of majority?" Marlbury slanted him a knowing look. "The shrew will refuse permission. Can't stand for someone else to be happy when she's not—and she's plain enough she has no prospects of her own."

"I thought of that. We're only half a day's ride from Gretna Green." Oliver drained his brandy and leaned back against the chair, the room spinning somewhat. "I'll whisk her away for a runaway wedding, no permission required. And when we're back, I'll take her to London. My brother *could* contest the wedding, I suppose, but Isabella is technically the son of a gentleman, and I doubt Henry will want a scandal attached to our name. No, he'll pretend everything was above board."

"It's risky."

"It is," Oliver conceded. "But not without its merits. Who else can I marry on such short notice?"

"The shrew will contest the marriage."

"No she won't—not if she doesn't want her sister ruined. By the time of the wedding, she won't have much choice. Of course, it would be different if Isabella were unwilling, but she is more eager than me to go ahead with this plan."

Marlbury threw his head back and barked laughter at the ceiling. "You dog. The shrew will be furious you've outdone her."

"She can be furious all she likes," Oliver said absently. "Isabella doesn't seem to think she will be any great impediment." He rolled his head, the room turning soft and hazy. This was how he liked the world: a little out of focus. A little out of touch. "You don't have to like it, Marlbury, but you can't stop me now." He reached for a decanter of wine and tipped it straight into his open mouth, letting himself sink further into the chair. Marlbury's father was currently in London on business and wouldn't be back for some time, which meant they were alone in the house. And free to drink as much of his father's liquor as they could get their hands on.

There were worse ways to spend an evening.

"When do you intend to do it?" Marlbury asked.

"Tomorrow evening. We'll travel through the night to Gretna Green and arrive back in the morning, already married. Then," he added, "I will have the unmitigated delight of writing to my brother, informing him of my marriage and my intention of calling on him with my new wife."

"And your new wife's sister," Marlbury said.

"Well, we shall see. Isabella said nothing about it. Perhaps she'd prefer to stay here." Oliver shrugged. The sister and her preferences didn't concern him so long as she did not make them his problem. "That is a bridge I will cross after the event."

"Well, good luck," Marlbury said with a snort. "Rather you than me."

Oliver lay back on the sofa, the world spinning pleasantly around him. Ever since coming to Bidlington Hall, his future had looked up considerably. Soon, he would have a wife with which to taunt his brother, and an inheritance to prevent him from having to confess to his inadequacies.

"I don't know," he said, letting his hand—along with the decanter of wine—fall against the floor. "I think this might be the best decision I have ever made."

Chapter Three

Emily's fingers shook as she smoothed over the paper in her hand. The letter had come addressed to a 'Miss Brunton', and she'd opened it without thinking. Now, she sank into the rickety chair by the kitchen table.

Darling Isabella, was scrawled across the top in messy, masculine handwriting, each word splattered with ink as though written painstakingly.

I'll see you an hour before dawn tomorow morning. Pack worm love and be ready to go at once. Remember tell no one; they will know all when we return.

Yours,

O

Emily's throat closed. Aside from the atrocious grammar and spelling—she presumed 'worm' ought to be 'warm'—the note made *O*'s intentions very evident: he was arranging an assignation.

The use of 'love' suggested Isabella was someone he was familiar with. Her beau—only this was no mere flirtation.

Tell no one.

Clearly Emily was included in this. Isabella had said nothing to her, only that she had a plan. Emily had believed that Isabella had perhaps secured an offer of marriage, or close to. Not a secret assignation.

Was this truly her plan? To allow herself to be ruined without consequence?

There would be consequences—Emily would be his consequence. For him to have sent this affectionate, careless note, he must care nothing for Isabella's character or what might happen to her if her transgressions ever saw the light of day.

Emily would not let that happen.

She clenched the paper in her hand, thinking hard. Isabella had not yet seen this; there was still hope. Emily would be the one to wait outside at dawn while Isabella still slept.

She crumpled the note into a ball and tossed it on the fire, where it landed on the embers and burst, briefly, into flame. Then she retired upstairs.

"Is everything all right?" Isabella asked as she huddled under the blankets in the bed they both shared. The air was cold; Emily's breath turned white in the candlelight.

Emily forced a smile she couldn't feel. "Everything is fine."

Emily barely slept as she awaited the morning. Just before dawn, she climbed out of bed. Isabella, unburdened by her foolishness, had slept the night through without stirring, and slumbered on even now.

All being well, by the time she awoke, Emily would have dealt with this latest threat to their happiness.

After creeping into her father's room, where she found a pearl-inlaid pistol she had been considering selling, she slipped downstairs through the dark. With a cloak over her head and a scarf wrapped around her neck and mouth—necessary in this weather—the amorous young man would no doubt think she was his sister. Then, when he got close enough, she would confront him.

She could picture him now, everything Marlbury had been. Arrogant, overbearing, cruel.

Shuddering, she crept down the stairs and out into the frigid night air. All at once, she was glad for her woollen dress, cloak and scarf, and wished she could go back to bed. Her head ached, and that faint feeling of being overworked and underfed plagued her again.

She shook her head, fighting to stay awake, and paced back and forth in the gloom. Dawn was still some minutes away, but the world was lightening every passing second.

If these were the conditions the gentleman thought suitable for seduction, he had a great deal to learn about his craft.

Not for the first time, she wondered who he might be. She knew everyone in the village, and no one had a name beginning with O. There was Maximus Orwell, she supposed, but he was pushing forty and although her sister could be flighty, she didn't suppose such a young girl would be interested in so old a man.

So who was he?

The sound of hooves clopping along the uneven cobbles of the street caught her attention, and Emily turned to see a large black carriage making its way along the street towards her. Four high-stepping horses drew it, and although she had occasionally seen Lord Rotherham pass through the village, she thought she had never seen such a grand coach.

Who could own such an ostentatious vehicle?

Emily stepped back, her numb fingers slipping on the pistol. She gripped it more tightly as the driver jumped nimbly down. In the light of the lamps, she saw he was her age, give or take a year or so, with a shock of curly blonde hair on his head and a startlingly handsome face. At the sight of her waiting, he broke into a grin.

"There you are," he said, his voice warm. "Have you been waiting long? No matter—I'm here now, love. Come, we must make haste."

Emily hesitated, the pistol still in the folds of her cloak. Isabella's lover was a lord—or close to. A gentleman of means. And if she confronted him here, with that enormous carriage in place to make a spectacle, someone would be sure to see.

After she had gone to such lengths to ensure there would be no scandal, she could not afford to allow him to cause a scene.

Seeing her hesitation, the man took her elbow. "Don't be nervous. You'll be comfortable, and I'm a steady driver. Hurry, before anyone sees."

Steeling herself, Emily obeyed the pressure of his hand and allowed him to hand her into the carriage. The door shut behind her, and she instinctively ran a hand over the smooth panel. No handle. No way out.

Breathe.

This was not the time to panic. They would presumably not be travelling far; there was no luggage on the carriage, and the note had not mentioned packing. Once they reached their destination, she would threaten him with the pistol and he would take her back home. Even a cad, surely, upon realising he had the wrong lady, would do that much.

She would make sure of it.

The carriage swayed as the man climbed atop, and a second later, the carriage lurched into motion. Emily assessed her surroundings. There was a heated brick and a pile of blankets; she would not freeze, at least. That was something.

Wrapping the blankets around herself, she sat back on the plush leather seats and waited for the inevitable moment of their arrival.

Three hours later, or thereabouts, they had still not arrived. They hadn't even changed horses. With every passing minute, Emily's stomach knotted with worry. This was not the quick trip she had been envisaging.

What could he be planning to do with her this far from home? Had he been intending to make Isabella his mistress? If so, then Emily had misjudged the situation; she ought to have confronted him there and then, even if it had risked someone seeing her, rather than allow him to cart her away like this.

Isabella would wake to find her missing. She hadn't even left a note.

It began to snow. Emily watched the spiralling flakes with dread. They had to have travelled at least thirty miles by now, and here the hedgerows were frosted with white.

Mr Pickett had been right, after all, and what terrible timing it had been. How would she get home now?

The road widened, and she caught a glimpse of houses, huddled as though in defiance of the weather. Another town—one she didn't recognise. Surely they would stop soon.

When they did, he would get the shock of his life.

She retrieved the pistol from where she had placed it carefully beside her and gripped it tightly once again. Let him face the barrel of a gun and realise the magnitude of his mistake.

They finally came to a halt, and after a second, she heard the man jump down from where he had been leading the horses. She pointed the pistol at the door as he approached.

A latch clicked, and the door swung wide.

"I," she said grandly, "am not Isabella Brunton, and you, sir, have abducted me against my will. What do you have to say for yourself?"

Chapter Four

Oliver was cold, hungry, and exhausted. Beyond the biting frost, he'd also been forced to endure a snowstorm, and he was not accustomed to handling a carriage of this size. His coat was sodden through, he had no desire to be amorous, and he'd been seized with misgivings about his entire plan.

And now he faced down the barrel of a gun.

Snow landed wetly on his hat, and his fingers felt numb. What he really wanted was a hot drink, a bath, and a bed. Preferably with a beautiful woman in it.

Not this woman. Isabella Brunton was a blonde-haired, buxom beauty. She had a wicked laugh, a sweet button nose, and was adorably flirtatious.

This lady had frizzy red hair that stuck out around her face, a sharp, angular jawline, eyes like gimlets, and a pistol. Pointed at his head.

He *really* needed that drink.

Holding both hands in the air, he stepped back to give her leave to descend the carriage. She did so, trailing one of the rugs as it half fell off her shoulder. With a curse, she shrugged it back on, glaring at him all the while.

"What the *devil* do you think you're doing?" she demanded.

"I might ask you the same question," he said, looking from the butt of the pistol into her face. He had never met Isabella's sister, but he could only presume this was the lady in question—and now he understood her reputation. "What are you doing here?"

"You *kidnapped* me."

He glanced over his shoulder at the blacksmith's forge behind him, where the bulk of Gretna Green's weddings took place. "On the contrary—you entered the carriage of your own volition."

"I would not have done if I had any inkling we were going so far."

"And I would never have taken you here if I had known who you were," he countered. "I intended to marry your sister, not *you*."

Her jaw dropped, shock written so plainly across her face, he could have laughed. "Marry," she repeated. "You were going to *marry* Isabella?"

"I can think of no other reason to take such a miserable trip across the border." He sighed, trying to think his way through the mess. In the dawn light, with the scarf and the cloak, he hadn't noticed it wasn't Isabella. That ought to be any man's first step in arranging a runaway wedding, but the fact of the matter was, he hadn't been expecting anyone else.

And she had climbed into the carriage under her own power.

"Well, this is a bloody mess," he said. "I presume you are the infamous Emily."

She blinked, and her fingers shook a little around the pistol. The next second, she adjusted her grasp. "You may address me as Miss Brunton. And yes, I am Isabella's sister."

"Miss Brunton." He swept off his hat and sank into a low bow, replacing it on his head with a wince at the cold. "I'm The Honourable Oliver Beaumont. Now we are both acquainted, let us get to the heart of the matter. Why are you here?"

"I received the note you were so obliging as to send my sister," she said, her face heating a little, fiery red giving her some wonderful colour that disguised the thinness of her cheeks.

"And you decided the best course of action would be to take her place," he said dryly. "No doubt you thought you would rather find *yourself* the wife of a gentleman."

Fire flashed in those eyes. He'd assumed them to be the same blue as her sister's, but now he rather suspected they were grey, like steel. "Your note said nothing of marriage."

He barked a bitter laugh before he could help himself. So, Isabella had kept their arrangement secret, and thus Miss Brunton had seen his note and assumed a mere assignation.

None of this explained why she had chosen to take Isabella's place.

"I need a drink," he said. "And these horses need a rest. I'll find us a nearby inn."

"Together?"

"Unless you would prefer to remain in the carriage?"

He could see from her face she did not. No doubt she was nearly as cold as he was, and just as exhausted. Against the paleness of her skin, her freckles stood stark like constellations. She was not soft or delicate enough to be pretty, but he conceded that the freckles were taking.

Not that it mattered one way or the other.

He gestured at the carriage, entirely out of patience. "Get in, or I'll leave you here."

She huffed in irritation, but climbed back inside. He slammed the door and went to climb onto the coachman's seat, every muscle in his body aching. If anything, the snow only came down faster. "Damn weather," he muttered, and flicked the reins.

The ride to the inn took around five minutes, which gave Emily just enough time to find her composure from where Mr Beaumont had disposed of it.

He'd been intending to bring Isabella to Scotland—most likely Gretna Green—to *marry her*. Marriage. Her mind felt as though he had dipped a spoon into her brain and twirled it around. All this time, she'd been assuming the worst, and he'd planned this.

Had she ruined everything?

Of course not, she told herself. *If he wanted to marry her clandestinely, he probably had evil plans for her.*

The Honourable Oliver Beaumont. If he was in the area, close enough that he might have met Isabella, the only person she could think of that he might visit was Lord Marlbury—a man who ruined women and abandoned them with heartless regularity.

If that was the case, Isabella would have known about the connection. For her to have continued to encourage him—and Emily was not so foolish as to think Mr Beaumont acted without consent—then the only explanation could be infatuation. Like countless women before her, Isabella had fallen prey to a set of devilish hazel eyes and artful curls, and that childish inclination had been enough to overpower every warning Emily could give her.

What a mess.

They rattled into the coaching inn, which, given the early hour of the morning, was not as busy as it might have been. Emily rejoiced silently; the fewer witnesses, the better.

Mr Beaumont hopped down and after a few moments' conversation with an ostler, he opened the door for her.

"Sister," he said pointedly, holding out his hand. His fingers looked reddened and sore from the cold, and after a moment, she placed hers atop them. His skin was just as chilled as it appeared, and she almost jerked her hand free again. Brows lowering, he gripped her tighter and tucked the same hand firmly in his arm.

"Breakfast is served in the taproom," he said conversationally as he led her towards the door. The building was small and ill-kept, though it looked as though it saw a great deal of traffic. The whitewashed walls were peeling, revealing grey stone underneath, and a great slab served as a front step, the middle dipped from where countless feet had stepped. The interior of the building was dark and smoky.

Mr Beaumont wrapped a hand around her elbow, shifting her to one side, and with a burst of irritation she noted it was a protective gesture; a drunken man staggered past them in search of fresh air.

"Careful, Emily," he said in a low voice. "One might think you'd never stepped foot in an inn before."

She felt her face heat at the derisive note in his voice. "Don't call me by my Christian name," she snapped. "It's not polite."

"What do you call your sister?"

"How dare you bring my sister up now?"

He gave her a little shake, eyes glinting. "What do you call her?"

"Isabella," she said, realising too late what he had been forcing her to come to terms with. Siblings, as they were pretending to be, tended to use their first names to address one another.

"Call me Oliver," he said, and released her, striding into the taproom as though he belonged there. She followed, hiding her reddened, cracked hands in her cloak. If anyone believed they were brother and sister, she would eat her bonnet—her bonnet which, thanks to the lateness of the hour last night, she had not put on. As she followed him further into the room, and sat in the chair he pulled out for her, she kept her hood up.

Even so, unruly curls danced from underneath it, frizzing from the cold and the wind.

Mr Beaumont—she refused to call him by his given name, no matter what liberties he thought he could take with her—made no comment and merely ordered a large breakfast. Sausages, bacon, eggs and ale. All things she was not accustomed to eating first thing in the morning. Or, of late, at all.

Sound from the other patrons cut through the silence between them. Emily merely gazed out of the window, doing her best to ignore her companion.

Eventually, however, she could no longer bear it. "Why are you marrying my sister?" she asked abruptly, turning.

His brows both rose. "Why not?"

"What do you mean? She is seventeen and has no dowry."

"I have no need for a dowry." When a buxom maid brought Mr Beaumont his ale, he winked at her, and Emily's ire rose like bile in her throat.

"How dare you make up to every pretty girl you encounter after claiming to intend marriage for my sister," she said under her breath.

His gaze flicked to her, as though he, too, was aware that she had condemned herself by not classing herself as one of the said pretty girls. He tipped the frothy concoction into his mouth, then made a face. "Tastes like piss." At her look of irritation, he sighed and rolled his eyes. "Your sister isn't here, and thanks to your hand in the matter, I'm not marrying her. What do you expect from me?"

"Some constancy! Fidelity, perhaps?"

"I'll save that for after I have a wife."

"And if she were here?"

He gave her a very pointed look. "If she were here instead of you, things would be going rather differently."

Her cheeks burned, but she resolutely refused to look away. "You are crude."

"And you are a prude," he said, almost in dismissal. "Eager to judge. Has no one ever told you not to throw the first stone?"

"Has anyone told *you* not to seduce underage girls?"

"On the contrary," he said, irritation flaring in his eyes. "I never seduced her. I courted her."

"You intended to abscond with her."

"I intended to marry her," he said, producing the words as though bored. "Hardly the same thing."

"And you might have done so honourably!"

"Oh?" He leant closer, bracing on his elbows. "And would you have granted me permission, Miss Brunton? As her guardian, would you have allowed me the privilege of marrying your sister?"

"I might have done," she said, honesty forcing the truth from her, "if I thought you loved her."

He canted his head, watching her as though he could read every flicker of expression across her face. "Would you believe me if I said I did?" he asked, sounding almost curious. "Would that absolve me of my sins? Or are you determined to cast me in the role of villain?"

"If the shoe fits," she said tartly.

"Well then." He leant back in his chair, the wood creaking ominously, and shrugged. "There's nothing more to say on the matter. But let me say this. I have never once lied to your sister."

Emily scoffed. "A likely story."

"I'm no monster. Your sister wants nice things, and I offered to provide them for her. A house, trinkets, a place in society.

It would have been the same as any marriage made for the purpose of marrying."

Emily reared back in her seat. "My sister *loves* you."

"Did she tell you that?"

"Not in as many words, but—"

"Then what do you know about the matter?"

"My sister would never marry a man she didn't love!"

"Then perhaps you don't know your sister," he said. "We have been perfectly clear with each other about what this is. Oh, she likes me well enough, but love? I don't believe she ever had any intention of loving me."

Emily shook her head. Isabella was not that materialistic. Yes, she wanted an escape from this life, but not with a near-stranger. Not with a man prepared to whisk her away to Scotland in order to marry her illicitly—she would never have done that unless she loved him.

"Don't look at me like that," Mr Beaumont said impatiently. "If she married me, she would have everything she wanted. London society, the association with my excessively titled relatives, and a house she could be mistress of."

Emily folded her arms, trying to ignore the sheer exhaustion in her limbs. She had been run down for so very long. "And what of you? What do you gain from the arrangement?"

"A wife," he said at once. "I have need of one."

Emily buttoned her lips as another maid brought their breakfast over, slamming the plates onto the table. Piles of sausages and bacon and fried eggs, the yolk breaking and seeping out across the grease. She stared, stomach turning. So much rich food—far more than she'd had in a very long time.

"There's bread coming," the girl informed them. A different wench from before, but just as comely. And Mr Beaumont seemed just as happy to grin up at her, handsome and boyish, full of charm and boisterous fun.

There seemed not a serious bone in his body.

This was what Isabella had wanted?

If so, could Emily justify standing in her way?

Chapter Five

Oliver tapped the table as he viewed the woman sitting opposite. What the devil was he supposed to do now? He had taken the wrong sister. By rights, he should ask *her* to marry him instead; it was the correct thing to do, unless he could return her home without anyone noticing her absence—an unlikely feat in this snowstorm.

And he did need a wife.

If Henry were here—and Oliver was damn glad he wasn't—he would have suggested marriage.

Oliver's gaze flicked down to Miss Brunton's hands. Poor, cracked things, blistered and almost bloody by the knuckles where the skin had split countless times. He could only imagine how painful they were.

"What is your age?" he asked.

She blinked, brows slashing down in a frown. He noticed she had done that often in the time since they'd met. Did she ever smile—or, heaven forbid, laugh?

"My age?"

"Yes," he said. "Your age. I'm three-and-twenty. There, now you have mine."

"Four-and-twenty."

Not in the first flush of youth, but perfectly acceptable. He disliked the prospect of marrying her, but this was what he got for attempting to behave clandestinely. "You must see what we should do now," he said.

"After breakfast, you will drive me home." Her gaze, almost silvery, flicked to him. "And then we will speak with Isabella about what she wishes to do."

He could imagine nothing more excruciating than that conversation. Miss Brunton had got it into her head that her sister was some sort of golden-haired angel, and nothing he could say could disabuse her of the notion the girl loved him.

Oliver knew better: Isabella loved nothing more than the idea of wealth. He was nothing more to her than a means of escape.

"The snow is coming down quite heavily," he said. "And the horses require rest before we can make a return journey."

"What are you suggesting?"

"I am not entirely sure when I might be able to deliver you home." He held her gaze. "In my original imaginings of the event, I had not intended to immediately travel back to Dalston."

"Then what do you propose we do?"

"If you were to marry me, that would solve our immediate problems."

"It would?"

"I would rather marry sooner than later, and it would preserve your reputation. I don't make a habit of ruining young ladies."

"No?" A flash of—was that disdain in her eyes? "I'm glad to hear it. But I have no intention of marrying you; I assure you, that would not solve any of my problems. Once the horses are adequately recovered, you *will* return me home, and I shall think of an excuse for my absence that does not involve feckless young men."

"And if we cannot return until tomorrow?"

"Then I pray Isabella will have the sense not to broadcast my disappearance."

He rested his elbows on the table, intrigued despite himself. "I am the son of an earl, Miss Brunton. Upon my marriage, I will come into a nice little property—"

"And now your reasoning for marrying becomes clear—"

"And I will be perfectly respectable. Yet you object to my suit."

"It is not the suit so much as the man itself," she said firmly.

"You object to my character?"

"And your morals."

"Are they not one and the same?"

"One can be morally upright and still disagreeable," she returned. "You, however, are neither morally upright nor agreeable."

Intrigued, he leaned forward still further. "A damning condemnation."

She scowled. "You don't seem enormously distressed by it."

"If you ever meet my brother, you will learn to have thicker skin than that. I have been described as morally corrupt *and* deficient in intelligence on more than one occasion." He shrugged. "There comes a time where no further insults have any sting. But back to the matter at hand. I would be gratified if you would do me the honour of marrying me."

Those silvery eyes rose to his face, and she looked a little as though she could not decide whether to be irritated or amused. "No you wouldn't."

"Excuse me?"

"You would much rather marry my sister if it came down to it."

"Of course I would," he said impatiently. "But she's not here, and you are."

"How gratifying." She shook her head. "But the answer is no. Do not ask me again, Mr Beaumont."

He shrugged; he had done his duty, and now if she returned home and was ruined, that was no longer his problem. "Then let the chips fall as they may. We will leave as soon as the horses are sufficiently rested."

Outside, the wind howled and snow battered the panes until they rattled. Emily glared at where Oliver now leaned against the taproom bar, talking and laughing uproariously with the proprietor. Evidently her company was too dour for him to take—which, although not an unusual conclusion for young men, did nothing to improve her mood.

He had no right to be so merry at such a time. After potentially ruining two people's lives, he ought to at least show some remorse, but apparently he had never heard of the word. The sight of it jarred; all she had known was responsibility since she was seventeen years of age. Yet here he was, wild, ill-mannered, feckless.

Selfish.

If she could convince Isabella not to be in love with him, and not to marry him, she would.

He took a long swallow of the amber liquid in his hand, his throat bobbing. If he were to be believed and his father *was* an earl, he certainly had a knack for adapting to his society—she could not imagine a gentleman this privileged had much to do with men like this. And yet he laughed among them as though he were one of them, as at home here as he would be in a drawing room.

No one would believe them to be siblings—he wore simple but expensive clothes, and hers was a thrice-darned gown she had extracted from her mother's trunks two years ago.

He was handsome, broad-shouldered, and had gold stubble across his jaw. She was dowdy and plain.

That oughtn't matter, yet for some reason it did.

She crossed the room to his side. "Mr Beaumont," she said, and he stopped laughing to glance at her. A roguish curl fell across his forehead, and it was irritatingly charming.

"Emily," he said, saluting her with his glass. "Have you come to hurry me along?"

"If such a thing were possible."

The innkeeper, a sturdy-looking man with sideburns down to his jaw, grunted. "Won't get far in this weather. I'd recommend you stay and wait for better conditions."

"Of course you'd say that," Oliver said cheerfully. "But you aren't the one going out in it, so it doesn't matter one way or the other."

The innkeeper shrugged. "Your funeral."

"Finish this for me," Mr Beaumont said, sliding the glass across to her. "It'll warm you right up." He winked, sliding off the stool. "I shall go in search of our horses and get things prepared for us."

Emily stared at the glass of liquid he had offered her. Brandy, perhaps? Wine? She couldn't be sure; it had been a long time since her house had held any alcohol to speak of.

"It won't hurt you," the innkeeper said, before moving on to serve another patron.

She took a tentative sip. Heat flared across her tongue, and a burning sensation erupted in her throat. Unpleasant—and yet oddly warming. The heat sank into her stomach, and she found it remarkably easy to take another sip, then another, finishing what little remained in the glass.

How irritating that Mr Beaumont was right—about this, or anything. She would much rather he were an irredeemable rogue and she could convince poor Isabella to fall in love with someone more worthy. Or, better still, no one at all.

She had just finished the glass when Mr Beaumont summoned her to the frozen courtyard. His enormous carriage stood alone on the cobbles; no other vehicles were, evidently, prepared to brave the storm.

Emily could hardly blame them. If their circumstances had been less pressing, she would have felt the same.

Mr Beaumont came to stand beside her, dressed in a large oilskin coat that was too large on his frame. "In you go," he said.

"Are you driving?"

"Alas yes. My pockets are not deep enough to convince a man to offer me his life."

"You exaggerate."

"Only a little." He grinned at her, the wind mussing his curls. "Hold on tight, darling. I can't promise you a comfortable ride."

"I'm not your darling."

"No, you're a thorn in my side," he retorted. "Come on, get in so I can take you home."

"Thank you," she forced herself to say.

He gave a rueful grin. "My damned honour," was all he said as he closed the door behind her. A minute or two later, the carriage lurched into motion, and they left the inn behind them.

Every part of Oliver was cold. He had paid a coachman a handsome sum for his oiled leather greatcoat, which deflected most of the precipitation—*snow, call it snow, you fool*—but his hands had clawed into icicles around the reins, and he was confident his nose was half a thought from departing his face entirely.

He ought to have just left her there despite her protests, marriage or no. He'd offered—it was entirely on her that she had refused him. Not exactly how he'd envisaged his first proposal to go, but never mind.

But no. She could not be prevailed upon to marry him, and for reasons beyond his understanding, he had agreed to brave the storm to return her home.

Henry would approve. And the thought made Oliver want to rebel. He was not a man who did the right thing for virtue's sake alone.

Damn it all.

More to the point, he had lost any desire to marry Isabella. If the girl *did* love him, that would make the entire thing uncomfortable. He had been certain she didn't, but Miss Brunton's insistence she did had shaken him.

Or, perhaps worse still, she might tell Emily she loved him so he would be forced to marry her, all while merely coveting the prospect of his inheritance.

He ought to leave the lot of them behind.

The wind blew drifted snow across the road, and Oliver squinted. Was that a corner coming up ahead?

The curve finally appeared to him, and he swore, hauling on the reins. The horses reared, trying to desperately to correct their course, but the wheels skidded against the slick ground, and momentum shot them forward. Too fast.

His fault, for thinking he might beat the storm.

His fault, for not seeing the approaching corner past the blizzard.

The horses tossed their heads, and the air burned his lungs as he drew in a deep, snow-filled breath. The countryside looked foreign, covered in white as it was. It was impossible to know where the road stopped and the verge began.

He cursed again, hands numb as he gripped the wooden bar before him.

The carriage shuddered. Tipped.

He knew the second it was beyond the point of no return. Time seemed to slow, thick as honey, as the carriage tipped. Past the howling wind, he thought he heard a scream. The horses whinnied, and gravity took hold of him, tossing him from the hard coachman's bench and headfirst into a snow-drift.

Chapter Six

Emily came to in aching, ringing silence. Her head throbbed. When she put a hand to her temple, her fingers came away damp. Dim light filtered through the window, which, she thought, gazed up at the sky. Already, snow covered the glass.

She, along with the brick—she suspected the source of the wound on her head—and the blankets were lying against the side of the carriage, which now faced down.

Everything felt too quiet, sound dampened by the falling snow. Her breath came in juddering fits—the only thing she could hear. Slowly, moving in a daze, she reassured herself that no other part of her was hurt. Arms, legs, torso. Only her head ached, sharp stabs of pain every time she moved. Her thoughts moved fuzzily about her head.

They had crashed. That was it. The carriage had tilted, and they had landed hard, and—

"Emily!" The sound was distant, but it cut through the ringing in her ears, and she moved her head, searching for the source of the voice. The door opened, letting snowflakes drive inside, and a head poked through. "Are you all right?" Mr Beaumont asked a little desperately, his voice tight.

"I—I think so." She sounded as dreamy as she felt. Surely, any second, she would open her eyes and find herself rattling back along the snowy countryside.

"Give me your hand." He opened the door wide and extended a hand, his entire demeanour thick with strain.

No, not strain. Pain.

When she didn't move, he added, "I'll pull you free."

She exhaled sharply, forcing away the fuzziness with sheer force of will. This would *not* get the best of her. All she needed was to approach the situation with a modicum of logic. A few truths were undeniable.

They had been in some form of accident.

The carriage lay on its side, presumably in a ditch.

She had hit her head.

It was snowing.

At least Mr Beaumont appeared to be, if not unhurt, then at least alive. That was something.

She looked up at him, at the way his form was already rapidly being covered by the falling snow. They could not remain here.

"Here," she said, finding the blankets and handing them to him. "We should think about staying warm. Do you know where we are?"

If he was surprised by the way she took control of the situation, he didn't show it. "I'm afraid not."

"Never mind. We'll have to walk until we find something, unless you think we can right the carriage ourselves."

"No." There was a trace of pained irony in his voice. "That, I fear, will prove impossible."

"As I thought." She put aside all thoughts of freezing to death. That was simply not an option when she had a sister to get back to. Instead, she gathered the blankets and handed them up to him. "We'll need these, then. We can put them over the horses. Are they all right?"

"I think so." He accepted the blankets with one awkward hand, then returned for her. Pistol in one hand, she clambered free with his help. The cold hit her anew, as did the wind. When she jumped down from the upended carriage, her feet sank into several inches of snow.

Mr Beaumont's face was, for once, utterly grim. And the carriage was ruined—on its side, several splintered pieces of wood jutting into the air. Perhaps, under other circumstances, it might have provided an imperfect shelter, but it would not have protected them against the chill for long.

And then there were the horses to think about.

She turned back to Mr Beaumont, a biting reflection of his driving jumping to her tongue—only to fade in the next second, thanks to the awkward way he held one arm. His lips were pale, and his hair was plastered against his head. Snow coated every part of him.

Her anger dissipated.

"You're hurt!" she exclaimed.

"Broken arm, I should think." He grimaced. "Hurts like the devil." His gaze caught on her head, and he swore under his breath, taking her chin with his good hand and turning her head this way and that. "What happened here?"

"I think one of the bricks hit my head."

He cursed again, and Emily was faintly surprised the snow didn't melt around the ferocity of his words. His thumb touched her cheekbone, his touch surprisingly gentle, and he wiped away a trickle of blood. "Can you still see straight?"

"Yes. I'm fine." She wasn't sure if she was, but they didn't have the luxury of collapse; with him in that state, he wouldn't be able to carry her to safety, or even lift her onto a horse.

"No you're not," he said, his voice low and ominous. "Neither of us are. We are in a storm and I have no bloody idea where we are, or if we're even in Scotland or England."

Emily shuddered, the cold biting at her elbows and nose. The throbbing in her head hadn't ceased with the chill; if anything, it was worse.

"Lean on me," he said, still with that grimness in his voice. "Let me get you to the horses." He wrapped a hand around her wrist to lead her to where the horses stood at the front of the carriage. They were all upright. Oliver had piled the blankets on one, and its pair had a hurt hock by the looks of it. The other two appeared unhurt but unsaddled and obviously spooked, eyes rolling. Snow settled on their backs.

There was no scenario in which they could ride these horses to safety.

To Emily's embarrassment, she found the simple contact of his hand around her wrist a source of reassurance. They were in this together.

"The first thing we ought to do is secure your arm," she said, trying to think. When her father had broken his arm, the physician had set the bone and tied it to a splint. There was nothing easily available to set the bone with here, but if she at least pinned the arm to his body, that would keep it still.

Mr Beaumont shook his head. "There's no—"

"We'll use a blanket for a sling. It'll be better than nothing until we can find a doctor."

"And you will be the one to do it?" he asked sceptically, the sarcasm in his tone belied by the sweat beading on his brow. "Darling, you can hardly stand up straight."

"Neither can you," she snapped. "And if we are to traipse through the countryside during a storm, we would be better off doing so in as full health as possible." Ignoring his irritated huff, she stomped to the blankets and, placing the pistol aside, shook one out. Impossible to get all the snow free, but she did her best, refolding it with shaking hands. He winced, and she winced along with him. "I'm sorry," she said, tying the two ends around his neck. "But we need to hold the limb in place."

He breathed harshly through gritted teeth. "It's fine."

She stepped back, admiring her handiwork. "There. That will suffice for the time being, I think. We should get moving."

"Wait." With his good hand, Mr Beaumont reached into his pocket for his handkerchief, drew it out and proffered it to her. "Here. For your head."

She debated arguing, but decided against it, and gingerly pressed the soft cotton against the point of pain on her head. Blood soaked through the material, watered down by the melting snow.

"I will take the gun for now," he said, picking up the pistol where she had deposited it, and tucking it into an internal coat pocket. "I at least have the capacity to carry it without alarming anyone we encounter."

Under any other circumstances, she would have been adamantly against Mr Beaumont taking possession of the pistol, but she saw the logic in it. And she didn't strictly know if it was loaded; it had served its purpose.

"I want it back," she said.

"Fine. Can you walk?"

"Yes." She didn't know if it was true, but there was little else she could do. With her head, and with the lack of saddle or bridle, she fancied riding would prove risky.

Mr Beaumont strode to where the reins still held the horses in place, and drawing a penknife from his pocket, he slashed through their bindings. "Here," he said, thrusting one set of reins into her hands. "I'll take the others. Follow me."

They began their miserable journey. All too soon, her feet felt like blocks of ice, and although Mr Beaumont was walking ahead, striding through the snow and breaking a path, the hem of her skirts soon became damp and encrusted. Ice bloomed on her lashes, turning them heavy with every blink. The tips of her fingers turned white.

Frostbite had not come to Dalston often, but she knew of it. The blackened extremities, nerves dead. Incurable. How would she provide for Isabella if she did not have her hands? It seemed an impossibility. Yet even her panic felt muted under the frozen weight of the world.

Behind her, the horse she led trudged with patient misery.

After what felt like hours—or perhaps even days—Mr Beaumont came to a stop ahead of her. "I spy a light," he yelled, pointing ahead. Emily squinted, but the snow was too thick to make out much of anything at all. He abandoned the horses and approached her, his face terribly pale, the tips of his hair white with frost and settled snow.

"A farm?" she asked.

His gaze flicked to her temple, then back down to her face. "Most likely. I don't know who lives and runs there, but I expect we will have to shelter as husband and wife."

"Not sister and brother?" she asked, already knowing it was fruitless.

"Such a story won't hold under close examination. We look and sound too dissimilar. The inn was one thing because we were two patrons out of many, but someone's home is a different story." He plunged a hand into his pocket once more and pressed something into her hand. When she uncurled her fingers, it was to see a ring. She glanced at Oliver, but he was already turning away.

"I can't wear this," she said. Her tongue felt too thick. "Oliver. I can't wear the ring you were going to give my sister."

"If you want them to welcome us, then you must."

She watched him stumble back to the head of his horses, fumbling for the reins with his good arm. Although she was in enough discomfort to classify as physical pain, he was in more so. They needed rest and refuge.

And he was right: under close examination, they could not pass as brother and sister. Their colourings were entirely different, and their accents; he had been born in the south of England and she the north. All the governesses in the world—and she'd only had two—would have been unable to banish the slight cadence to her words. He was quite obviously a man of fashion; her dresses were many years out of date and heavily patched.

They did not look like they belonged together in any capacity. But certainly not as siblings born equal.

With clumsy fingers, she slid the ring on her third finger and returned to trudging through the snow towards the lights. They gleamed, golden and warm, between the driving snow, and it seemed to her weary eyes like a haven.

Please say this is an inn. If there were an inn, they might have the chance to hire a room, or even rooms. Perhaps hire a carriage to take them back to Dalston as soon as the snow cleared.

What would Isabella be thinking about her absence? She ought to have left a note, but she had not thought she would be gone at all. All she'd intended to do was threaten him and return to bed.

She had the oddest, overwrought temptation to weep.

Finally, they reached a small track leading off the road that widened into a courtyard. There were what appeared to be barns to one side, and a large stone house on the other. Not an inn—decidedly not. But it was shelter, and she would accept anything under any terms to escape the ferocity of the snow.

Ahead of her, Mr Beaumont dropped the reins of his horses and reached for her arm, dragging her close to him. "Knock," he advised her, voice ragged with exhaustion.

She raised her fist to do just that, but the door swung open of its own accord, and a plump-faced woman stared at them both with utter astonishment.

"Mercy me," she said, glancing between them both, and Emily felt a burst of relief that they were, at least, within the bounds of England. "What a pair of sorry-looking folk."

"My wife and I had a carriage accident," Oliver said, and Emily did her best not to flinch at the word 'wife'. "Is there anywhere to shelter our horses?"

"He has a broken arm," Emily said. She couldn't quite bring herself to say the word 'husband'.

"Oh you poor lambs. Of course, you must come in at once." She held the door open, and the delicious scent of roasted meat filled the stone hallway. Emily's clothes dripped miserably across the floor. Their host shut the door firmly behind them. "Gregory," she hollered. A lean man appeared in the doorway. Like her, he appeared in his forties, his build defined by years of hard labour. "There are four horses in the yard. Stable them, if you please. We can put the two mares in a stall to share tonight, if needs be. Now, you come this way, my dears." She led the way down the stone hall, then right into a dining room. Like the hallway, the floor was made up of large stone flags, and Emily found herself grateful for the lack of carpets. Four children stared at them with wide eyes from where they were seated on a bench by the table, which groaned with food. Emily's stomach gave a large gurgle.

"I don't suppose you might call for a physician?" Oliver asked, his voice a little faint. "And a change of clothes. I have some money—"

"We don't need money to help folks in need," the lady said firmly. "Though I don't think we'll get a physician to you in this weather. But there our stable hand, and he knows his way around a broken bone. Seems every year, a cow or horse breaks something and he has to set it."

Oliver's face turned near white in the firelight, and he swayed on his feet. Emily felt a burst of pity for him.

"Do you have anything for his relief?" she asked, one eye on the children, who were looking at them avidly. "Laudanum, perhaps? Or even just some brandy?"

"We'll have something." The lady led them forward in a decisive swish of her skirts. "Now, you're very fortunate that we have a spare room. Don't often do, except my eldest recently married." She cast a glance at them both. "I'm afraid the bed is narrow, and—"

"Quite all right," Oliver gasped. "I'll sleep on the floor."

"No you won't. Not in your condition. I'll sleep on the floor," Emily told their kind hostess. "If there's a truckle bed of some description. Or I can take another room entirely. I'm almost unhurt, so—"

"There'll be a bed somewhere, I'm certain of it." Their hostess led them up a set of narrow stairs to a small, neat room with one slanted wall of the roof, and a window inserted into it, looking at the sky. A single bed lay underneath it, and a heavy set of drawers were set against the opposite wall. Aside from a threadbare rug and a painting of a pig beside the door, the room was empty.

"I'll fetch you some clothes to change into," she said. "Clean and dry, that's what you need. And I'll ask my old man for a bottle of something to take the edge off. And a tray, before the youngsters eat it all." She beamed with such good humour and kindness, Emily could do nothing but smile back. "My name's

Susan Chambers, by the way, and my husband is Gregory Chambers."

"Mr and Mrs Oliver Beaumont," Oliver said before Emily could speak—fortunate, for the name sounded entirely more natural on his tongue than it would have on hers.

"But please," Emily said, with all the smiling goodwill she could muster, "call me Emily."

"Right you are, ma'am," Mrs Chambers said. "I'll be back in two shakes of a duck's tail." She closed the door and whisked herself away, leaving them alone.

Chapter Seven

Oliver stared at Emily, her curls a dark brown from the melting snow, her face flushed from the sudden heat. At least her lips held colour now—small mercies. Now they were closeted in this farmhouse, he had doubts about his plan. The prospect of having his arm mauled by a farmhand who knew how to set animal bones made him feel as though his nerves were on fire.

"Are you all right?" Emily asked, her brows drawing together. There was still a hint of dried blood on the side of her face, and a large purple bruise. He wondered idly where his handkerchief had gone.

"Define all right." He reached out his good hand to brace against the wall. "I'm alive."

"We need to get you out of that coat and shirt," she said, starting forward, but he stepped back.

"Absolutely not. I refuse to let you manhandle me."

"Don't be ridiculous. I put your arm in a sling, didn't I?" Somehow, despite her obvious discomfort, she had the gall to look put out by his refusal. "I can help."

"I would rather you made no such attempt," he said stiffly.

She rolled her eyes. "Oh, very well. It's your arm."

"I'm well aware of that."

The door opened, and Mrs Chambers bustled back in, the children behind her, peering in. Oliver grimaced. He'd been around children plenty enough; his sister's son was an unruly chap, always running off to cause mischief. But he would much rather his suffering had no audience.

"Here," Mrs Chambers said, laying two piles of clothes across the narrow bed. "I'll get working on a tray to bring you when you're decent."

"Would it be possible to have a little assistance?" Emily asked, and the saccharine note in her voice ought to have been the warning he needed. "My husband's clothes will have to be cut off in order to free his arm."

"Oh! Of course, my dear. I'll send my husband up. Come with me, and I'll get you nice and dry in a jiffy." She beckoned Emily out of the room, and although Oliver should have felt relieved by the fact, he felt a little panicky. Pain, he knew, was causing his mind to work overtime, coming to countless irrational conclusions. What if something were to happen to her out of his sight?

His head ached. He felt hot and cold all over.

"Look after her," he called to Mrs Chambers, who clucked reassuringly and offered him a kind smile. It ought to have reassured him, appeased his concerns, but all he could see was the bruise on Emily's face.

While undoubtedly she should take some responsibility for their predicament—if she had not interfered, he might have been happily married and ensconced with an agreeable woman by now—he had caused the accident.

Her welfare entirely depended on him. And if these kind people saw through their lie, if she were more hurt than she appeared, then—

The door opened once more, and the same thin man from downstairs entered the room. "Right, my lad," Mr Chambers said with a friendly grin. "Let's get you out of them wet clothes before you catch your death. The missus said you needed 'em cutting free."

"Regrettably," Oliver said.

"Shame to ruin these clothes, but best to get you out of them." He held up a bottle of what appeared to be whisky. "Here, let's get this down you first. Warm you up and make the experience a mite less unpleasant."

Only a mite—but that was enough for Oliver to grab the bottle and upend it in his mouth. Burning liquid sloshed down his throat. He swallowed several mouthfuls before Mr Chambers motioned for it back. Reluctantly, Oliver did as instructed.

"Don't want you to have too much, or you'll feel it tomorrow morning."

"Of the two evils, sir, I rather suspect that is the lesser," Oliver said.

"Oh, call me Gregory," Mr Chambers said cheerfully. "We don't stand on ceremony much around here."

"Then please call me Oliver."

"Right you are, Oliver. Now"—he dragged a chair to the centre of the room—"I recommend you sit on this. Never mind the cushion—what is wet will dry, that's what I say. And I don't want you fainting on me."

Feeling more than a little faint, Oliver sank on the chair as instructed.

"Don't mind me," Gregory said as he began plucking at the knot of the string. "Might as well preserve this blanket as well as possible. Your wife fashioned this for you?"

"Yes. Emily."

"Nice name, Emily." Oblivious to Oliver's flinch, Gregory tossed the blanket aside and began cutting through the coat, the greased material evidently a challenge. Agony seared through Oliver, and he gritted his teeth, doing his best to ignore the blackness on either side of his vision.

The whisky had set the room spinning, but didn't feel as though it had numbed all that much of the pain.

"Another drink," he gasped.

Gregory brought the bottle to Oliver's lips and tipped. Oliver eagerly gulped another few mouthfuls, only coming up for breath when the older man drew the bottle away. "That's enough for now, my lad. You'll want more when Old Tom comes to set the limb."

Yes, by the sounds of it, he very much would.

Gregory returned to his sawing. "Been married long?" he asked, as though they were in a drawing room over tea rather than in this bare, pitiful room with Oliver's broken arm swinging sickly within the confines of his clothes.

"Not long," he managed.

"Ah. Thought you had the look of newlyweds. Well, if you want my advice"—Oliver most certainly did not; the last thing he wanted right now was a well-meaning lecture about how best to conduct a marriage—"then you'll take each day as it comes. Listen to her. She might have her nagging complaints, but sometimes she's right, and you've got to respect it. A happy wife makes for a happy life."

Gregory finally tugged Oliver's coat free, and Oliver decided the best course of action was to pass out from the pain.

Emily paced the confines of the small hallway, glancing at the closed door before pacing resolutely away again. She'd eaten, changed into a thick dress that was far warmer than any she owned, and now all she had to do was wait for the stable hand to set Oliver's arm.

The silence from inside the small bedroom had her irrationally certain that he had passed away, thus taking with him her best chance of returning home promptly. She felt sick and dizzy with worry.

"You'll wear a hole in the carpet," Mrs Chambers said with a trace of pity. "Here, come and sit with me. You'll feel better for it. All that traipsing through the snow."

Emily had given a highly abridged account of how they had come to be stranded, including their reasons for travelling in such appalling conditions. Her story had not involved a runaway wedding, but it had involved them being married only a week or so. Partly because she didn't want to stray too far from the truth, and partly because she did not think she could accurately portray the role of well-established wife.

At that moment, the door opened and the stable hand—a pleasant-faced man named Thomas and referred to as Old Tom—emerged. "He's out," he said to both Emily and Mrs Chambers. "Passed out when Mr Chambers tried cutting his coat away from his arm. Nasty inflamed, it was, but it should be sorted now. A blessing he weren't conscious for it, if you ask me." He dipped his head in what appeared to be an uncomfortable nod, then headed for the stairs. A moment later, Mr Chambers emerged.

"I imagine he'll wake in the morning with a bad head," he said, and gave an apologetic smile to Emily. "My apologies, ma'am."

"Not at all." Emily drew the shawl she'd been lent around herself. "May I see him?"

"You can, but there ain't much to see."

Perhaps not, but Emily would rather be present when Oliver awoke, so she could tell him the story they had concocted for the sake of their kindly hosts. They were honest, God-fearing people who would be scandalised at the prospect of sheltering two unmarried people in the same room.

Guilt clawed at her stomach at the thought of deceiving the people who had taken them in, whose clothes she wore on her back.

"There now," she heard Mrs Chambers say to her husband behind her. "You leave them be."

Emily shut the door on the family and stared at the bed. The way Oliver lay, sprawled across the pillow with his hair wildly mussed, made him appear as though he had tumbled into bed after some debauchery.

Someone, likely Mr Chambers, had changed him into clean, dry bedclothes that hid his poor arm.

For a long moment, she stared down into his face, relaxed and unconscious. The golden stubble on his chin, the chaos of his curly hair. She'd always assumed curls were angelic, but there was nothing angelic about this man. Despite his youth, there were still sharp edges to him.

An idle lord, yes, but not one without his own form of bitterness.

She dragged a chair closer, the room seeming as though it was spinning. The nausea in her stomach still hadn't eased, and she closed her eyes for a second.

When she opened them again, she found Oliver watching her with an expression of consternation. A headache pulsed at her temples.

He attempted to rise, and she pushed at his shoulder. "Be still or you'll hurt yourself."

He blinked, gaze a little cloudy, and eventually focused back on her. "I was rather hoping it was all a bad dream," he said, with a return to the slightly dry drawl she'd become accustomed to. "I presume your presence, and the fact I'm mildly inebriated, is a sign that it is not."

"How is your head?" Emily asked. "Mr Chambers said you would wake with a bad head."

Mr Beaumont snorted. "Perhaps if one never drinks. He allowed me only a few swallows."

"I take it you are accustomed to a great deal more."

He looked at her steadily. "If you are inclined towards judgement, I suggest saving it for another time."

"I hardly see the need to argue with you," she said, smoothing out the unfamiliar skirt. "Now we're here, in this condition, there's not much we can do but make the best of it."

His gaze landed on the side of her face. "How do you feel?"

"Perfectly well, thank you."

He snorted, but instead of responding, pushed himself into an upright position despite her protests. "Where is the truckle bed? Have you requested one?"

"Not for you," she said calmly.

"As the gentleman, it is my prerogative to bear the discomfort."

"Oh, is that what you mean by 'gentleman'?"

"And here I was thinking you wouldn't argue with me," he returned. Despite herself, she felt a smile twitch at her lips.

"Mrs Chambers asked how we met, and I concocted a story of you courting me and us marrying in a perfectly sensible way after the reading of the banns."

"How very proper of us."

"I thought that was better than claiming a runaway marriage."

"And such a story would be unnecessary, seeing as you are of age," he added. "Very well. How long have we been married?"

"Not long. Weeks, perhaps? I said nothing about where we live," she added, feeling suddenly defensive. "So we can claim wherever you choose."

"I hardly mind. We can say Dalston if it pleases you."

"Nothing about this situation pleases me," she snapped. "Moreover, I know nothing about the process of marriage. You, as the expert in the matter, should be in charge of deciding these things."

"I, an expert?"

"More so than I," she said, curling her fingers in her skirts. "After all, I have yet to meet a man worth marrying, and I do not expect to."

"Intriguing," he murmured, leaning forward, his gaze fixed on hers in a way that made her stomach drop. "Tell me, who was he? The man who broke your heart so admirably?"

Chapter Eight

Oliver knew the moment he'd asked the question that he had misstepped. The whisky was to blame, or perhaps the aching in his arm; either way, he had erred. Emily's face flushed, and she glowered at him, her jaw locking. Her grey eyes flashed. If she could have eviscerated him where he lay, no doubt she would have done.

"What is there to say that my resolution is due to a man?"

He held up his good hand in a placating gesture. "Forgive me."

She rose, her back stiff as she strode to the window and stayed there, staring at the snowy, grey world that lay outside. Dusk would fall soon—perhaps it had already fallen—and already the light was indifferent. Still, it was sufficient to show the way her shoulders hunched and her hands clenched; he doubted it was because of the cold. The last vestiges of daylight illuminated the gleam of pale skin at her neck, but cast her hair into the deep red of autumn leaves, near blending with the gloom. She didn't look away from the frigid glass, but he saw her shiver.

Regret, a sensation he was rather unused to, made its presence known. But what the devil was he supposed to do? He hadn't known when he teased her that she was going to react in such a way. But his better judgement notwithstanding—he did on occasion have a better judgement—he wanted to know her story. There were so many scattered pieces of her life she had already shown him; he wished to put them together so he might understand the whole.

But he had gone about finding out the wrong way.

He pinched his nose. "Miss Brunton," he said.

Silence.

Ignoring the dizzying pain in his arm, he pushed himself up, swinging his feet out of the bed. His stomach revolted, but with some force of will, he was able to stand. The whisky, he imagined, was helping more than he wanted to admit.

"Emily," he said again.

"Leave me be. I don't want to speak with you."

"I'm sorry."

She remained silent, hugging herself now, those thin shoulders tight. He waited, rolling to his toes and back again, but she made no move to say anything further, or to so much as glance at him. So he retrieved the blanket from the bed and slung it over her shoulders, made clumsy by the use of only one hand. Her small hands came to grip the edges, pulling it tightly over herself.

"I'm going to find Mr Chambers and investigate the possibility of more whisky," he said, retreating. "And a truckle bed. For me. Don't argue the point. You'll find I'm remarkably stubborn when I have cause to be."

Her sigh sounded as though it came from deep within her. "You ought to take the bed."

"I told you not to argue." He made for the door. "Come down when you're ready," was all he said as he slipped through.

Emily stared at the frozen glass. Soon, the candle would go out and she would be plunged in darkness, but she didn't think she'd mind. Maybe she wouldn't notice. Maybe if her world were black, it would ease the aching emptiness in her chest.

She didn't think she loved Lord Marlbury any longer, but thinking about marriage—*her* marriage—made her think of all the hopes she'd once had. Her innocence, her optimism. Marlbury had exposed her to the world's cruelty, and soon after he abandoned her, her mother had died, and her father had wasted away.

Love, it seemed, was not the pure, sweet thing she had dreamed of in youth.

No, it came with barbs; either it cut you, or it lingered long enough for the wound to turn rancid. Her parents had loved one another, and that love had ruined her father.

She didn't know how long she stood there, absorbing the cold until it sank into her bones, but eventually darkness fell, and when the door opened again, her entire body felt stiff. Her head pounded, and nausea swirled in her stomach.

Oliver carried a candle with him, and when she turned, she could see its light flickering across his face. She half expected him to say something, but instead he directed Mr Chambers to place the truckle bed on the floor, as far from the bed as was possible in this small room.

As Emily watched, feeling numb, Mr Chambers built the fire, setting it going merrily, and a maid arrived with her arms full of blankets.

"Thank you," Oliver said as he gestured for the blankets to be placed on the bed. No wink this time, she noted. Perhaps even he accepted that inside another man's household was a very different place than the tavern. The girls there accepted and wanted his winks, perhaps even supplementing their income by selling their bodies to the highest bidder. And the maid here merely worked as a maid.

Or perhaps he was as tired and done in as she felt.

Finally, Mr Chambers and the maid left, and Oliver turned back to face her.

"I told them you were feeling unwell," he said. "Mrs Chambers has a tray of food waiting for you."

She shook her head, the room spinning a little. She was so *tired.* All her life, it seemed, she had been tired. "I'm not hungry."

"You haven't eaten for hours."

"I have eaten more today than I ever have before in a single day." That might not be true, but it was close enough. "I just want to rest."

"Then rest, but come closer to the fire." Without reaching for her, he beckoned her closer, until her fingers burned from the heat. "You must be frozen."

She didn't have the energy to explain that she rarely built up the fire to this extent at home, or that they rarely lit a fire in the bedroom. Instead, she allowed him to guide her down to the truckle bed. Her fingers curled in on themselves. She didn't even have her anger at him any longer.

"I spoke to Mr Chambers," he said. "The nearest posting house is ten miles away. I must have taken a wrong turn in the blizzard. Fortunately, the snow appears to have stopped. Tomorrow, I'll ride out with Mr Chambers and assess the damage done to my coach." He winced. "My *brother's* coach. He won't forgive me easily."

"Your brother's? I assumed it was your own."

"No, I took it when I left him last. He has others, though, don't worry." He slanted her a long look, as though waiting for her to pass judgement. But she simply didn't have the emotion in her anymore. "We had an argument, and I left angry."

"What did you argue about?"

"His expectations for me. Among other things."

"Other things such as your inheritance?"

"His wife has an independent fortune—it belonged to her late husband—and she is the one bestowing the inheritance on me. I only receive it once I marry, and while my brother wished me to wait, for various reasons I had rather the happy event occur sooner than later."

Of course he would; what man did not want a fortune?

"And so you stole your brother's carriage and seduced my sister."

"I stole my brother's carriage and crashed it," he said. "Not my finest moment, I'll agree—you have not seen me at my best, Miss Brunton. But I did not seduce your sister."

Small mercies, she supposed. If she could trust his word—and she found she did, oddly enough.

"And as proof of my honour, what little of it remains, I will do my best to return you home as soon as the snow stops. Hopefully that will absolve me in your eyes, if not my brother's."

"Perhaps," she said. "If you are successful in your attempt. How are the horses?"

"One has lost a shoe and another has a sprained hock, but they seem to have escaped remarkably unscathed, according to Mr Chambers. I'll take a look at them in the morning." He gave her a sharp-eyed glance, as though seeing through her lacklustre conversation to the exhaustion that lay underneath. "Oh, and Mrs Chambers provided some bedclothes for you."

Emily touched her head and winced. How could they ever repay this family? "How generous of her. If you could—please tell Mrs Chambers I have no need for dinner. I would rather just sleep."

"Of course." He rose, the colour somewhat restored to her cheeks. "I'll knock before coming back in, I assure you."

To her surprise, she believed him, and although they were set to share a room, she had no fear that he would take advantage of her in the night. In part because doing so would be harder with a broken arm, and in part because he had shown her surprising consideration over the past few hours. "Thank you."

After he left the room, she undressed quickly and clambered into the nightclothes, freshly laundered and rough to the touch. With Oliver having placed all his nightclothes and other things on the truckle bed—no doubt by design—she gave in and took the other. The pillow was cool against her cheek.

As she closed her eyes, she wondered what things would look like when she finally did return home. Whether Isabella would ever forgive her, or if their lives would be irrevocably changed.

Chapter Nine

When Oliver awoke the next morning, his entire body felt as though someone had run him over with a horse. While his arm most certainly hurt the most, the truckle bed—or, perhaps, being thrown from his carriage—had done untold damage to his back. That was what he got for trying to be the gentleman in the situation.

And yet, more fool him, he would do it again.

He stretched, ignoring the low, steady ache in his arm, and rolled awkwardly out of bed. Emily must have already left while he was sleeping; he was alone in the room. A good thing too: being unable to dress and undress himself, he had slept in his shirt and breeches, and was now unacceptably rumpled.

When he made it to the window, however, all thoughts of clothing left his head.

All that greeted him was a world of white. A carpet of snow blanketed the land, glittering in the frosty sunlight. Beautiful, perhaps, but thick enough that the roads would not be clear for some time. They were trapped here.

If Emily had already risen, then she must have seen this already. He wondered how she had taken it. Not too hard, he hoped. This would be a blow to their plans, but she had sustained a blow to the head, and his arm was equally an impediment. A few more days of recovery would do them no harm.

After combing his hair and disguising the wrinkled state of his shirt as best he could, he left the room. One hand outstretched for balance, he made his way along the uneven wooden floor to the narrow, rickety staircase. The scent of smoke greeted him, and by the time he made it to the giant flagstones that marked the first floor of the house, he felt as though he had entered another world entirely.

The stairs emerged in the dining room, where a large fireplace puffed smoke and too many children dashed around an enormous table. One of them—a girl looking to be about twelve years of age—attempted to set each place as her siblings raced around the furniture in overwhelming mayhem.

One of the little boys, five or six at a guess, skidded to a halt in front of Oliver and stared up at him with wide eyes. "Are you the gentleman what came last night?" he enquired.

"I am," Oliver said, and as his stomach gurgled again, he glanced apologetically at the girl setting the table and added, "I'm famished, I'm afraid."

Footsteps sounded, and he turned to find Emily in an apron several sizes too big carrying a large dish into the room. At the sight of him, she stumbled, almost tripping over a flagstone, and she recovered, eyes wide.

"Oh," she said, regaining her composure and placing the dish on the table. When she uncovered it, she revealed a plate of steaming bacon, and his stomach grumbled. "You're up."

"It seems you've been up longer than I have," he said gruffly, noting the way her cheeks flushed from exertion. Except for the bruise on her temple, the cut seeming almost swollen, she appeared well. Still, the sight of the wound bothered him. "Is there anything I can do to help?"

"Help?" She blinked, and he almost wanted to laugh. Lord, what an impression he'd made on her if she found his offer so outlandish.

"Yes, Emily. Help. Assist. What would best help you?"

"By the looks of your face, sitting down," she said sharply, taking his good arm and guiding him to a chair. "If you didn't feel up to rising, I could have brought a tray up."

"I fear I'm a poor invalid," Oliver said, patting her hand. Her fingers curled under his, and she jerked back. "I dislike being left alone in empty rooms. Besides, I came in part to find you."

Those silvery eyes searched his, and she remained silent until Mrs Chambers bustled into the room, carrying another platter. At the sight of him, she let out a squawk. "Lawks, you're up already, Mr Beaumont! I wasn't expecting to see you out and about so soon, what with that arm of yours. Your wife has been a great help in the kitchen."

Emily flushed a little, glancing sidelong at Oliver as though she feared he would chastise her for helping. Instead, he felt the full weight of the burden his presence here must be on these people. Emily could cook, at least. But what could he do? Nothing useful—that had always been the problem.

"Sit with your husband there, love," Mrs Chambers said, not seeming to notice the way Emily hovered awkwardly beside him. "I'll handle the rest. You've done more than enough already, especially considering your condition."

Oliver gave her a piercing look as she slid along the bench beside him. "Does your head hurt?"

"Rather less than your arm, I fancy," she said, frowning at his concern. "I'm not a delicate flower, you know."

"I know that, but it doesn't mean you're immune to all injury. A brick hit you, darling. It's not nothing."

"Truly, I'm fine," she said.

Frustrated but unwilling to push the subject, he turned to the children. "What are your names?"

"I'm John," the youngest boy said, sticking out his chest proudly. "I'm five." To prove it, he held out five chubby fingers.

"And you can count!" Emily said approvingly. "Very well done, John."

A girl with flaxen pigtails and her mother's rounded cheeks looked at her hands. "I'm Judith," she said.

"Judith is six," John informed them both.

An older boy stuck out his hand. "I'm Peter. Ten."

Oliver shook the hand with as much sober dignity as he could summon. "Hello, Peter. I'm Oliver."

"And that's Sarah, but she's too scared to speak to you." Peter jerked his thumb at the eldest girl, whose face was practically purple with the force of her blush. "She's twelve."

Mrs Chambers re-entered the room with a large skillet filled with fried eggs and a loaf of fresh bread. As though this was a well-established routine, Peter took the bread from her and began cutting generous slices.

"Here," Mrs Chambers said, placing the thickest slice on Oliver's plate. "You'll need feeding up after that accident, love. And you too, Mrs Beaumont." She deposited another thick slice on Emily's plate.

"Emily, please," Emily said weakly.

"Then you can call me Susan." The front door crashed, and there was the sound of boots cracking against the stone. Mrs Chambers lifted her head. "That'll be your father," she said to her children, and they all settled neatly in front of their plates.

Mr Chambers entered the dingy dining room and paused by the fire to toss another log into the greedy flames. The walls were singed with soot, telling Oliver the smoke puffing into the room at regular intervals was not a rare occurrence.

"Everywhere's frozen up," the lean man said as he took his seat at the head of the table, rubbing his hands.

"What about the animals?" Mrs Chambers asked, coming to brush her hand across her husband's shoulder.

"All fine. They'll be glad to get back out into the pastures, but they'll do for now." Mr Chambers looked across at Oliver. "Your horses are recovering well, too. I've put a poultice on the sprained hock, but the blacksmith won't be able to get here any time soon for the shoe, I reckon."

Mrs Chambers leant over the table and began spooning portions of food onto each of their plates, beginning with Oliver and Emily. Along with their bread, they got three rashers of bacon and three eggs, and Mrs Chambers set some tea to steep.

The children immediately began to dig in, all talking over each other. Beside him, Emily ate quietly. As Mrs Chambers supervised little John, and Mr Chambers fielded Peter's questions about working in the fields, Oliver leant in closer.

"How early did you rise to help with breakfast?"

"As early as I would usually rise," she said in a prim voice.

"Is that designed to make me chagrined?"

"Are you capable of chagrin?"

"Only on special occasions," he said, and dipped his bread into the runny egg yolk. "You should have woken me."

"For what purpose? Can you so much as boil a kettle?"

The obvious answer was no—he had never boiled anything in his life—but he disliked the thought of being deemed incapable yet again. "I imagine I could have done with instruction."

She winced as though something pained her. "I would rather not have to endure instructing you."

"That was rude." He took some jam, placed a dollop on his bread, and offered some to her. "You know, we really ought to be nicer to one another."

She flushed, practically snatching the jam from his hands. "I am perfectly nice to you."

"Mm, I suppose you *did* sit by my bed last night," he mused, lowering his voice and watching the blush spread across her face. There was something deliciously appealing about the sight. "Smile, darling. Mrs Chambers is watching." Then, just because he could, and because he wanted to, he took Emily's hand and brought it to his mouth. Emily's fingers flexed against his, and her cheeks burned.

Mrs Chambers chuckled. "You must be proud of your wife, Mr Beaumont. She knows her way around a kitchen, that's for certain. She will keep you an excellent house."

Emily retrieved her hand, tucking it on her lap, and Oliver grinned. "I couldn't agree more," he said. "I am extremely fortunate in my choice of bride."

Chapter Ten

After breakfast, Emily fled back to their bedroom, and Oliver followed her upstairs, shutting the door behind them. Food seemed to have done him good; although he still held his arm stiffly, he seemed rather more robust than he had been.

She could not say the same for herself.

"Are you all right?" he asked.

"I'm fine."

"So you keep saying." He reached for her, and she flinched back, but he only caught her chin. A frown darkened his face as he examined her temple. "I wish I could have prevented this," he murmured. His thumb brushed her jaw, a gentle touch he appeared to have done entirely unconsciously, and Emily held still. Warmth bloomed where his skin touched hers, and she wanted to find an excuse for this sudden awareness. Perhaps it was that she was afraid of him. Or merely that someone had not touched her in this way—tenderly, as though she might break underneath him if he was not careful—in such a long time that she had forgotten how it felt.

Oliver didn't seem to notice, his gaze still fixed on her temple. He was not very much taller than her; a few inches at most. With the way he leant in, breath dancing across her face, he was almost close enough that she could kiss him.

Just as he had no doubt kissed Isabella.

That thought made her pull away. His hand dropped to his side, and she took another step back. Distance—they should have distance between them. When they returned to Dalston, if Isabella still wanted him for a husband, they would marry. Emily could not risk becoming too involved.

"I should—" She didn't know what she should do.

"You should rest," he said firmly. "I'll see to the horses and the carriage. Help me into my coat, and I'll investigate to see how matters stand."

Emily fetched the greatcoat from the corner of the room, pistol heavy in the pocket. She concealed the pistol under some blankets, though it had been some time since she had suspected Oliver of doing anything to act against her.

Oliver let out a sigh at the sight of the ruined material. "I paid a pretty penny for it, and now look at it." He hissed a breath as she draped it over his shoulders, feeding his good arm through the remaining sleeve. "Ah well. This is the price of my own foolishness, as Henry would be quick to tell me." His gaze travelled across her face, and she could have sworn something like concern flittered in his eyes before he offered her a rakish grin. "Now, wife, shall we?"

"There's no need to pretend when we're alone."

"But it's such good fun, don't you think?" He gave a roguish wink, and Emily was disgruntled to notice it was rather more pleasing to be the recipient than to watch him wink elsewhere. He took her arm, tucking it in his elbow as though they were about to promenade rather than venture back downstairs. To her horror, she discovered she rather liked the press of swell of his biceps against her fingers, and worse, enjoyed his teasing familiarity.

Evidently her head was disturbed. She could only pray she regained her sense soon.

"Sit in the drawing room awhile," he said when they were downstairs. "Rest, Emily, if you can stomach the word. I'll be checking up on you." He hesitated as he released her, and she hoped he wouldn't kiss her hand again—once had been quite enough. More than enough. Disturbingly pleasant, in fact.

"Don't hurry back," she said. "I won't miss you."

"You make for a cruel mistress," he said, but his eyes laughed at her. Before she could protest, he had vanished, and she was left to make her way to what passed for a drawing room—or perhaps a parlour. The two youngest children sat with their tongues out, tracing their letters.

The peacefulness of the household reminded her of quiet evenings around the fire when she was a child. Her father had always played with her and Isabella, often while her mother reclined on the couch with a book. The fire roared, and she sat by it, letting its warmth sink into her. Her head pounded, and she did her best to ignore the pain.

Despite her best efforts, however, her headache only worsened, as did her dizziness. By the time Mr Chambers and Oliver returned to the house, over an hour later, she felt positively unwell.

A frown darkened Oliver's expression as he took in her face.

"Are you tiring Mrs Beaumont out?" Mr Chambers demanded of his children, only to be received with choruses of *no*.

Oliver made his way to Emily's side, taking her arm and guiding her to her feet. "You look pale," he said.

"If you ever believed you were charming, you were mistaken."

"Are you well?"

"A headache, that's all." One so bad that she felt as though her head would throb so badly, it might split and spill her brains on the floor.

And then she would vomit all over them.

Oliver's hand tightened on her arm, and she realised she was swaying. "Emily," he said.

The door opened, and Mrs Chambers bustled in. "Oh, my dear," she said after taking one look at Emily. "Back to bed with you. I recognise a poorly face when I see one."

"Here," Oliver said, propping her arm over his shoulders and wrapping his good arm around her waist. "Let me help you."

"I don't need help." Emily tried to blink away the brightness of the room. "A sit-down is all I need. A little quiet."

"I'll decide what you need." He sounded stern, and she didn't have the strength to resist him as he half-carried her upstairs to the small room they shared. There, he laid her gently down on the bed, and as her aching head met the coolness of the pillow, she let out a little sigh.

"Truly, I'm all right," she said, but it was a relief to be upstairs, a relief to be able to close her eyes.

"I'll make you some nice hot broth," Mrs Chambers said.

"Oh, you shouldn't," Emily attempted to say, but her tongue tripped over the words.

"Nonsense. And after you did so much to help out this morning. If I had known—but never mind. You stay right there." She pulled out the covers and wrapped them around Emily in a motherly gesture that made her eyes sting. "I'll be back directly." On her way out of the room, she exchanged a murmured conversation with Oliver, but Emily couldn't hear it, and she had no energy to ask.

The bed beside her dipped. "You ought to have told me you were feeling so wretched," Oliver said. "I wouldn't have left you alone if I'd known. And you got up to help with breakfast, too."

"I wanted to help," she mumbled.

"Well, you've helped enough. Now, I suppose, it's my turn." His cold hand pressed against her forehead. "Sleep. I'll make sure everything is all right."

She had to concentrate on the words to make them happen. "I don't think even you can guarantee that."

"Then we shall both discover what I'm capable of."

In all his twenty-three years, Oliver had rarely been called upon to be the man in charge. He had gone as far as to avoid all sense of responsibility.

But here, with Emily unconscious and breathing softly beside him, what else could he do but step up? There was no one else to, and he had promised her he would make everything all right.

Once he was certain she would not wake, he went in search of Mr Chambers, finding him in his study. Papers were piled everywhere, and the sight made Oliver feel vaguely ill; even a farmer could not get by without knowledge of his letters.

"Ah, Oliver," Mr Chambers said, an unlit pipe in his mouth. "How is she?"

"Not good. I need a physician."

Mr Chambers removed the pipe from his mouth. "That bad?"

"She collapsed. If she's hurt—" He couldn't allow himself to think of it. "I can't let anything happen to her."

"Aye, I understand that, but you saw the roads—they're all but impassable. You can't get a cart down them."

A strange desperation came over Oliver. "Then I'll walk if I have to. Just tell me where the nearest physician is."

"Five miles along, in the nearest village." Mr Chambers sighed and shook his head. "I can't go with you, son, but if need be I can spare a horse. We've a carthorse that might make it through these drifts, and could probably bear another person on the way back. But there's no guarantee Mr Winters—that's his name—will come with you."

Oliver would force the man if need be. All this was new to him, but when he closed his eyes, he could see Emily's pale face and hear his own voice promising her he would show her what he was made of.

He hardly knew what that was—nothing good, he was certain. But he had to try.

"I'll take it," he said. "And thank you."

"I wish you'd wait for the snow to melt."

"I can't. She hit her head in the carriage—and she's so stubborn, she wouldn't tell me she was feeling ill until now." He dragged a hand through his hair, scraping it back off his forehead. His arm ached, but he fancied he could ride so long as someone helped him on and off.

No one had looked out for Emily in a long time, or so it seemed. It was about time someone did.

Responsibility sat strangely on his shoulders, but for once, though urgent, it wasn't overwhelming. He could do this.

"When can you have the horse ready?" he asked.

"I'll get him saddled up now." Mr Chambers clapped him on the shoulder. "God help you, lad. You'll need it."

Chapter Eleven

When Emily next opened her eyes, it was to see a handsome gentleman leaning over her. He had sandy curls that clung damply to his forehead, and hazel eyes that contained hints of green amongst the brown.

Could she be dreaming? No one this handsome existed in her daily life. Any second now, she would wake up in her bed with Isabella.

Pressure on her hand. Slowly, as though she moved through treacle, she glanced down to where she found his fingers wrapped around hers. He was holding her hand.

What an odd dream.

"You're awake," a male voice said.

Was she? This didn't feel how she associated being awake to feel. Her surroundings were wrong, too. And who *was* this man? She blinked, trying to bring him into focus.

"Emily," he said, and brought her hand to his lips. Everything about him looked *cold.* As though he had brought winter inside with him. "Emily, can you hear me?"

She blinked at him, puzzled. Confused. Some part of her mind recognised this man, but he had not imprinted himself on her so deeply that she would recall him no matter what. All her thoughts felt fuzzy.

Finally, a name came to her.

"Oliver," she croaked.

Relief spread across his face like fallen snow. "Thank heavens. I thought you'd forgotten me." There was something a little unsteady about his voice. She frowned at it, the world slowly coming back to her in bits and pieces. Fits and starts. She was Emily Brunton, and for some reason she was lying down on this bed instead of doing something useful. There were dishes to scrub and eggs to collect and so, so many rooms to dust. Cooking to do, fires to light, and budgeting their frugal income. They couldn't afford coal.

Oliver pressed on her shoulder. "No, Emily," he said, oddly gentle. "Don't get up."

Her tongue felt too thick in her mouth. "But there's so much to do."

"Nonsense, child," another voice said to her left. A female voice this time, motherly and anxious. "There's nothing you need do but feel better."

"I—" She couldn't collect her thoughts enough to get the words out. "Isabella."

"She's at home, waiting for you. Us," Oliver corrected a little too quickly. "She's all right."

More memories filtered through the haze in her mind. Oliver kidnapping her, trying to marry her—or rather, Isabella—and trudging through the endless snow to get here. They were pretending to be man and wife, and there was no guarantee that Isabella was fine, because if this much snow had fallen here, then it would have fallen back at Dalston, and Emily didn't know if there was enough food in the house to see them through. The chickens would continue laying, of course, and there was flour and salt and some yeast that she had picked up the last time she had gone into the village—but Isabella had never made the bread.

Isabella, Emily was starting to realise, had done very little around the house. But that only meant she would find it much harder to do everything now.

She closed her eyes, and Oliver squeezed her hand again.

"I fetched the physician," he said, leaning in closer so she could feel the hot brush of his breath against her skin. Her head throbbed. "He said you have a commotion of the brain and recommended willow bark for pain relief. And rest. But you'll be all right."

"The . . . physician?"

"Yes. I rode out in the snow." He shuddered, and she felt another burst of cold air from him. "Horrendous weather, but it was worth it." She heard that tinge of panic in his voice again, and opened her eyes to find his face just above hers, brows drawn over those bright eyes.

"Oh," she mumbled.

"More tea," Mrs Chambers declared, and bustled out of the room. Everything fell silent, but for the crackle of the fire. Emily stared up at Oliver, who sat back, his mouth a hard line.

"You wouldn't wake up," he said. "Mr Winters said you would be all right when you awoke so long as you rested, but I thought—" He shook his head. He looked older here, and she had the oddest inclination to reassure him. All this worry over *her.*

"I don't understand," she said. "You rode all the way out in this weather for me?"

He dropped his hand onto his lap. "What else was I to do? I said I would make it right, Emily."

"But your arm."

"I'll admit, it was a dashed uncomfortable journey," he said with a quick smile that didn't reach his eyes. "But Mr Winters took a look at my arm and said he couldn't have done a better job with the splint, so that's something. And it was worth it for the reassurance that you'll be all right."

Mrs Chambers re-entered the room, a tray in her hands and the promised tea atop it. "Here," she said. "I've got to get back to the house, but you let me know if there's anything you need."

Emily looked into Mrs Chambers' kindly face, and she felt a surge of guilt and affection so vast, it threatened to swallow her whole. "I'm so very grateful," she said, her voice cracking.

"Nonsense, child. You get better, you hear?" She bent and kissed Emily on the cheek before bustling to the door and leaving quietly.

Emily looked at Oliver. "And to you," she said quietly. "I am grateful. You—we barely like one another."

"Speak for yourself," he said with a hint of that roguish charm. "You are growing on me by the day."

"You make me sound like a fungus."

"A fungus wouldn't insist on making breakfast for the family while she was suffering from a brick to the head, so that is a most unfair comparison."

To her surprise, Emily cracked a smile. "I suppose I shall attempt to be more fungus-like, then."

He adopted a shocked expression. "Was that a *joke?* You truly must have hit your head."

"Very funny."

"Thank you—I like to think so." He took her hand again, toying with her fingers as though the gesture were perfectly natural. "How badly does your heart hurt?"

"Only a little."

"For you to admit any pain at all must mean you are in agony."

She rolled her eyes, which did nothing to ease her headache, and closed her fingers around his. "Help me sit up, please."

"As you wish." He slid a hand under her shoulders, and she did her best not to notice the warm press of his palm as he levered her upright. Her head pounded, and at the look on her face, Oliver leaned over to a case on the table she hadn't noticed before. "Willow bark," he explained, measuring out a little of the powder and handing it to her. "In case you have a fever. And for the pain."

At home, she had a similar little medicine box, although its ingredients had all run out some time since. After accepting the little spoonful of powder and the water to wash it down, she rested against the bed's headrest. Oliver fussed, rearranging the pillows, and when she frowned at him, he raised a brow.

"Not had someone look after you before? It's quite simple. All you have to do is sit back and let it happen, then thank me. A smile is appreciated, but optional."

All her previous amusement and humour vanished. Her chest felt too tight. When *was* the last time someone had looked after her? Not since her mother had died, that was for certain—Isabella had been too young to care for anyone at first, and then . . . Well, Emily had got into the habit of not letting her weaknesses show.

But she recalled how it felt to be cared for—the memories were quieter now, faded against the everyday worries of her life, but still there. Her mother's cool hand on her forehead. Feeding her broth. Curling up with her on the sofa, telling her endless stories as the fever sent her imagination soaring.

But back then, she had been a child, and her only responsibility had been to grow up healthy and strong. Both parents had been around to guide her.

Embarrassingly, she found tears start to her eyes, and she did her best to blink them back. This was not how she behaved. She did not have the time and space in her life for weakness.

"Emily?" Oliver looked as though he wanted to reach for her, but thought better of it. "What did I say? I'm sorry."

"I'm just thinking about my childhood. Isabella." She didn't dare give him too much of herself. "When you marry her, please don't introduce her to Lord Marlbury."

"Marlbury?" His face creased in confusion. "What's wrong with Marlbury?"

Everything. She closed her eyes, knowing she had already revealed too much with her request. "Nothing. It doesn't matter."

"Are you acquainted with him?"

In the most intimate of ways—along with half the girls in the village. "It doesn't matter," she repeated, more forcefully this time. "I should never have said anything. Thank you again for fetching the physician for me."

"I must now take him back," Oliver said. "In the meantime, I forbid you to leave this bed."

Something sparked inside her, past the misery that came from being so exhausted and aching—a certain awakening. Curiosity about what it could mean to be commanded, and how it might feel to command.

No, no, *no.*

She shook her head, dislodging the thought. Such things did not belong attached to Oliver of all people. He was destined for her sister—her *sister.* And she was destined for no one at all.

Marlbury had made sure of that.

Oliver watched her as though he could read every single one of her thoughts, perverted as they may be. His throat bobbed as he swallowed, and a line appeared between his brows.

"Forgive my wording," he said. "But I mean it. Stay where you are, Emily. *Rest.* And feel better soon." He raised a hand as though to brush it across her face, then let it drop and strode from the room.

Chapter Twelve

When Oliver returned, he ate a warming dinner with the family—precisely what he needed after such a long, frozen journey. Night was already settling over the land by the time he ventured upstairs with a pack of cards. Emily was just finishing the tray of food Mrs Chambers had brought her earlier.

She saw him and smiled, and his stomach gave an alarming twist. "You're back," she said. "Did the physician get home safely?"

"He did. And so did I." He held up the cards. "Do you fancy a game?"

She raised her brows. "Of what?"

"Whatever you like. Vingt-un? Commerce? Loo? Whist?"

"You know all the games, I take it." She settled herself more comfortably against the pillows. "Why not whist?"

"As my lady wishes." He settled himself beside her and dealt, the movements familiar by now. "Have you played before?"

She made an inarticulate sound in the back of her throat. "Our circumstances are unfortunate now, but I did not grow up in a barn, Mr Beaumont."

"You strike me as a very proper young lady."

Her cheeks reddened, and she steadfastly did not look at him as she thumbed the worn corner of her card. His father would have noted the movement, told Oliver to memorise the individual appearances of the cards and what they were so he might tell others' hands. Oliver attempted not to watch, rejecting his father's teachings, but the progress of her chapped fingers over the frayed corner proved too mesmerising to resist. "Not as proper as all that, I assure you."

Intriguing. But he knew better than to push, so he merely played the first card. "Then I take it you had a happy childhood?"

"Mm." She played another card, following suit. "For a time."

"A time?"

"My father and mother loved one another," she explained, seeming to disappear inside herself to a different place, one that held nothing good. "And they were happy together—my father, the country gentleman, and my mother, the city lady. I used to want to love the way they did."

Sensing they were on the brink of a confession, Oliver stilled, not wanting to do or say anything that might persuade her not to confide in him.

The silence stretched between them, and he cleared his throat. "But now you don't?"

Emily glanced at him, her eyes like the grey of an approaching storm, then looked away. "My mother died, and my father lost himself in his grief. Such a love—and such heartbreak. I think that was when I realised love could be poison."

Oliver almost recoiled. "Poison?"

"Do you not think? When one loves so deeply, they lose their own sense of self. Oh, my father loved my mother. He would dance her around the room, kiss her hand as though they were meeting for the first time, and deliver outrageous compliments. They were utterly in love, and when he lost her, he was utterly broken." She pressed a hand to her chest. "I was seventeen, and were it not for me, we would have lost everything. The servants stayed only because I ensured their wages were paid. And when there was no more money, I was the one to speak with them and let them go."

"Emily—"

"It rather taints the happy childhood memories, don't you think, knowing what comes after?"

Their entire acquaintance thus far, he had considered her plain, but there was something captivating about the fierceness of her expression now. "And that's why you have no intention of marrying?" he asked.

"In part, yes. Why should I offer myself to someone who could ruin me so desperately? I have no intention of falling in love with a man who could leave me and destroy what remains of my life. My father was miserable until he died, and I want none of it." She met his gaze square-on. "So no more talk of marriage, Oliver. Not for me. I won't marry, and that's the end of it. Be content with my sister, if she should still want you."

Isabella. He had almost forgotten about her; she hardly seemed to belong in this farmhouse. If he had been travelling with Isabella, he could guarantee she would not have tramped across the snowy road without complaint. She certainly would not have risen early with a head injury to make breakfast.

Isabella posed herself as a doll, content to be put on a shelf.

Oliver was no longer sure he wanted to put her there.

"Emily," he said, unsure how to broach the subject, but knowing he needed to, at least a little, dispel the illusion that Isabella was an innocent, virtuous, selfless sister. "When your mother died, what did Isabella do to help you?"

"She was ten years old—she did nothing, and I would not have asked her to."

He took her hand in his, wishing he could ease the pain of her poor chapped knuckles. "And when your father died? That was only a couple of years ago, was it not?"

"When she was fifteen, still a girl." A frown touched Emily's brows. "She is my sister, Oliver."

"Her hands did not look like this," he said softly.

"Of course they didn't. I would never have allowed it. Don't attribute our situation to her lack of initiative. I sheltered her and gave her everything I could. Why should we both suffer the folly of our father?"

"Why should you take the burden entirely on yourself?" he returned.

"Because I am the elder," she said simply. "And because I love her."

His chest twinged, and he fought to keep his anger from his face. When Isabella had mentioned her father dying, the implication had been that nothing much had changed. She had posed it as though she and Emily were equals, yet her hands had been soft, her clothes warm and elegantly made up, if a few years out of fashion.

She had never sacrificed herself for Emily, but it seemed as though Emily had done nothing but sacrifice.

"And when Isabella marries, what will you do?" Would she continue to live in her forgotten, rotting house, scraping for every penny so she might survive?

The picture pained him.

Gently, she withdrew her hand from his. "Don't pity me, Oliver. I'll be fine."

"The same fine you were when you nearly collapsed because a brick hit your head?" he demanded hotly. "Forgive me for wanting something better for you."

"We can all want something better for ourselves." She tilted her head a little. "Tell me about this brother you're fleeing from. Is he stern? Cruel?"

"I can see what you're doing, changing the subject in order to distract me."

"Is it working?"

"Are you certain you wish to know about Henry?"

"I find myself curious."

"About him and not me?" He clasped a dramatic hand to his heart, but when she remained unmoved, he sighed. "My brother is the eminently more responsible and respectable son, and he will inherit the earldom when my father passes on. He is ten years my senior, and he can be stern, but not cruel." Oliver sighed. "My father neglects all responsibilities where possible, and so my brother picked them all up. He wants me to do the same."

"Then why don't you?"

Despite himself, Oliver's ears flamed. He disliked the thought of losing whatever regard she might now hold for him, but the thought of lying to her—or playing his inadequacies off as mere carelessness and indifference—seemed equally as insupportable.

"It's not as easy as all that," he said, testing the words. "I find myself—I am ill-suited for most occupations."

"And why is that?"

He sucked on his teeth, but the worst that could happen was she would look at him with disgust, and surely that was not so bad. Bearable. "I struggle with writing," he said. "Reading, too. The letters, the words . . . Everything feels muddled in my brain when it comes to putting it on paper. I'd much rather do my thinking with my hands."

"Your hands," she repeated, looking at the hands in question.

"Being a gentleman's son doesn't involve much of that," Oliver said, sighing. "If I were the firstborn, it wouldn't matter so much, I expect, but I'm not."

"I imagine eldest sons must read and write, too. Estates require maintaining, and there are expectations." Emily frowned across at him. "Does your brother struggle with this?"

"No, and my sisters are voracious readers and letter writers. They think me indolent and lazy because I rarely reply, but doing so makes me feel . . ." It made him feel stupid. Most of his life, he had been made to feel a fool—and so he had played into it. At least then they thought he was a fool because he chose to be, not because it was born in him.

"You could tell someone," she suggested.

"I have," he said, forcing something approaching a smile. "I've told you."

Her eyes widened a fraction. "No one else?"

"I would rather my wider acquaintance is unaware of my shortcomings." He sighed, running a hand through his hair again. His childhood tutors' frustrations all played back across his head. They berated him for not trying, for refusing to learn, all while the words tangled in his head, all sense wrung from the letters.

"Your brother might understand," she said gently.

"My brother believes that sheer dogged will is enough to achieve anything one puts one's mind to, and if I fail at that, it is simply because I am not trying hard enough. Failure is weakness, and he does not allow for weakness. Thus, you see, he would have no sympathy for my predicament." He lay across the bed, angling himself to partially conceal his face and any vulnerability he felt. "When I have my estate, I will hire a steward who will do all my letter-writing for me. I shall dictate, and he shall write and read them for me, and no one need be any the wiser. I have thought it all through."

"And so you will live in fear all your life of someone finding out?"

"No one will think twice about it, darling. A man of means may be eccentric. It is only a man reliant on others who lives in danger of discovery."

"I doubt many people view it as the deficiency you do."

"You may be right." He offered her his most charming smile. "But I intend never to find out."

That night, Oliver sat at the edge of the truckle bed, his candle flickering and the sound of Emily's slow breathing filling the air. Of everyone in the world, he had confided in Emily.

And she had not looked at him as though he were deficient. A miracle. She had not judged him. She judged his excesses, yes—he had done plenty of things that he knew she would condemn, and harshly. After all, he was his father's son.

But she would not judge him based on something he could not help.

What on earth was he supposed to do with that?

He stared at her red lashes, tipped blonde. Those constellations of freckles, sprinkled so liberally across her nose and cheeks. Objectively, he knew, she was not pretty. Her mouth was too small, her nose too sharp. Her jaw too pronounced and her brows too severe.

And yet she did have beauty—the kind that only made itself known after looking. Eyes that could look like damnation or starlight. A smile that changed the entire contours of her face. The candlelight burnished her red hair and turned her skin to silk.

He wanted her.

Not in the way a man usually wanted a woman—the way he had half-heartedly wanted Isabella after she posed herself seductively before him. He wanted Emily *despite* all the reasons she had given him not to want her. Forbidden fruit, all the more desirous for being out of reach. He did not need to have her, and she certainly did not need him, but he hungered for her all the same.

Resigned, frustrated, unable to slate his lust, he lay on the bed and attempted to think of anything but her soft mouth around his cock, or the way she might look divested of her clothes, thighs wide to accommodate him.

He failed.

Just like everything else worth having in this world, she was destined never to be his.

Chapter Thirteen

When Emily woke, she was surprised to find it was morning and she had slept all through the night. Her head still ached, and the nausea hadn't abated, but despite Oliver's presence in the room, she had slept all through without fear.

Then again, perhaps that was less surprising—since her mother's death, she had slept in the same bed as Isabella near constantly. At first for comfort, and when the money began to run out, for warmth.

Now, it was alien for her to sleep in silence, without the reassuring sound of another person's steady breaths.

Oliver was no longer asleep now, however. Instead, he lounged across the bottom of her bed with discomforting familiarity. Or rather, she suspected she ought to find it discomforting.

Instead, she merely sat up, her stomach roiling. "What are you doing?"

"Did you know you snore?"

"I do not!" If she did, Isabella would most certainly have complained.

"No, you don't, but it would have been exceedingly amusing if you had." He sat up with some effort, and she saw he wore nothing but a shirt that looked remarkably worse for wear. He glanced down at it and grimaced. "Yes, I know. I look like a regular ragamuffin."

Actually, he looked somewhat debauched, but rather than disgusting her, it made her stomach give a disconcerting lurch.

No doubt an after-effect of her knock to the head. Bricks could do that, or so she hoped.

There was a patch of skin visible at the base of his neck, lighter in colour than that of his neck. Ordinarily, he wore a cravat, but that must have become too creased to be viable.

Her cheeks heated.

Either Oliver didn't notice or he made a valiant effort not to show it, because he merely said, "I hate to bother you, darling, especially when you're ill, but Mr Chambers rose early and is in the fields, and I would much rather you were to do this than Mrs Chambers."

"Do what?" she asked suspiciously.

He gave a rakish grin. "Undress me."

Shock punched through her, along with more of that liquid heat. Oh, she had undressed a man before, but only with one purpose in mind. And that was not—she could not—

"Nothing too scandalous," he hastened to reassure her. "I would do it myself, but my arm is too great an impediment." His grin didn't reach his eyes, and she realised suddenly that he was probably in a great deal of pain. After his ride through the snow yesterday, he had likely jostled his arm, and now it would be feeling all the worse for it.

"What would you like me to remove?" she asked dubiously.

"Merely my shirt. I have another ready, courtesy of our hosts." He nodded at his truckle bed. "All you need do is draw it over my arm in a manner that doesn't cause me to collapse on the ground in a mess of tears and expletives. I would, of course, be most grateful."

Yes, in the absence of Mr Chambers, the next logical person to help him would be her. And it wasn't as though she had never seen a male body before. Her fingers tingled, and she curled them into fists.

This was a practical matter. Nothing more.

He raised his gaze to her, half self-deprecating, half amused. "I know there is nothing you would like to do less, but I am prepared to beg you in order to remove this monstrosity from my body."

"It *is* a little rumpled," she allowed.

"Never has such an understatement been uttered in my life. I have never been so attired, Emily, and it is harming my ego to no end. The things I have endured in this shirt are not to be spoken of again, and I must wear something clean for the sake of my dignity if nothing else."

Emily pressed a hand to her mouth, suppressing a laugh. "How dramatic you are. Very well. Come here." She beckoned to him, and he came closer, shuffling until he sat beside her, his legs dangling over the edge of the bed, his face turned in her direction. His broken arm had been strapped to his torso, underneath his shirt, and he held himself stiffly.

"This may hurt," she warned.

"I'm ready."

She reached down to the hem of his shirt, which lay untucked. Her knuckles grazed the material of his breeches, and she exhaled before easing it up over his stomach.

Skin. She did her best not to notice, but that was almost impossible when he was so close, heat soaking into her. With her other hand, she reached around him a little, ensuring the shirt didn't catch on his arm as she continued to draw it up.

He remained utterly still, not even seeming to breathe as she reached his shoulders. The muscles of his stomach were tense, she saw as she glanced down, and there was a tantalising line of hair leading down into his breeches.

She swallowed.

The last man she had seen divested of his clothes had been Marlbury, but they had both been seventeen, just coming into adulthood. This was very different—Oliver had left boyhood behind, and she had not known how very different a man would be. Slightly more filled out, though Oliver was by no means as bulky as some men could be.

He reached his hand out and gripped the shirt, tugging it free of his head. Emily jumped, relinquishing her hold, and flushed. She had been staring. Like some kind of lovestruck fool, she had been gawping at this poor man when all he wanted was her assistance.

"I—" She cleared her throat. "Do you need anything else? How is your arm?"

"Uncomfortable, but it's well secured." He rose, the shirt in one fist, and she glimpsed his back—the dip of his spine and the shifting muscles of his shoulder blades. Her mouth was dry, her heart pounding too fast. "I'm sorry," he said, not facing her.

"No, no. Do you need me to—"

"No," he said quickly, his back still to her as he picked up the new shirt and shook it out. "I can manage."

Well, she *had* hardly helped. It was hardly surprising he didn't want her to stare at him any longer. How humiliating—she had always assumed she was better than this, but this morning she had been so utterly unprepared for a man in her space. A man, moreover, requiring her to take off his shirt.

With some visible difficulty, he wiggled into the shirt and tucked it into his breeches—Emily averted her gaze for that—and eventually stood mostly decent again.

"I'll ask Mrs Chambers to bring you some breakfast," he said, finally turning, a slight flush on his cheekbones. So she had embarrassed him too. Wonderful. "Until later." He gave an oddly formal bow and left the room.

Emily put her head in her hands.

Oliver stood with his back against the door, breathing slowly.

What had happened to the shrew he had been so unwilling to consider marrying? Nothing about her had changed, but waking to the sound of her soft breaths had been akin to torture, and she hadn't flinched at the prospect of removing his shirt.

No, if anything . . .

He couldn't afford to think about that. That way lay nothing good. She was strictly off-limits, and if he convinced himself that she wanted him in any capacity, it would be so much harder to hold back.

No, he would have to be a gentleman about this. And under no circumstances ask her to remove another item of his clothing. That had been a mistake, if his body's reaction was any indication.

Squaring his shoulders, he approached the stairs, determined to find some chores he could do before going back to visit Emily. When he did, he wanted to appear perfectly normal. That way, she would not think he was placing undue emphasis on what had passed between them.

If he was lucky, she would not have noticed how much he had enjoyed her removing his shirt.

What he really needed was a release. But, at a push, hard labour would do.

Anything to take his mind off how much he wanted the prickly, unapproachable, unexpectedly appealing lady in the bed upstairs.

Chapter Fourteen

The next few days passed uneventfully. Emily remained in bed, in part because she had no desire to leave, and in part because Mrs Chambers and Oliver insisted on it. While he left on occasion to visit the household and help with chores, he still spent most of his time with her, either reading or playing cards.

By the end of the third day, she was heartily sick of whist and Vingt-un, and was relieved to wake the next day to a clear head and hunger pangs.

Finally.

Oliver still snored in the truckle bed, so she dressed as quietly as she was able, hoping not to disturb him. Although he had treated her precisely the same as he always had since the shirt-removal incident, she couldn't get the image of his torso from her mind.

That little line of hair snaking down to—

She shook her head, trying to force the image from her head as she slipped from the door. But she had only reached the dining room when Oliver tumbled down the stairs after her, resplendent in shirtsleeves once again. His hair was carelessly dishevelled in a way that made every muscle in her body tighten.

"Emily!" he said, coming to a stop before her. "What are you doing out and about?"

"It's about time I had some fresh air."

"Outside? But it's freezing." His eyes narrowed. "I don't like it."

"You don't have to," she said. "I'm doing it anyway."

He clucked his tongue in irritation. "You are *incapable* of rest."

"I've had three full days of rest, Oliver, and if you force me back upstairs into that tiny room, I might lose my mind."

He heaved a sigh. "Fine. In that case, allow me the honour of showing you around. You'll need all your wits about you to escape Clarabella."

"Who on *earth* is Clarabella?" she asked, mystified.

"You'll know when you see her." He grinned and released her arm. "After breakfast, Emily."

"I don't appreciate this ordering me about you're doing."

Mrs Chambers rounded the corner from the kitchen, and Oliver immediately shifted his hold on Emily, drawing her closer against his body. The sudden proximity and his warmth startled her that she didn't move away, not even when he rested a light hand on her waist. Her face flamed. Being touched like this made her feel dizzy all over again, but this time she suspected it had nothing to do with being hit in the head with a brick.

Drat it all. She'd thought she'd overcome this strange fascination with him, but here she was, her heart fluttering as though she were seventeen all over again.

She stepped back, and Oliver let her. "I'm feeling much better," she announced, trying to look utterly unperturbed. "I'd like to go outside today."

"Oh good," Mrs Chambers said, and beamed at Oliver. "Doris will be glad to see you."

"Doris?" Emily stared at Oliver. "First Clarabella, then Doris."

"Ah, you'll like Doris," Mrs Chambers said, "but Clarabella is a nasty piece of work. You watch out for her, now." And then, as if she had not said something utterly bemusing, she bustled past Emily and into the parlour.

Emily rubbed her temples. "Am I still dreaming?"

He laughed. "Have some toast, and I'll show you."

After breakfast, little John threw himself affectionately into Emily's lap. "Did you know Clarabella chased Mr Beaumont half across the yard?" he asked.

Emily glanced at Oliver. More and more intriguing. "I did not," she said.

Oliver heaved a mock-pained sigh. "You've ruined the surprise." To her, he added, "Clarabella is a pig."

"I named her," John said proudly.

"She sounds as though she might be a delight, but she is a menace," Oliver said, his mouth twitching as though he could not quite keep hold of his straight face. "That beast ate one of my boot's tassels."

Emily had another strange desire to laugh. Oliver sparked that desire inside her more and more the longer she remained in his company. "Serves you right for wearing such expensive boots in the farmyard."

"I knew you would take her side!"

Emily could not hold her smile inside any longer. "Have you yet to make peace with poor Clarabella?"

"Poor Clarabella? I have to take my life into my hands every time she is released from her pen."

"Clarabella likes *me*," John said, snuggling closer. Emily, who had not been subject to the unconstrained affection of small boys before, and who found she liked it very much indeed, held him tighter. "I think she doesn't like Mr Beaumont."

"That much is obvious," Oliver said, and held out the affected leg, boot sans one tassel. "I even bribed her with a carrot, but my overtures were ruthlessly overturned."

"Perhaps she doesn't like carrots?" Emily suggested.

"She eats rotten turnips," Oliver said. "The idea that she could dislike carrots is preposterous."

John squealed with laughter, both at the sight of the afflicted boot and the exaggerated woe in Oliver's voice, and Emily chuckled. Oliver looked rather overtly pleased with himself.

Mrs Chambers summoned John to do his letters and plied Emily with warm layers galore—mittens and cloaks and scarves—until she was so thickly bundled, she could barely see. Then, when both Oliver and Mrs Chambers were satisfied she would not catch hold, he offered her his arm.

"Allow me."

She stepped outside on his arm and inhaled deeply. In Dalston, not a day went by without venturing outside at least once, either to the market or some other shop in the village, or else feeding the chickens and tending to her little vegetable garden with whatever skill she possessed.

So far, she had mastered potatoes, turnips and cabbages, and thought she could go the rest of her life without eating more of any.

"How very gallant," she said as Oliver supported her.

"It may surprise you to learn that I *was* taught how to be a gentleman."

"Did you forget or merely disregard those lessons?"

"You wound me! One must first know the rules in order to break them."

"If you expect me to be impressed with your flagrant lack of respect for rules, then you have missed your mark."

He shot her a mischievous glance. "Why, darling, I didn't think I was *capable* of impressing you, but I'm pleased to learn I was wrong. How, pray, could I achieve such a notable event?"

"You're being ridiculous," she said.

"I'm not! If I *could* impress you, I should make the attempt immediately."

She didn't say that he had already impressed her with the readiness he had thrown himself into the hurdy-gurdy lives of these people; how stoic he had been in the face of his injury; how selfless he had been when he had ridden out to find a physician for her. If she did, she would be voicing things that she didn't dare acknowledge even to herself.

"It is an impossibility," she said.

He clasped his hand to his chest. "Shall I ever recover from this blow to my heart?"

"Your self-esteem, perhaps. Your heart remains untouched."

"Does it?" He turned to her, eyes gleaming with an oddly golden light today, like tiger's eye. "Perhaps I find your cruelty refreshing."

Her heart skipped a beat, and she told it very firmly to stop.

"We barely like one another," she reminded him.

"As I have told you before, that is no longer true. You may not like me, but *I* like *you*. You may deny it all you like, but there's no hiding from the truth." He turned her, leading her around the house to the back garden, where chickens fluttered and pecked in a vegetable patch, which sported the winter vegetables of leek, winter cabbage, and sprouts. "Now," he said, stopping by the gate, "let me introduce you to Doris."

With a squawk, one of the chickens abandoned the soil she was pecking in and ran headlong for them. Oliver opened the gate, beckoning Emily inside, and bent to greet the bird. He stroked her head and picked her up, cradling her in his good arm. Her feathers were brownish bronze, and she had beady black eyes.

"Hello, Doris," Emily said, removing her glove so she could better run a finger along Doris's clipped feathers. "She likes you," she said to Oliver.

"That's what one gets for feeding the chickens. I also have it on excellent authority that Doris loves everyone. She's an anomaly among chickens—she enjoys being held."

At the sight of Oliver crouching in the dirt, holding a chicken of all things, speaking about them as though he were intimately acquainted with them, made a lump form in Emily's throat. "Have you kept chickens before?"

"Not in the slightest, but John has been keeping me apprised." He grinned up at her from where he crouched. "And I haven't been spending *all* my time with you, you know. Sometimes I've even been helpful."

Who was this man? Certainly not the same one who had taken her to Gretna Green. "Did you enjoy helping out?"

"On occasion, when it involved chickens and pigs and horses. I used to steal away into my father's stables all the time. Asked the head groom to take me on as a stable hand. He never did, but he let me pretend sometimes."

"You wanted to be a stable boy?"

He shrugged, and Doris fluttered in protest. "It seemed a simple occupation. Every boy loves horses—and very few like expectations."

Oliver did not strike her like every boy. His childhood could not have been happy if he'd sought solace in the stables.

"If I could be a farmer's son, I would be," Oliver said, letting Doris go.

She nudged his shoulder. "You like mud that much, do you?"

He laughed, nudging back, and her stomach fluttered the way Doris's feathers had. "Come on," he said. "Let's brave Clarabella and see how the road is doing. I think the snow is melting."

Yes, the snow. The road. Soon, they would be leaving here, and all these confusing emotions would stay behind. All this was merely a product of their proximity; once she had some space and time to herself, she would come to her senses.

Back around the other side of the house, Oliver checked the gate to the pigpen was closed, and led her down the driveway to the road. As before, spread between the hedges, the dent where Oliver and his carthorse had passed a few days prior now partially refilled.

This time, however, there was the steady drip, drip, drip of melting snow. It would not be long now until the road was passable enough for them to walk it, if they so chose. Not that much longer until other vehicles could potentially pass by.

Their adventure was nearly at an end.

Oliver took her bare hand in his; she'd failed to replace her glove. She'd always hated her hands—scrubbing sheets and pots with their caustic soap always made her skin chap and crack, but he touched her as though she were made of glass.

Even Marlbury had not made her feel delicate before.

She ought to pull free, but it had been such a long time since someone had comforted her, she couldn't quite bring herself to retreat from his warmth. She was a cold hearth, and now finally there was fire.

At what point was this wrong?

She closed her eyes.

"Emily?" he said softly.

She was relieved to be returning home—Isabella needed her, and she needed to find her equilibrium again. No more handsome gentlemen and long-forgotten desires.

"I expect we'll be able to leave tomorrow," she said, pulling her hand free. Something in the region of her chest hurt, and she steadfastly didn't look at his face. What she needed from him now was his levity, an assurance that he felt nothing at the prospect of them parting. Then she could convince herself that she, too, felt nothing.

But he just stared at her steadily, as though he was searching for the right words to say.

A hoarse, squeaking bellow sounded from behind them. The moment shattered, and when Emily turned, she almost laughed.

A large, pot-bellied pig stood in the centre of the yard, a gate behind it swinging open. Its head swung low, and it made another furious grunting sound that made the hair stand up on her arms.

She had seen plenty of pigs in her life, but she had never seen one that so embodied the concept of rage.

Oliver let out a laugh, and shifted his hold on her hand, gripping her more firmly. "This is Clarabella."

"So I'd presumed." She tensed as the pig grunted again. "Will she chase us?"

"Almost certainly. When I give the word, run, or she will be sure to eat an item of your clothing."

She could not have done this with anyone else. And even though the pig had to be two hundred pounds of solid muscle, something airy lifted inside her—the opposite of the dread that had been plaguing her just moments ago.

"Ready?" Oliver asked.

Clarabella glared at them both. If Emily's imagination were a little less logical, she might have thought her eyes gleamed red. She squeezed Oliver's hand. "Ready."

Clarabella put her head down and snorted.

Oliver launched forward. "*Run.*"

Chapter Fifteen

This was, regrettably, not the first time Oliver had run from a pig. This pig, in particular. Clarabella was surprisingly fast, but although she was an ornery demon, she never did any damage that he could see—except to his boot. And, as John liked to point out, that was entirely his fault for his boot having tassels in the first place.

Beside him, Emily let out a shocked laugh as she slipped and skidded across the ice. Her face had regained some of its colour, and he found himself captivated by her.

Her laugh. He hadn't heard her laugh before—not like this, as though she had no choice but to be happy—and he felt as though he would do almost anything to hear it again.

If the only impact he had on her life was to remind her how to have fun, then he would consider it a job well done.

Her hand in his, he dragged them both across the yard. Clarabella charged from behind, and Mr Chambers emerged from the side of the house.

"Who let the pig out again?" he yelled into the air, and lunged after the disobedient swine.

Oliver was breathless with mirth and exertion as he pulled Emily around the side of the house, ignoring the ice underfoot until it finally got the better of him. His legs slipped out from under him, and he twisted, jerking Emily with him. Unable to use his other hand for balance, his shoulder crashed into the wall. Emily lost her balance entirely and landed headfirst in a snowdrift.

The world swayed. Pain erupted from his arm, and he gritted his teeth through the first few waves as he sought to steady himself enough to assist Emily to her feet. Only, by the time he had regained his equilibrium, she was already back on her feet, her hair wet with melting snow.

"Are you all right? Your head." He reached for her, but she laughed, backing away with her arms raised.

"Stop fussing! You're like an old lady."

An accusation he could say with certainty had never been levelled at him before.

The pain in his arm finally eased to manageable levels, and he bent, scooping a handful of snow and tossing it at her. She coughed in shock, but then a wicked light appeared in her eyes, and she acquired a handful of snow of her own. However, instead of tossing it into his face, she came closer, holding the snow aloft like a threat.

"Emily—" he started, but he didn't get any further before she took the handful of snow and shoved it down his neck. The icy cold sank into his bones, and drops trailed down his back under his shirt. Her laugh broke free, and before he could help himself, he caught her wrist, tugging her closer.

How could he ever have thought her plain? The chaos of her curls vied against the vivid flush of her cheeks. She could have been a fairy from the glens. Wild, utterly untameable, and as likely to curse you as kiss you.

He very much wanted to kiss her.

Half-melted snow slipped from her cheek. He looked from it to her eyes. She was still smiling, but her laugh had faded into something he thought he could read—he hoped he could read.

"Your laugh," he said, his voice low and intense. He wanted to say something to ease the tension, but nothing came to mind. All he knew was this fairy of a woman was close enough to taste, and he craved to know how she felt against his tongue.

She scoffed, her eyes searching his. "There's nothing special about my laugh."

"Rare things are always precious."

"I laugh," she insisted. "You make it impossible not to." As she said the words, her brows drew together.

"No, don't frown." He released her wrist and brought his thumb to the faint line the expression produced. "Not today. Not now."

"Oliver—"

He slid his hand to her jaw, waiting for the moment she pushed him aside. He was playing with fire, he knew, but he couldn't help herself. If she told him to stop, he would, but until then—so long as she gave him permission . . .

His thumb traced a path to her lips, and her breath shuddered.

"Tell me to stop and I will," he said, his voice rough. "Tell me to go inside and never approach you like this again, and I *will*, but damn it, Emily, I want to kiss you."

"We can't," she whispered.

His thumb traced the line of her bottom lip again. "Is that a no?"

She blinked, melted snow gathering on her eyelashes. Her fingers closed around his shirt, but instead of pushing him back, she merely held on, her knuckles turning white. He waited, giving her time to tell him to stop.

Instead, she closed her eyes.

He leaned in, pressing his mouth to her temple. Her fingers traced up to the bare skin of his neck. He shivered.

"I would like—very much like—to kiss you," he said, speaking the words against her skin. "Will you allow me that honour?"

She tilted her chin up to him in invitation. But he didn't dare move until she whispered, the words barely audible, "What are you waiting for?"

He almost groaned with relief as he took her mouth with his.

This was not his first time kissing a lady. London and Oxford had been rife with ladies eager to be kissed, and he had practiced his art on their willingness. Before, it had been perfectly pleasant. Enjoyable. A precursor to other acts that he enjoyed still more.

This was his first time being annihilated by a kiss.

Perhaps it was the degree to which he had wanted her before they reached this moment. He could not recall this level of need before—he had needed to feel the way her lips moulded against his, the way her mouth opened to accommodate him. The wet heat of her tongue against his.

By God, he had dreamt of this, in that vague, unsubstantiated way a man fantasised about a woman he could never have—and none of his imaginings came even close to the reality. His attraction to her had come on so suddenly, he couldn't pinpoint the moment he had gone from thinking her plain to thinking her beautiful, in her own way.

He wanted to see every inch of her—but not in a merely carnal way. She kept secrets behind those big grey eyes, and he wanted to uncover them all. He wanted to know all of her, every piece that she did not give up so readily.

There was no reason to his desire.

All he knew was he burned for her. Soft lips, warm skin, a tongue that teased at his, mimicking acts he had no doubt she knew intimately. He cupped the back of her neck, desperate to drink more of her in. Her hands gripped his coat more firmly, tugging him closer.

Hearing her laugh had been the thing to undo him. Not practiced seduction—no, it had been the sound of her joy. A woman who laughed not because she ought, but because she couldn't help herself.

"Emily," he murmured against her mouth before sinking into another drugging kiss. Without meaning to, he ground against her, his hips pinning hers to the wall of the house. The accompanying rush of desire, of pleasure half unrealised, left him dizzy.

He was but a man, and there was only so much blood his brain could stand to lose until thinking became an impossibility.

She froze under him.

He had thought nothing could stop him, but that was enough; he shoved back, panting. They stared at one another. Her lips were red, her eyes luminous. Tendrils of wet hair plastered to the side of her face.

She was everything that was lovely.

"Isabella," she said. One word, and it was as though someone had tossed a bucket of cold water over his head, drenching him. Desire faded, replaced by an understanding that made him grit his teeth.

He could not marry Isabella.

When he had felt nothing for anyone else, it had been an easy decision. She wanted a wealthy husband and escape; he wanted a pretty wife and to hide from his responsibilities. Neither had wanted to be better than their circumstances had made them.

Now, everything had changed. He did want to be better—Emily made him want to be better. He wanted to make her laugh, to ease her burdens and care for her in ways no one else had.

He did not want to marry Isabella.

No, he *could* not. No man could stomach marrying one sister when he craved the other. Any respect he might have had for Isabella had disintegrated after learning how absolutely she had taken advantage of Emily.

"Emily," he said, not knowing how to tell her, but knowing he must.

"We must think of Isabella." Emily paced past him, the ice preventing her from striding. "She deserves better than a sister who would betray her in this way."

"You haven't betrayed her, Em."

"How can you say that when I kissed the man she is going to marry?" She touched her lips. "I *asked* you to kiss me."

"If you want to get technical about it, darling, I rather suspect I begged."

"What do the nuances matter when the action itself was so cruel?"

"She doesn't know, and she won't. And besides, it doesn't matter—"

"Of course it matters!" She placed the back of her hand against her forehead in a gesture of frustration. "How could I have been so selfish?"

He almost laughed at the idea of Emily being selfish when it was Isabella who had been selfish all their lives. And now he was being selfish, because he wanted everything.

"Listen to me," he said, reaching for her arm and tugging her to a stop. She looked up at him, cheeks flushed and eyes shining with shame. "It doesn't matter what you do or don't do, or how you behave, because I can't do it."

"What do you mean? You can't do what?"

He took a deep breath. "I can't marry Isabella."

Chapter Sixteen

The words sounded as though they had come from far away. She grasped them, struggling to make sense of what he had said. When she'd first heard of the match, she had been disappointed, but now she knew better—she knew what sort of man Oliver was, and what a good husband he would make.

She could not allow any man to break her sister's heart the way Marlbury had broken hers.

"Don't say that," she said, the words thick. "You have to marry her. You *promised*."

"I did, before I knew what it was I was promising." He gripped her hand, but she tugged it free. "But we are not engaged. There's nothing between us but—"

"But *your word*."

"We made idle plans when I thought money alone could bring harmony to an ill-suited marriage. That is all, and nothing more. There is no formal agreement, no arrangement, and what little expectation there may be will soon be repaired. I'll admit my actions are not what I might have hoped they would be, but that does not make your sister an innocent maiden left to perish in her own grief."

"An ill-suited marriage?" She remembered Marlbury, those heady summer days where he had wooed her with sunshine and his father's whisky. He'd promised her love and fidelity, and with him, she had thought she had a future. Happiness.

That had lasted just a few weeks, but in her young mind, she had spent a lifetime in his company.

She recalled the way he had lain her back on the picnic rug and pushed her skirts up to her waist, kissing away her protests and telling her love made him do it.

Love made him do so many things—and she had welcomed it, believing that this was the highest form of adoration.

But that had not been the worst part. No—that had been later, when he had stopped coming. And then, when she had cornered him, desperate and heartbroken, he had attributed his lies to her consumption of the whisky. Told her that she could never be tempting to a man like him; compared her ailing charms to those of other girls who had pleased him better; claimed that she was delusional to think he would ever want to be with someone like her.

Isabella could not suffer the same.

"Yes, ill-suited," Oliver said, frustration in his voice now. "And ill-conceived. After so long in my company, do you truly think I am well matched with your sister?"

"You thought so yourself before we kissed!" she snapped. Shame sank deep inside her, turning desire to ash. In that moment, when he'd been standing over her, she'd been reminded of how it felt to want something—for so long, she had not allowed herself the luxury of need, but it had found her then. Need and heat.

Marlbury had seduced her with pretty words and promises, but Oliver had made her feel as though he wanted her just as much in return, and the feeling was intoxicating.

She shut it down.

"The kiss?" He tossed up his hands. "The problem is not that we kissed, Emily. It's that I wanted to kiss you. I have been wanting to kiss you for days now, and if you do not think that an impediment to your sister's happiness, then I do."

Emily covered her face with her hands. This was her fault. *She* was the impediment to Isabella's happiness; if she had not got in the way of Oliver's plans, Isabella would be married by now—and yes, seventeen was too young for marriage, but Oliver was a good man, far better than she'd imagined. Her sister would have been cared for.

An impatient sigh, then Oliver's hand wrapped gently around her wrist. "Emily," he said, soft again. "You can't blame yourself for this."

"On the contrary. Without me, none of this would have happened."

"Your sister would have been desperately unhappy, as would I." His thumb swiped across her skin, and she remembered belatedly that she had not replaced her glove since stroking Doris. "Time has been her enemy, not you. I arrived in Dalston angry at my brother and determined to spite him, and Isabella was a means to that end."

"You wanted to marry so you would not have to admit to your deficiency," she said, muffled through her hands.

"Yes, true. And yet I would not have confided that truth in her the way I did to you. Now I've had some time to think and reflect—and be here, with nothing to do but help with the chores and speak with you—I see how much of a damn *fool* I was."

"Isabella deserves better."

"Perhaps," he said, his voice wry. "But I fancy she will find herself someone new in time, and will spare me very little thought. If I were a pig farmer, no matter how handsome, she would not have looked twice. Believe me when I say she doesn't love me. And she knows I don't love her."

Isabella, that conniving? Could she believe it? Isabella had never wanted the life they shared, and if she had come across Oliver in Dalston, so evidently a gentleman, young and handsome and ready to be flirted with—was it so surprising that she had taken the opportunity fate had presented to her?

It was just . . . Emily had seen the glow on her face when she came back from meeting with him, and she had recognised it; she had worn the same one when meeting Marlbury.

She freed her wrist from his hold and paced away from him. Distance, that was what she needed—distance and clarity.

"Em," Oliver said, pleading now. "Even if she had intended to fall in love with me, she barely saw me. I have spent more time with you than I ever did with her, and are you in love with me?"

She whirled. "I am not my sister! Nor am I seventeen."

"That doesn't change reality. I saw her a handful of times, barely so much as kissed her, and I hardly promised her the world. We talked of a runaway marriage and of coming into my inheritance, and I assure you that is what she loved far more than me."

Emily pressed a hand to her chest, feeling the rapid pounding of her heart. Fear coursed through her veins, that Isabella might endure the same things she had—but reason and logic soon took hold. When she had been with Marlbury, she had sneaked away to spend every second of every sunlit day with him. Their mother had, in retrospect, been ill, and no one had paid attention to her comings and goings. There were no chores, no responsibilities, and her governess paid far more attention to her sister.

The same could not be said for Isabella now.

Emily had lain with Marlbury, several times, offering him her body as well as her heart. He had promised her everything, and she would have taken him for her husband even if he *had* been a pig farmer, because love did not come armed with conditions.

"For the first time in my life, I feel as though I have a purpose, being here," he said. "Working on the farm, *doing* something worthwhile with my time. It is a new sensation, admittedly, but one I enjoy. Isabella wants me to be an idle lord whose purpose in life is to buy her pretty dresses and take her to elegant balls. But that's not the life I want."

"Then what *do* you want?" A new fear entered her heart, and her next words were jagged and sharp. "I won't marry you."

He held up both hands. "Did you hear me asking you to? One kiss does not a marriage make. Besides, you told me you had no intention of marrying. Love is poison, remember?"

She let out a sigh of relief, her shoulders loosening. If he was telling the truth and Isabella didn't love him, she might be disappointed by his changed mind, but at least she would not go through the same heartbreak she had.

Love *was* poison.

She prayed if Isabella ever came to love, it would be in moderation, and when she was old enough to truly comprehend the risks.

"If Isabella does love you, you ought to keep your promise to her," she said.

"Is that what you want?" He came to her now, cupping her face in his hand and looking deep into her eyes. His were every colour under the sun, split through with gold. "Even if it makes her unhappier in the long run?"

"I—" This came too close to telling him everything, and she didn't know if she was quite ready for that. She felt raw, as though he had taken a knife and carved her open. But he had confided in her; perhaps she could do the same, at least a little. "I loved someone once. I thought he loved me in return, but he was—he was cruel, and he left me when someone new caught his fancy. He broke my heart, and my mother broke my father, and I refuse to let Isabella go through anything similar."

Oliver's eyes darkened, but his hand remained gentle on her face. "She won't. I swear it."

Strangely, despite everything—he was Marlbury's friend, after all—she believed him. "All right."

"Tell me something." He inhaled deeply, as though steeling himself, then said, "Was it Marlbury?"

The air rushed from her lungs, but she had given him too many clues; of course he had put them together. There was no point lying to him now. "Yes," she said.

"Did he hurt you?"

"Only with his lies."

Oliver nodded, a precise gesture, as though he wanted very much to say more, but held himself back. "What happened?"

She shook her head. "Not now."

"Later?" When she didn't respond, his gaze searched her eyes, as though he could prise the answers from her that way. "Let me help you, Em. I know you may not have the best opinion of me, but I want to be there."

Just as he had sat by her bedside when she'd been ill.

How could she deny him this?

"All right," she said, the words a promise. "Later."

Chapter Seventeen

Later came around torturously slowly. After her confession that Marlbury—the same Marlbury whom Oliver had spent any number of drunken hours with—had been the one to ruin Emily's hopes and dreams—he found himself unable to sit still. While she helped inside the house, he rubbed down the horses with his good hand, ignoring the ache in the other.

No wonder she had responded so badly to Oliver's declaration that he wouldn't marry Isabella. If only she could see her sister for who she was—a conniving, selfish girl who was far more invested in looking out for herself than for protecting Emily. Not once had Isabella asked Oliver to take Emily with them once they were married. He had presumed they would, but that had never been a condition of their marriage. All she had daydreamed about was visiting London and keeping a carriage and all the new gowns and shoes she would buy. If he had insisted on Emily staying in that empty old house on her own, he had a sneaking feeling Isabella would agree.

Perhaps with the intention of sending Emily some of her pin money—but he knew that such resolutions would have fallen by the wayside quickly enough.

And that was the kind of wife he had been happy to accept.

What folly.

After dinner, Oliver endured several hours in the drawing room until Mrs Chambers finally sent Emily to bed, and he followed on her heels.

Later had arrived.

He wanted to miss none of it.

Only when he closed the door behind them did she turn to look at him, sinking onto the bed and bracing herself against her hands. He meant to ease into the subject slowly, gently, to reassure her that he would not judge no matter what had happened between them.

Instead, he said, "Did he force you into bedding him?"

She blinked, clearly flummoxed, then shook her head, a slight smile springing to her lips. "Ah, so you know I lay with him, then."

"I suspected." He had for a while now. "So he promised you marriage in exchange for that? And then abandoned you?" He paced about the room, trying and failing to shelve his anger. This was no place for it, but he despised any man who took advantage of a woman in such a way.

With Isabella, he had offered her marriage, but he had said nothing of love, and he had not taken her innocence.

"Do you think less of me for it?" she asked, watching him.

He stopped. "No, not in the slightest."

"Even though I am a woman who has been compromised?"

His laugh was short and harsh. "Then I suppose so have I. Do you think less of me for it?"

"No." A frown touched her brow. "Although I would have done if you'd seduced my sister."

"I suspect it would be more that she would have seduced me," he said dryly. "But fear not—her virtue is safe."

Emily nodded slowly, looking down at her fingers, splayed on her lap. "Marlbury didn't get me with child, if that's what you're wondering," she said. "We weren't careful—back then, I didn't understand the need to be, and I hardly thought it mattered, seeing as I believed we would be married. After he left, I worried I might be, but . . ."

But her bleeds had come.

"When I knew I wasn't, I cried for three days," she said, her voice matter-of-fact. Oliver ached for her. "But in time, especially after Mother's death, I was relieved. I didn't have the time for ruination."

"God, Em," he murmured.

"I don't need your pity." She met his gaze, her expression unyielding. "I made a mistake and I believed him, but those days are over."

In other words, she had no intention of giving herself to anyone else.

Not marrying, he could understand, in a way—if she feared falling in love, she wouldn't want to expose herself to something that could so risk that aim. And although he had seen some excellent examples of happy marriages with his siblings, his parents stood as proof that not all unions were felicitous.

But he did think it sad that she would never open herself to physical affection. The way she had kissed him—she had hungered for it. That had not been the kiss of someone who disliked such things.

"All right," he said, and came to sit beside her on the bed. "I don't pity you. But you are limiting yourself, darling."

She raised a brow, and he wanted to laugh at the sudden chill in her expression. "Are you suggesting you think marriage the only course of action open to me?"

"You misunderstand me entirely." He possessed himself of her hand and kissed the back of it. "You may remain a maid for the rest of your days if you so choose. What *I* am saying is that you should not let Marlbury deny you future joy." He turned her hand over and kissed her palm, waiting to see if she would push him away. "Future *pleasure*."

Her fingers clenched, but she didn't pull away. "What are you saying?"

"Well, we have already established your sister doesn't love me and I don't love her, and we will not be marrying." He turned his attention to her other hand, and she allowed him. "I enjoyed kissing you, and I rather suspect you enjoyed kissing me. So, I have a proposition for you."

"You would like to ruin me?" she asked, the wry note in her voice not quite disguising its breathiness.

"Fie, how ungenerous." He laughed against the tips of her fingers, then drew them gently into his mouth, sucking them deeper. "I'm asking for another kiss, Emily. Just one." He looked up at her. "What do you say?"

The problem was, Emily wanted very much to say yes.

The sensible part of her brain warned her that such things were dangerous—she knew better than to give herself to a man, even one such as Oliver. But she had spent seven years being nothing but sensible, denying herself everything she could ever want. For seven years, she had been drowning, everything good sinking to the depths of the ocean. When Lord Marlbury had left her, she'd thought he'd taken her desire with him. All that had been left was dust and her broken heart.

This man had reassembled those broken pieces. Finally, for the first time in years, she felt like flesh and blood again.

What was the harm in giving in? Allowing herself one bright moment before she returned to the drudgery of her life? If she refused him, he wouldn't go home and marry Isabella; all she would be doing was denying herself.

She had been so tired, so cold, for so long.

"A kiss?" she asked.

"Nothing more."

"A kiss always leads to something more."

His eyes sparked, and she knew he wanted to. But all he said was, "Only if you choose it to."

This didn't have to change anything. There could be intimacy without affection. After all, Mercy Briggins had been known to take the blacksmith's son here and there to mutual satisfaction until she'd married, and neither had seemed to pine after the other.

If Mercy could do it, why could she not?

"I would never hurt you the way Marlbury did," Oliver said. "And I mean that whether you allow me to kiss you or cast me from your sight." At the twitch of her lips, his own smile broke free. "Which would look odd, but I assure you, it's not unheard of between married couples."

"I could hardly send you away here."

"There's a perfectly serviceable sofa downstairs. I assure you, I've slept on worse."

"With a broken arm?"

"It barely hurts any more. I'd be perfectly comfortable."

"Are you *trying* to convince me to send you away?"

"Of course I'd rather stay." His grin turned lopsided and charming. "I would *rather* kiss you right here on this very comfortable bed, but I'll settle for sleeping elsewhere if that's what you'd prefer."

"You," she said as severely as she could, "are a terrible flirt."

"And here I thought I was rather good at it."

She gave in and laughed, one hand covering her face. How he achieved this, she didn't know; how could he make her laugh with such *ease*? When so much of her life had felt like darkness, he came along with the light.

His smile faded as she looked back at him, and her stomach tumbled at the expression in his eyes. Deep, dark, the colour of midnight.

"What do you want, Emily?" he asked, and heaven help her, she was tempted. There was nothing but the light of a candle between them, no one to witness them but God himself, and she suspected He had already forsaken her.

Could she be selfish?

She was beginning to think she could. Just for today.

As though sensing her amenability to the proposal, he brought his thumb to her mouth once again, the rough pad scraping across her bottom lip. It oughtn't to have been so appealing, and yet she was instantly burning, too hot even in the cool of the room.

"I won't do anything until you tell me I can," he said. "You have the control."

Victor Marlbury, the man who had broken her heart and taken her virtue, had never asked for her permission in this way. He had taken her capitulation as consent, and she had thought that was love, that overbearing need.

But she saw the same need in Oliver even as he waited for her response.

How could she have denied him?

The control was in her hands, and she would take the reins.

"You can have your kiss, and more," she said, her heart pounding with the thrill of finally giving in to the inevitable. This was objectively a terrible decision, but it was hers in a way that very little else in her lonely life had been, and she was determined to hold on to it.

Isabella would never know that for one night, Emily craved the man she'd intended to marry.

Later, she knew, Emily would feel guilty, but she refused to allow guilt space in her mind for now. For once, excitement tingled to her fingertips. She was really going to do this. No one had coerced her into it; she had decided of her own volition.

If she was careful, she could have both. Pleasure and control.

"But," she said, "there must be rules."

Chapter Eighteen

Oliver stared up at Emily's downturned face. Rules. Of course she wanted rules—she was a woman for whom very few things had been within her control. This, if she was to engage in this, must also be.

Understanding that in a logical, intellectual way was very different from the reality, however.

His heart gave a kick in his chest—nerves, anticipation—and he nodded. He would give her whatever she needed, and he would take whatever she offered; there was no other way for this to go.

"Very well," he said, retreating to his bed to put distance between them. As far as was possible, they should both have clear heads. "Tell me your rules. I warn you now, there's very little you can tell me that would make me not want you, but I assure you, if I'm not comfortable, then I'll say."

She nodded, lacing her fingers together. "My first rule is that there is nothing between us but mutual pleasure and satisfaction."

"Understood."

"My second rule is . . ." Her gaze darted to the side, and she looked as though she steeled herself. "I will not remove all my clothes. I know pleasure can be achieved without a full loss of modesty."

"Ah." He did his best to keep his expression neutral. He had offered her a kiss; she was offering far more. Much as he wanted to see her bared for him, he could not push her. "What about mine?"

"Your clothes?"

"Yes. What are your preferences?"

"I—" She hesitated, glancing at his crotch, and his cock responded, swelling in anticipation of something he couldn't even be sure would happen. "What are you comfortable with?"

"Everything," he said immediately. "I would prefer to be unclothed unless you dislike the thought of seeing me." He wagged his brows at her, and she laughed again, shaking her head.

"I have no objection."

"Well, then. Anything else?"

"We never tell Isabella of what occurred between us," she said immediately.

"That goes without saying. What happens between us in this room stays in this room."

"Yes. And after—after we are done, I would prefer it if you didn't . . . That is to say, I would like for you to immediately take your bed."

For a long moment, Oliver said nothing. He'd had a few dalliances where speed was of the essence—all lifted skirts and muffled gasps and few kisses. On the surface of things, he didn't know why he reacted against doing the same with Emily.

Perhaps because he had an intellectual and emotional connection with her—he was accustomed to being used for sexual gratification by near-strangers. But for someone he knew to treat him like that stung in an odd, indefinable way.

Yet what else had he been expecting? She'd said it herself: this was all pleasure, no intimacy.

He could do that.

At least, he thought he could.

"I want to be in control," she said, and it felt as though the words had left her like an exhale, as though she had needed to say them for so long, they had burst free without her permission. "And for you to submit. To me."

Now *this* was intriguing.

"Very well," he said. "Then you will be in control. You will lead the way, and I will follow. Teach me, Emily. I will be your most avid student." Finally, he rose, coming to kneel before her in a demonstration of submission. Her breath hitched as he took her wrist in his hand and kissed her inner arm. "Tell me what you want from me," he murmured, pressing the words into her skin. "Tell me, and I'll obey." A sharp intake of breath told him how much she liked that, and he continued. "Does that please you, darling? Having me on my knees for you?

Willing to do anything you command?" Finally, he looked up at her in time to see her blush. She had such delectable colour, and he wanted to kiss it from her.

There were so many things he wanted to do to her. That he wanted her to *ask* for, to command him to do.

Things he wanted her to do to him.

He kissed her wrist one last time, then released her hand, standing before he got carried away. "Would you like to change before we begin? If so, now is your chance. I will wait over here; call me when you're done." Without giving her time to object, he strode across the room and faced the wall. They had done this a few times over the past few days, and the rustling clothes had always been akin to torture, but it felt different this time. His skin heated, and he felt the urgency of his arousal pulsing through his body.

Lust took on a new edge when it was like this—when he was getting so much, yet being denied so much at the same time. His urgency came from needing to make the most of this moment before it inevitably passed.

Once he took her back to Dalston, he expected he would have to leave and never see her again. These were the last few days in her company; if he didn't embrace everything she offered him now, he would never get another chance.

Some part of him, buried so deep it was more instinct than rational thought, knew that he could not bear that eventuality.

"I'm ready," she called, and when he turned back around, it was to see her in a nightgown that devoured the shape of her body, rendering nothing visible but the pearled nub of her nipples. No matter what she pretended for the sake of indifference and control, she wanted this, too.

Her gaze moved down him, lingering on the unavoidably visible bulge at his crotch. "Are you not undressing after all?"

"I thought you might wish to do that yourself. If you recall, you started once before." He remained where he was, though he wanted nothing more than to stride over to her, to take her in his arms and bury his face in the loose, static curls around her head.

He wanted, he wanted, and he would never stop.

But she needed to feel as though she was in control here, and so he would take a step back and let it happen. "Whatever you choose, Emily," he said when she didn't immediately speak. "This isn't about my tastes. I'll have you any way you let me, whether it's naked or clothed, on my knees worshipping you or if it's against the wall. Against the bed. With my eyes closed." He grinned at her. "In fact, that might be rather nice. So, what is it to be?" He spread his hands, gesturing wide. "Tell me what you want, Em."

She inhaled, her cheeks hollowing as she considered, then she looked back at him. "I would like you to kiss me."

Finally. Finally. Moving slowly, he stepped closer, bridging the distance between them, and slid his good hand into her hair. She didn't want romance, didn't want affection, but he couldn't stop himself from kissing her the way he wanted to. Not as though she was another conquest, all pretty lips and swaying hips, but as though she was Emily Brunton, the lady he had been sharing a life with for the past few days.

Emily Brunton, whose strength made him want to be stronger. And whose weakness made him want to shield her from the world and everything it had done to hurt her.

Being around her made him want to be a better man, and he expressed that the only way he knew how—through his mouth. He kissed her deeply, slowly, urging her to soften under his touch, to let him in, to kiss him back with equal intensity.

And she did. Devastatingly. She razed him to the ground and built him anew. He had been aroused before, but as she gained confidence, flicking her tongue against his and arching her back, she brought him to ruin.

And he welcomed it.

"Your way," he said. "We do this your way. And if you ever need me to stop or slow down, all you need do is tell me. I might want you, but that doesn't make me an animal." He caught her face with his good hand, looking down into her eyes so she would know he was serious. "Understand? I want only what you will enjoy."

"I want you to enjoy it, too," she said, reaching down between their bodies to cup his erection.

"That is not a concern." No, his concern was that he would hold out long enough to give her what she needed.

His concern was that he would not know well enough what she needed, and she would be too proud to tell him. His concern was that she would not know what *she* needed, having never given the consideration any thought.

More than anyone else he had ever been with, it mattered to him that she enjoyed herself.

She drew back, and he watched. They should blow the candle out, he knew, but he would miss the lustrous gleam of her eyes, and the gleam of red in her rampant hair. Though her body was still a mystery to him, he would miss the little he could see.

"This is a first for me," she said. "Being in control."

He brought his mouth to the curve of her neck and kissed her there. She quivered under his touch, and he thought he would be half mad before the night was out for certain.

He didn't think he cared.

"Then explore all you like," he murmured. "Use me as you will, and promise me you won't hold back."

A pause, as though she was weighing up her desires against her sense of what she ought to want. Then, finally, she nodded, exhaling as though in relief. "I promise."

What power came from control. Emily had never known it before. When she'd been with Marlbury, it had been so very different. He had always taken the lead, and she had followed, not even considering that she could say no. He had never offered the reins to her. Never once implied that her pleasure would come first.

Oliver had not hesitated. He had demanded that she *use* him, and the words had sparked a new fire inside her. She felt almost giddy with the force of her desire, so much greater at the prospect of control than it had been at the prospect of yielding it.

His erection pressed into her lower stomach as she kissed him again, sliding her hand into his hair and tightening her fingers into a fist. He made a muffled groan, that erection throbbing against her, and she felt an answering pang of heat between her legs.

"Where do you want me, Emily?" he murmured against her mouth. "Tell me what you want."

This time, she didn't even have to consider it. "Stay still."

"Yes, ma'am."

She reached up to his cravat, unfolding it and putting it on the bed. Next, she unbuttoned his waistcoat. He helped her shrug it off, but he made no attempt to assist her in taking off his shirt. His damaged arm lay underneath it, in a sling against his body, and she frowned at it.

"I don't want to hurt you."

"If you do, I'll tell you."

She sucked in a breath as she looked at him, taking him fully in, without shame, for the first time. He was pale; so much of his body had clearly never been exposed to the sun. Soft, light hair dusted lightly across his chest and down his navel to his breeches, and the bulge there, clearly outlined by the soft fabric.

Yes, she could be certain that he wanted this. Out of curiosity, she pressed a hand against that bulge, pleased by his slight intake of breath. She traced him, exploring. So different from Marlbury, both in length and width; she had not known there could be so much variation.

"You see," he said, his voice a little more strained now. "You are not hurting me."

She leaned up to kiss him again, still sliding her fingers up and down his erection. "Be quiet," she whispered against his mouth. His answering smile pressed into her lips, but he did as she commanded, even as she painstakingly unbuttoned his falls and slid his breeches down his legs.

His erection bobbed eagerly in the air, as though seeking the warm pressure of her hand once again.

For a long moment, she just looked at it, amused with the way it hardened just from her gaze alone, veins bulging along the side and a tiny bead of moisture at the tip.

When she brought her hand to him again, he let out a harsh sound that made her feel as though she were flying. Taking her time, she explored him by candlelight and touch, smoothing her fingers over the soft skin. His sac, hanging underneath, the skin firming as she took him gently in her fingers and squeezed.

He released another ragged breath, but said absolutely nothing, remaining utterly still as she brought her fingers all over him, learning the touches he liked and the ones he didn't.

When she brushed her other hand across his nipple, he twitched in her hand. An answering throb echoed between her legs. Already, she knew she was slick with desire.

"Get on the bed," she told him, and he didn't hesitate, crossing to the bed and lying on his back. Another thrill ran through her as he watched her with hawk-like focus, waiting for her next instruction.

This man, stronger than her by far, lay motionless, *waiting*.

He would do whatever she asked.

Anticipation buzzed through her like lightning.

His acquiescence was the reason she felt no compunction about fetching her shawl and folding it. "I'm going to place this over your eyes," she explained as she brought it to his face. "Let me know if you can still see anything."

There was a spark in his eyes before she covered them, and his hand twitched from where it lay on his stomach. "As you command," he murmured. When she had secured it in place, he moved his head back and forth. "I can see nothing."

"Good." Stepping back, she reached for the hem of her nightgown and pulled it over her head. The cold air bit at her naked skin, and she ran a self-conscious hand over her ribs. Too many years of not enough food had left their mark; she had never been voluptuous, but hunger had stolen all her lushness, and this week had not been enough to repair the damage. Her breasts, always small, were practically nonexistent, and she could count the ridge of her ribs, pressed against the jut of her hipbone.

Men did not lust after her the way they had lusted after other young ladies—after Isabella, even.

Oliver wanted her even knowing that she didn't possess curves, but she couldn't bear the vulnerability that came from revealing everything to him. All the things Marlbury had praised about her body, hardship had stripped clean away.

She would not allow the past to take the present from her.

Oliver's hand twitched slightly as she knelt on the bed, the mattress dipping under her weight. For once, she didn't move quickly. With Marlbury, they had always been eager to take advantage of what little time they had—and so often, they had so little time. Snatched moments together that had felt like glimpses of sunlight on a cloudy day.

She placed a hand against Oliver's stomach, and his muscles contracted.

"Emily," he said on a rasp. "May I touch you?"

She considered his words, and his hand clenched into a fist at the silence. But still she waited until she was sure of her answer. "Not yet."

His frustrated groan came with the edge of a laugh. "Cruelty incarnate."

"Am I?" Next she placed her palm against his thigh, and saw the way his muscles rippled all the way up his body. "Hand above your head."

He made no objection, raising it until his fingers locked around the metal bars of the headboard. "Is this to your liking?" he asked, and she smiled, though he could not see—that smile was for her and her alone.

"Yes," she said, and moved, straddling his thighs. He released a long, sharp huff of air. Almost a sigh, but not quite. A gasp, an exclamation of surprise and pleasure. He twitched again, but despite the dampness between her own thighs, she moved slowly, sliding her hands up his legs to the sharp arrow of his hipbones. The taut flatness of his stomach. His breaths came fast as she deliberately skirted where he wanted her the most.

But although she could sense his impatience, knew implicitly how very much he wanted this, he made no attempt to move his hand or free his eyes. In yielding to her, he had given her his word, and she could see now he would not break it. Relief burned in her heart at the realisation. Part of her, even now, had been preparing for the inevitable moment he broke her trust. She had been guarding herself against the prospect of hurt, even as she bared herself to him.

In silent thanks, she bent and pressed her lips to his ribs. His every breath, deep and shuddering, lanced through her, a pleasure of its own though he hadn't so much as laid a finger on her.

Slowly, she kissed down his torso until she was at his very tip. He made a muffled sound of what could only be described as despair.

She raised her head. "Do you want to stop?"

"No. Please, don't stop." His chin rose, and his lips parted as he took a breath. "Do whatever you choose with me."

"You're enjoying this?"

"The most exquisite of tortures."

Another smile touched her lips. He compelled so many from her.

She slid her hand up and down his length, savouring the feel of the soft skin over the hardness. The bead of moisture that emerged from her ministrations. His back arched and he let loose a whispered curse that near singed the air. He smelt of salt and musk and something undeniably *Oliver* that made her press her thighs together.

This was not new to her—Marlbury had guided her hand on him, that and more, but it had always been a dynamic of him dictating her motions to her.

Now, she could choose her own pace, whether to use one hand or two, and she experimented, listening for the changes in his breath.

"Emily," he said. Close to a beg, half a groan.

She slid her hand along his length, letting it join her mouth, and his hips thrust. "Keep still," she told him.

"Is that a command, my lady?"

A command. A shiver ran through her. "Yes."

"Then I shall endeavour to obey." This, it seemed, was delivered through gritted teeth. "Though you try my patience."

"I have a suspicion you are enjoying your patience being tried." Before he could answer, she brought him again into her mouth, and he gave up on words. His hand was white-knuckled around the iron bars now, his body trembling as he attempted to do as she'd commanded. The sight of him, prone before her and utterly under her control, sent another burst of need through her, and she climbed up his body, setting overtop him, her knees pressed against his side.

"Tell me if you are close," she said, and wrapped her fingers around him. But instead of sinking down on him as he had no doubt expected—and wanted—she slid him through her folds. Again and again, back and forth, right where she needed him. She had never done anything like this before, but she liked the power of it, the sensation of him pleasuring her through her own hand.

The little of his skin she could see through his blindfold was flushed, and his breath came hot and fast. Heat flooded her body at the sight of his undoing, the tiny sounds he did his best to withhold. Faster than she ever thought possible, she too found herself at the brink.

"Emily," he groaned. "Let me—"

"Wait."

Once more, he did as she commanded, and she leaned down, one hand on the pillow by his head, the other between her legs, and pressed her mouth against his. He met her eagerly, hungrily, kissing her as though he had no other desire in his body. When she let out a mewling cry, her climax drawing near, he swallowed the sounds.

Still, he did not remove his hand from the iron of the bed. Her nipples scraped against his chest, just above where his injured arm lay, the friction sending sensation zinging through her, and at the spike of pleasure, she knew what she wanted.

"Touch me," she said with the last of her air, a woman drowning.

He moved, reaching blindly for her, finding her face first and cupping it, to her surprise, with tender gentleness. Then he slid his hand down her throat to her chest, to her breasts, first one then the other, squeezing her nipple as she brushed his erection through her folds one final time.

She shuddered apart.

Oliver held her, his own muscles drawn taut, his own desire tangible even when she was lost in the midst of hers. She tasted his lips, his tongue, allowed him to draw her into his mouth, to muffle her cries as her arms shook. He wrapped his arm around her as she caught her breath, boneless, the tail end of pleasure still ricocheting through every limb.

"Shh," he said, and she realised she was shaking still.

Splaying both hands across her chest, she braced herself, then took his hand in hers. "Touch me here," she said, bringing that hand between her legs, allowing him to feel her slickness for himself. His fingers hesitated only for a second as they glided through her folds.

"Emily," he said hoarsely. "You're beautiful."

"You can't see me."

His lips curved. "I know."

A ludicrous thing to say, probably a compliment he had bestowed on countless other lovers—yet still a different sort of warmth bloomed in her chest.

A dangerous warmth.

To prevent him from saying more—or perhaps to prevent herself from feeling more—she finally positioned him at her entrance. There, she hovered, waiting for some sign that at this crucial moment, he would force himself inside. One thrust would be all it took; she was wet enough that there would be no real obstacle.

His fingers trembled against her sensitive pearl. His jaw feathered, and the light flickered. The candle was burning low, and she drank him in while she had the chance.

The light vanished, plunging them into darkness, and she sank all the way down in one smooth motion, seating him fully inside her.

Chapter Nineteen

Oliver did not think he had ever before known the true meaning of pleasure. Now he did, and its name was Emily Brunton.

She rose above him, invisible in the dark yet still known to him. Every slide of skin and flesh against his fingers was another form of bliss as she rode him hard, not giving him the luxury of gentleness. He found he didn't want it. Let her take her pleasure from him—he would give it, willingly. Anything she wanted, however she asked for it, words or actions.

He wanted nothing more in the world than to please her. If he'd had his way, he would have chosen to please her in this way for the rest of their lives.

The thought shocked him, but it was true—if she had asked him to, he would have married her in an instant. All his reasons for not marrying Isabella did not apply when it came to Emily. He respected her, wanted her, cared for her. If this was not love, then it was at least some form of affection, enough that he prized her happiness above nearly anything else.

The best thing a man could do was marry a woman who would make him better, and after only a few days in her company, he knew she would do that.

If she had been amenable, he would have taken her back to Gretna Green and brought her back to that shoddy inn so she could claim him as her husband. Lying flat on his back as she plunged her body down him, over and over again.

He craved nothing more than to belong to her. To be hers.

An impossible dream, yet one he could not quite dismiss.

As pleasure wracked his body and his soul, he imagined waking up beside her in the morning, her hair a tangled mess, face devoid of its usual reserve. There, he would make love to her—or rather, would offer himself so she could make love to him.

He had grown accustomed to wanting nothing, to his detriment, but he had found something he wanted now, in this quiet room with this wild woman, and had no idea how he might take it.

How did one woo a woman determined not to be wooed?

She would insist on this ending when she returned to Dalston, and he would deny her nothing, because he could deny her nothing, and he would have to find a way to live with it.

He slid his hand down her body, finding that little nub of nerves between her legs and pressing, testing the pressure, listening to the way she bit back her gasps. She was not an expressive lover, but she knew passion. If he had more time, more opportunity, he would have found a way to know how it felt when she let go of her every inhibition.

If only she trusted him enough for that. She trusted him enough for this—to render him blindfolded and to ride him with those eager, desperate motions. A woman left to the mercy of her own abandoned libido. He didn't know how long she had been denying herself her desires, but he wished she would let him see those parts of herself instead of hiding, even now.

He wished he could push her over that edge into wanting him as much as he wanted her.

Above him, her breath hitched once again, and pleasure spilled down his spine, tightening in his balls. Perhaps it was a good thing she wasn't outwardly expressive, or he might have embarrassed himself too early. Still, he had to try and force himself to wait. He would wait as long as she needed.

If he could.

She panted harder. He already knew his every breath was ragged. With every bounce, she dismantled more of him, and there was no guarantee the aftermath would put him back together again. Just like the kiss, she ruined him in new and rare ways.

Was this what making love felt like?

He wished he could look into her eyes and see for certain how she felt. Whether it mirrored the way he was feeling now, the emotions too large for his chest, or whether she had carved away that part of her heart, discarding it as worthless.

He had never hated anyone as much as he hated Marlbury for breaking her so thoroughly.

He felt rather than heard her throw her head back. Her knees pressed more firmly into his sides, and her thighs quivered. Her hips ground against him, and he was buried so deeply inside her, he thought he might never find his way out.

"Oliver," she gasped. His name, slipping from her lips in supplication.

He gritted his teeth, trying to hold on for her, needing to wait. For a reason he couldn't articulate, even in the privacy of his own head, he needed her to do this. Needed it in a desperate, urgent, overpowering way that made no sense, yet couldn't be denied.

He needed to feel her let go when he was inside her.

She drew in one last shuddering breath, and he felt her come apart. Squeezing, trembling, her movements jerky. And though it near killed him, he stayed still, let her take her pleasure however she chose, even though he was so close—so, so close, on the verge of spilling himself inside her.

He closed his eyes, though he could see nothing, and gritted his teeth. The pressure in his spine built. Heat surged through him.

"Emily," he grunted. "I need you to—"

He needed to say no more. She slid from him like water, and mere seconds later, his climax overtook him. Her hand, small and cool against his urgent heat, wrapped around his erection, urging every last drop of seed from him. When he had finished turning himself inside out, she released him, and he lay back.

That had been . . . devastating.

They both lay together for a moment, each catching their breath. Her body pressed against his, skin to skin, and he let himself appreciate the moment for a little longer—it wouldn't be long now. She had what she wanted from him.

By God, she had torn him apart.

"I presume the candle has burnt itself out," he said into the darkness.

"Yes."

"I'll need some light in order to clean myself up." He cleared his throat, trying not to feel too awkward. Ordinarily, in situations like these, where they had no connection beyond what they had just done, he left and endeavoured never to see her again.

He had no idea how to transition back to something approaching friendship.

How did one become friends with one's lover?

His hand twitched, and he wished he could reach for her. Give them both some space after the event where they could find some equilibrium.

Perhaps he was a romantic after all. What a galling realisation.

Her hand brushed his shoulder, then found his jaw. She cupped his cheek, then turned his face so he was facing her. The first bump of her lips in the dark was clumsy, but she soon found his mouth, and kissed him long and deep. "Thank you," she whispered.

He exhaled a sigh of relief and kissed her back. "If you would like a repeat performance, all you need do is ask." He smiled against her mouth, feeling the way her lips quirked in response. Being blind had its obvious disadvantages, but it had distinct advantages, too. In the absence of sight, his other senses had risen to the occasion, and he was conscious of all the places they touched.

He could feel the press of her hand against his skin, his stubble against the chapped scrape of her callouses.

"In fact," he continued, "I would prefer to do it again if at all possible."

Her chuckle shivered across his skin as she leant back. "I was worried you might not like it."

"My tastes are adaptable. This was a first for me, but I wouldn't object if that were the only way I were to experience the event from here on in. And if you would prefer further control—to tie me to the bed—then, darling, you can have me like that whenever you choose."

"You talk as though it's nothing."

"It's not nothing," he said gently. "But truly, I enjoyed this. And you. I want everything you see fit to give me until our time runs out."

He sensed rather than saw her smile drop. "That will be soon."

And there it was. Reality, lodged like a stone in his boot. Uncomfortably pressing, unable to ignore for long. This was not their life; soon they would be leaving.

"It will," he said.

"Perhaps even tomorrow."

"Perhaps."

The mattress shifted as she moved off it. He heard the scrape of material against skin as she no doubt found her nightgown and covered herself up. "Thank you for the opportunity to explore this," she said after a moment, touching his leg as though to assure them both of her gratitude. "I truly did have a wonderful time."

And it will not be happening again.

The unspoken words hung between them. And really, he shouldn't have been surprised.

He sat up, removing the blindfold from his face. There was little more light without it, and he balled it in his fist, trying to force the awkwardness away. This was what she had asked for. He knew going in what she wanted from him.

"Tell me something," he said, halfway across the room to his bed and the bowl of water that waited on the sideboard. "Was this enough to get it out of your system, Emily? Are you satisfied now?"

She hesitated. "Yes."

"Liar," he said under his breath, quiet enough that she didn't hear him.

The sound of her slow breaths haunted him as he lay awake, the ache in his chest reminding him that not all ailments could be cured by time and rest.

Was this enough to get it out of your system?

The words played around Emily's head as she listened to Oliver's slumber. Early dawn light slipped past the shutters, bathing the room in grey, and she lay alone in her bed.

Just as she had requested.

At first, she had sunk into sleep without issue, but now she lay awake, mulling over everything that had happened, trying to convince herself that she had made the right decision.

This was one thing, this pleasure, but she could never marry the man her sister had aspired towards. That would be a betrayal too far. And so it only made sense that she keep Oliver at bay, and more importantly, kept her heart out of matters.

No intimacy. No emotions.

No thoughts about it happening again.

Even if the thought of the way he had submitted made heat bloom between her legs. As though she weren't already sore from the way she had ridden him just hours earlier.

No, it was very much not out of her system.

But it would be, soon enough. Once she returned home and picked up the threads of her old life, she would forget this ever happened. It would be as a dream to her—a pleasant dream that only visited at night, when the rest of the world was asleep. And perhaps she would never forget, but she would live—she would *survive*—and that was the only thing that mattered.

Chapter Twenty

To Emily's mingled disappointment and relief, the next day dawned mild. The temperature had risen overnight, and the snow had half melted already, the dark bark of trees stark against the stone grey sky, and grass poking through the shovelled lawn.

By the time they had finished breakfast, Mr Chambers confirmed that a post chaise had made its way past them.

"I reckon the snow's softened enough that it'll clear within a few days," he said as he kicked his boots off.

They all listened to the steady pitter-patter of melting snow from the roof.

Emily did not especially enjoy the cold under ordinary circumstances, and she especially did not enjoy this stage of the snow cycle, where everything turned mushy and damp—the sort of damp that tucked itself under collars and up sleeves. Colder, in some ways, that the crispness of freezing.

A temperature England excelled at.

Oliver looked at Emily from across the table. "Is the road traversable if we were to walk?" he asked.

"Walk? To the nearest village? You have ten miles to go, lad!"

"By the time we arrive, the snow might have melted enough to hire a coach."

Mr Chambers eyed Oliver dubiously. "Perhaps, but mark my words, you'll end up staying there overnight before you have a chance of getting out."

"I don't mind," Emily said hastily. "It's just we should get back to my sister. She'll be worrying about us."

At the mention of Isabella, Oliver's face went perfectly blank.

Neither of them had discussed the previous night yet, but they would have to acknowledge it. A small, jealous part of Emily was glad he would not be marrying her sister, but thinking about Isabella meant thinking about what they had done.

Isabella would never know. But Emily still felt guilty.

Even so, she could not stop sneaking glances at Oliver. And she had felt his eyes on her more than once, too.

"We were hoping to send Old Tom along in the cart this afternoon, if you can stand to wait that long," Mrs Chambers said. "That is, if the roads are looking well enough. It's a rickety old thing, mind, the cart."

Oliver swept them a formal bow. "I'm assured it can be no worse than my carriage, ma'am, and we're most grateful to you for all your generosity."

"Now then." Mrs Chambers blushed and flicked a tea-towel at him. "You're too handsome for your own good, Mr Beaumont, and that's the truth. Is there anything else you need before you go?"

"Going already?" John's small face fell. "But the snow hasn't fully melted yet."

Oliver tugged affectionately at one of his ears, and Emily absolutely refused to let her heart respond to the gesture. "We have to get back to our family," he said. "So they can spend time with us, too. But we've had a wonderful time being here with you all."

"We have," Emily said warmly, trying to ignore the full-body flush that suffused her when she thought what kind of wonderful time she'd had under their roof. Under the cold light of day, it felt sordid and deeply, overwhelmingly improper.

She loved it.

"And we'll miss you all," she added, trying to bring her mind to more suitable breakfast table matters.

"Will you come back and visit?" Sarah asked.

"My family lives a long way south of here," Oliver explained. "I don't know when we'll next be up in these parts."

Never, was the answer. Without being married, they could never return. Although she wished she could, if only to repay them for their generosity.

"Don't you pester them," Mrs Chambers said now, shooing her children away from the table. "They can't promise anything, I'm sure, and we wouldn't want them to, either."

Oliver's foot nudged hers, and his knee slid along the side of her thigh. Though no one else could see the gesture, it made her face flame, and she coughed into her tea.

His knee nudged her again, more insistently this time, and she caught the corner of his smile as mopped up his egg yolk with a slice of bread. Biting back a smile of her own, she nudged him back and glanced out of the window at the rapidly melting snow. The air temperature was positively warm now, and the trees and hedges were all bare.

By tonight, most of the snow would be gone, she suspected. And by this afternoon, enough of the road would be passable for them to make it to the nearest village.

Her heart squeezed at the prospect. The sooner she returned home to Isabella, the better. Her sister would probably be hungry and cold, whereas Emily had been warm and well-fed these past few days. Not to mention partaking in—well, Oliver.

On the other hand, she didn't want to leave. This had been a delightful interlude, and once she left, she would have to face the reality of everything she had done, and a life she had to endure, not enjoy.

The Chambers enjoyed their life. They had enough, and they had each other, and they were happy.

If only Emily could have faith she might one day have such a thing. But fate did not smile kindly on her, and even now, she had a prickling feeling behind her shoulder blades that something was about to go terribly wrong.

The next village along was called Bridekirk. After they assessed the roads and confirmed they could make the journey, all that remained was for them to gather what few things they had and bid their hosts goodbye.

"I will send someone for the horses and carriage," Oliver told them as they gathered in the hallway. "And recompense for the cost of stabling the horses, of course."

"Aye, you worry more about getting yourself settled. We'll do fine here," Mr Chambers said.

"You look after one another now, duck," Mrs Chambers said, embracing Emily. "And don't you worry about thanking us. It was a pleasure and a joy to have you around. Wasn't it, Gerald?"

Her husband nodded, clapping Oliver on his good shoulder. "We hope someone would do as much for our daughter and her husband, that's for certain. Take care of that arm, lad."

"I will," Oliver said.

"Do you have the money to repay them?" Emily asked in a low voice after they bid the children goodbye and crossed the yard to where the cart was being set up. Clarabella, to Emily's relief, was firmly locked away.

"Whether I do or not, Henry does. He'll send the money over regardless. It's what's right; he would never leave a debt like this unpaid."

"Would you?"

Oliver grimaced, glancing up at the heavy clouds as though daring them to rain on him again. "Not if I can help it." He adjusted his injured arm, wincing as he did so. "If Henry does end up having to fork out for this, I'll pay him back."

"With your allowance?"

"Well . . ." He kicked at the ground, looking almost bashful—and at anyone but her. "I thought—this morning, I thought I might approach my brother and ask him for help teaching me the things a landowner ought to know." The tips of his cheekbones pinked. "I will marry at some point, and when I do, I will come into my inheritance, and I ought to know how to run it. Properly, without relying on a steward for everything the way my father does."

Emily paused, realising the enormity of this confession. For the entirety of the time she had known him, he had posed his brother as some sort of tyrannical figure, but now Oliver intended to go to him, cap in hand, and ask for help.

She touched his unwounded arm. "I think that's an excellent idea."

"You haven't met my brother." His half-smile didn't reach his eyes. "He doesn't have the best opinion of me—there's a good chance he will turn you away."

"Or perhaps your brother loves you," she said, leaning her cheek against his shoulder for a heartbeat, "and wants the best for you. Perhaps he wants *you* to find the best for yourself."

"Perhaps."

They reached the cart. Oliver helped Emily climb into the back, and Oliver followed clumsily, trying to avoid knocking his bad arm. Six days into healing, and she could tell it still pained him, even if he did his best to hide it from her.

She wished she could magically make it better. Unfortunately, that was not how the world worked.

They settled themselves against the side of the cart amid bags of grain and old pieces of straw as Old Tom flicked the reins and urged the donkeys at the front into motion.

All around them, the melting snow dripped and pattered, and the watery sun bathed them in its indifferent light as they waved goodbye to the farm that had housed them for so long.

Oliver's warmth pressed into her side, a reminder that no matter what, she couldn't ignore his presence. They were soon to bid each other farewell, and the thought made her stomach twist a little.

This is what you wanted.

"What do you intend to do once we reach Bridekirk?" she asked.

"I doubt there's much to be done." He took her hand, enfolding her fingers in his. "It'll be too late to easily travel back to Dalston, so I'll take a room for the night—or two—and after a hearty breakfast tomorrow, I'll hire a carriage to deliver you home."

If she wanted, she *could* insist on separate rooms, or for him to deliver her back to Dalston tonight. He watched her as though he half expected her to demand such a thing.

One last night together. Would that be so bad? Isabella needed her, but what was the difference between late one night and early the next morning? Isabella was not an early riser; she would barely notice the difference.

"All right," she said, and his shoulders relaxed a fraction.

"Do you regret it?"

She eyed their linked hands pointedly. "If I did, do you think I would be here like this with you now? No, Oliver. I don't regret it." She felt as though a door in her mind and body had been opened. Things would perhaps have been easier if it had remained shut, but when had the best things in life ever been easy?

"Good," he said, exhaling. "Then I don't have to, either."

"What made you change your mind about me? When we first met, I don't suppose you intended for this to happen."

He grinned, the contemplation sliding from his face to be replaced by wickedness. He unhooked his fingers from hers, then slid his palm against her cheek. His thumb brushed her lower lip, the way it always seemed to when he wanted to entice her into doing or saying something inappropriate. No one had ever made her feel like this before. "Not when we first met, admittedly," he murmured, leaning in. "But darling, may I remind you that on occasion of our first meeting, I had just been driving for hours through the night and you held a gun to my head."

"After you ushered me into your carriage thinking I was my sister!"

"Not my finest hour, I'll admit. And yet, I can't bring myself to say I'm sorry for it. Are you shocked?" He brushed his mouth over her cheek, and she threw all resolutions about kissing, and the quantity thereof, away.

One more night, one more room, one more time.

"Very shocked," she told him. His nose brushed hers. They swayed with the motion of the cart. A stray piece of straw poked her in the back, and she knew the steady breeze had turned her neat bun into a frizzy mess. Yet for all that, she felt overheated, her skin sensitive under her clothes.

"Liar," he whispered, pressing his lips to her neck.

She shivered. "What if Old Tom sees us?"

"He's not looking," Oliver said. "And he appears to be as deaf as a post."

"Don't point out his deficiencies when he's driving us."

"The horses are driving; he's merely pretending to guide them."

"Much you would know on the subject," she retorted, her words breathy at the feeling of his mouth moving against her skin. He kissed her pulse point, trailing his tongue up the column of her throat.

"I like it when you're shrewish," he said, looking at her again, hazel eyes sparking. "I like it rather a lot."

"You might be the first person to have said that."

"Then I can say with utter certainty that everyone else in your life is an idiot."

She laughed, dizzy with pleasure from the ridiculous compliment.

Foolish, a voice in the back of her head said. *This is how it always starts.*

He dragged his mouth along her jaw. "I liked it when you blindfolded me. I would like you to do it again tonight."

"Is that why you intend us to stay overnight in Bridekirk?"

"Not the only reason. But I can't deny it was a factor." He looked at her with lust-drunk eyes. "Do you object?"

"I said once."

"Then tell me to arrange two rooms for us, and I shall."

She wouldn't. They both knew they had come too far for that; if she had intended to turn him down and reject him, she would already have done so.

"I'm glad," he said into the silence, his voice sinking lower. "I'm not ready to lose you yet."

A shiver rolled over her skin. "You shouldn't say things like that."

"Why not, if they're true? I know you won't let me do the honourable thing, so let me do the dishonourable thing instead." He flashed her another wicked grin. "Or rather, let me convince you to dishonour me thoroughly. However you would have me." He slid his hand to her waist, urging her onto him. She slid her knees either side of his thighs, perching atop his legs as though they were in a bed, or a chair, not in the bed of a cart rattling slowly along a winter road. "You may choose the means, so long as you choose me." His hazel eyes speared her. "Just for tonight."

She braced herself against his good shoulder. "Just for tonight," she agreed.

"I know better than to try and keep you any longer." He urged her down for a kiss, and she allowed herself to sink a little deeper into him. His good hand reached up her side to cup her breast, and she bit back a gasp, glancing to where Old Tom sat before the horses, oblivious.

Mischief sparked in Oliver's eyes, and when she shifted, she felt his arousal underneath her. How was it that in such a place, at such a temperature, her body could still respond in this way? As though he sparked a storm within her, and she crackled with lightning and thunder, an excess of sensation that made her fingers burn with the urge to touch him.

"Go on," he murmured, his voice hypnotic. "You know you want to."

She threaded her fingers through his hair, and he released a long breath as she dragged his head back. Then, just as he had done to her, she kissed along his throat, ghosting her lips across his Adam's apple, the tendons that tensed at the press of her mouth. She let herself taste his skin, and he bared his throat to her the way a rabbit might offer itself to the wolf.

"Admit you want this," he said to the sky, his voice so low she almost felt rather than heard it. "I know you do, but I want to hear you say it."

She tightened her hold on his hair, relishing the way heat leapt into his gaze, the way she felt his pulse speed as she pressed her fingers against the hollow of his throat.

"Will you beg?" she asked, tugging him back to face her.

"On my knees, if I must." His breath warmed her lips. "Whatever it takes. I can be patient. With you, darling, I can be as patient as you need."

"A rash promise to make," she said, and kissed him again.

Chapter Twenty-One

Although Emily did nothing the remainder of the journey but tease Oliver almost past his endurance, he insisted they eat a small luncheon before going up to the room he had hired for them.

"Believe me, we'll need to keep our strength up," he said, procuring them a table and platter of cold meats and cheeses. "And you should have some ale."

She wrinkled her nose suspiciously. "Why?"

"Call it a rite of passage."

"Will I like it?"

He grinned. "Almost assuredly not."

To her credit, eyes blazing on his, she raised her tankard to her mouth and took a large swallow. Then she coughed, placing it back on the table so firmly that the liquid spilt across the sticky wood. "That's vile."

"That's the spirit," he said, taking another gulp.

"Do you truly enjoy drinking that?"

"Enjoy is a strong word," he said. "I suppose it's all part of an inn's charm, drinking something that more resembles piss than anything close to human consumption."

She looked at him appraisingly. "You are more vulgar when in a place like this."

He winked at her. "Naturally. A man ought to fit in with his surroundings."

"What about when you're with your peers in a drawing room? Are you more refined then?"

"I rarely find myself in respectable drawing rooms."

"How about disrespectable ones?"

"What do you think I was doing in London all that time?" When she looked at him, her expression caught somewhere between amusement and horror, he nudged her knee with his foot. "I mostly spent my time in places such as this. Coffee houses. Gentlemen's clubs, that sort of thing."

"Ah," she said. "You were a degenerate."

"Has it taken you this long to come to that conclusion? For shame."

"You can only have yourself to blame."

"Are you suggesting I have behaved like a gentleman during the entirety of our acquaintance?"

Colour ran up her neck to her cheeks. She was positively delectable when she blushed. "Well," she said. "Not the entirety of our acquaintance."

"Mm, can you recall a specific time in particular I was less than gentlemanly?"

"Oliver," she hissed.

"No one can hear us," he said, settling back into his chair. "Eat up, then we can retire upstairs." At the poorly concealed irritation on her face, his grin widened. "Cheer up, darling. Once you have me in your bed, I'm sure you can punish me all you like."

Her eyes held a thousand promises, and all of them made his blood heat. "Oh don't you worry," she said, the words faintly threatening. "I will."

If Oliver had thought that having kissed Emily several times, he might ever *not* lose his mind when she kissed him, he would have been very wrong. Of course, some of that could be attributed to the fact he had been aroused for so long. When she met his tongue with hers, he wanted to groan in relief. This was almost too much, and yet he would never have enough.

When did lust become obsession? And how long before he crossed from one to the other?

He suspected he might already have made the leap.

"Where do you want me?" he asked against her mouth. "And how?"

She pushed at his shoulders, forcing him back to the bed-posts. "Stand there," she instructed. "Take off your clothes."

Well *this* he delighted in. "Yes, ma'am."

Her cheeks pinked at his immediate subservience. Aware that she was watching him, and with every intention of provoking her interest, he removed his cravat and carefully placed it to one side. Then he unbuttoned his coat, fumbling with the buttons somewhat thanks to his one inoperable hand. After undoing that and his waistcoat, shrugging it from himself a little awkwardly, he contrived to tug his shirt over his head.

All that remained were his breeches.

She watched, chest rising and falling, her eyes tracing across every line of his body.

"Do you like what you see?" he asked, oddly desperate for her answer, her validation. It didn't matter how he had been received before; he wanted *her* to approve.

"I do," she said, her gaze flicking back to his and softening a fraction. "Do you need help with your trousers?"

Of course he *wanted* help, but she had asked him to undress himself. "I can do it."

"Go on then."

"As you command, my lady." He unlaced them, then drew them down his legs, letting his erection spring free. She was still fully dressed, though he could see the slight outline of her nipples behind the material of her dress, and the awareness of his vulnerability made desire pulse through him. His cock twitched. She tracked the movement.

"Well?" he asked, cocking an eyebrow. "What next, my lady? Do you wish for me to be on the bed so you can ride me again?"

"No." She sat on the edge of the bed, drawing her skirts up and removing her shoes. Then she rolled down her stockings and glanced back at him, mischief and intent in her eyes. He thought then that he might be lost. Forever was a long time, and yet he suspected he had already given it to her.

No—she had taken it when he was not looking. And by God, he had not been a man until she had made him into one.

She knotted the stockings together and approached, taking his one good arm and drawing it behind his back. From there, she tied his wrist to the bedpost. Then she took a blanket from the bed—a rather ragged, worn thing—and wrapped it around his upper chest, tying it in a knot behind the bedpost, holding him upright.

From there, she surveyed him, lips pursed, and he strained to be closer.

"Emily," he said.

"Can you break free?"

"If I tried, I expect I could. Do you wish me to try?"

"No." Her frown lightened, and she smiled. "I think this is precisely where I want you."

"Helpless before you?" He swallowed as she removed a pillow from the bed and placed it on the floor by his feet. Surely she wasn't about to—

"Yes," she said. "That. Now." She rested one hand against his thigh, and he sucked in a breath. The anticipation made him feel as though he was walking on air, as though he might be struck down to earth by lightning any second, but heaven above it was worth it. "I have not done this for a while. Give me instructions if I don't please you." She cast him a long look from below, the angle making her eyelashes look as though they almost reached her brows, and he thought it would be a miracle if he survived this. "But this is not all I intend. You may not finish."

Now that would be the greater miracle.

"I will try," he said.

"Do not try." Her fingers squeezed his thigh. "Succeed."

He had barely a moment to prepare himself before her lips slid down on him and all thoughts emptied from his brain. Against his will, his hips bucked, wanting more of that sweet heat, but she pressed that hand into his thigh in a silent command. He gathered himself enough to obey. Her mouth was heaven—hot and wet, her tongue caressing him as she slid slowly up and down. The slightest accidental graze of her teeth sent shivers through him. Heat barrelled down his spine, and he stiffened, his hand curling into a fist behind him.

If he really wanted, he could escape. She had not tied her knots tightly—either she did not know how, or she wanted to leave him this small freedom. The *ability* to disregard her wishes.

Perhaps that was the greater show of control.

She cupped his balls, squeezing softly, and he made a sound partway between a whine and an anguished groan.

"Slow," he gasped. "This is—" His head fell back against the post. She was turning him systematically inside out, and he could do nothing about it. He *wanted* to do nothing; this was the singular greatest pleasure he had experienced thus far.

His knees trembled. She glanced up at him from where she knelt, that delectable mouth curved into a knowing smile. "Slow?" she echoed, and licked the sensitive skin right at the top. "Are you certain?"

"If you wish me to keep my word to you, then yes." His knees buckled as she treated him to another long lick, as though he were a delicacy she was only just experiencing. He cursed, low and under his breath, and when she chuckled, he cursed again, louder. "Have mercy on me."

"Mercy." She rested both her hands on his thighs and looked up at him, a vision of such sensuality that he groaned aloud again. "I don't think I will. Remember your promise, Oliver."

When she lowered her mouth on him again, he knew it was a challenge.

He was almost certain he would fail.

What man could succeed in the face of such provocation? He wanted her too badly, and the hot slide of her tongue was a pleasure so great, he thought it might stop his heart.

"Please," he said, the words slipping free. "Please, Emily. Slow, slow. Go slowly now." He shuddered as she brought him to the edge, then paused, testing his restraint. Gritting his teeth, he held back with every ounce of his being.

"Hm?" She pressed a kiss to his hipbone. "What did you say?"

"Please, Emily." It was as though he had been on the edge for so long, he had forgotten how it felt not to be seconds away from spilling everywhere. "Please, darling. Have mercy on me. Let me taste you. Let me touch you. Please, go slowly."

A smile spread across her lips. "I like it when you beg." She took him in her hand. "Do you want me to stop?"

"No." When she pumped her hand, he near whimpered. "Perhaps," he said, tugging at the restraints just enough that he *felt* as though he was trapped there. His entire body trembled with the force of sensation—the pressure in his wrist where he was bound, the press of the blankets wrapped around his chest, holding him in place. The solidity of the bed behind him. At least it was not a flimsy thing; he had faith it would catch him if his knees gave out.

"I am so—" A gasp shuddered out of him as she paused again, right on the brink, sensing from his body language when he would pass the point of no return and stopping just before it. She was an adept student, and he was more than happy to be the means by which she experimented.

Again and again, she denied him just before his peak, until he felt as though she had melted him into a puddle of wax. Eventually, she raised her head.

"Now," she said, "it's your turn."

Chapter Twenty-Two

Emily hadn't intended to yield any part of herself to Oliver. She had enjoyed teasing him, enjoyed it so much the steady ache between her legs had turned slick, her arousal smearing every time she moved. The urgency to appease her own need rose—but more than that, she wanted to reward Oliver for allowing her this. For enjoying it, even, when it was all done at her whim.

His eyes pierced through hers, the pupils blown so large his gaze was near black. "My turn?" he rasped.

In answer, she reached behind him and fought with the knots; his squirming had tightened them, but not irreparably so. Then she stepped back and began to unlace her dress. Her heart hammered. Her fingers were slick with nervous sweat.

This had never been part of the plan. Yet he looked at her with such hunger.

"Don't touch me," she said. "Not yet."

His face was flushed, but he merely stared, watching her as though if he did so much as blink, she would disappear. "Your wish is my command."

Finally, she finished with her dress, pushing it down her legs. There were so many more layers for a lady to remove, but though she saw his fingers twitch as though he longed to assist her, he made no movement to help.

That was good. Good.

She inhaled sharply as cool air finally hit her skin. Her nipples, already peaked, pinched still further. Oliver looked at her face, and then, as though her silence were permission enough—and indeed it was—he turned his gaze down the rest of her. She had to stop herself from covering all her most intimate places—her breasts and the thatch of reddish-brown hair between her legs. The press of her ribs against her skin. The hollow of her stomach.

But Oliver's expression didn't change. If anything, it grew sharper. And his erection twitched, as though it sought her.

"Oliver," she whispered.

His gaze snapped back to her face. "Please," he said, and although she had enjoyed making him beg with her mouth, this was different. Deeper, so much more viscerally needy. "Please, Emily. Let me touch you."

Eyes still on him, she lay back against the covers, opening her legs to give him a view of what lay between. He sucked in a quiet breath, and it was as though with that single gesture, he had sucked the air from the room. She felt hot all over.

"Here," she said. "You may touch me."

He closed his eyes briefly, as though thanking some unknown gods for her benevolence, and knelt at the end of the bed, his good hand fastening around her thighs. His skin was not tanned, but the contrast against her extreme paleness—she was so white there the veins shone blue under her skin—made her stomach flip.

He pressed his lips in a chaste kiss against her inner thigh, then looked up at her through his golden eyelashes—searing, molten. "I am your servant, Emily. Tell me what you need."

"I—" She knew men used their mouths on women, and Marlbury had even mentioned he would like to try it, but at seventeen, she had been too afraid to let him near her. It seemed wrong, somehow. A level of intimacy too far.

Only he had convinced her to use her mouth, and she had enjoyed it more than she had thought she would. Although he appeared to hold the power—and indeed he held her hair and made use of her—she had been the one to dictate his pleasure. It had been her actions that had made his eyes roll back in his head and his jaw drop and his seed to spill.

But in the end, they had never gone beyond that; he had never used his mouth on her, and she had never asked him to.

But with Oliver, it felt different. With Oliver, everything felt different.

"I want you to use your mouth," she said.

"Have you ever had this before?" he asked. She shook her head. "Then I will do my best to please you. Guide me if I do it wrong."

He brought his lips between her legs and licked.

At the first touch of his tongue, she cried out. Her clutching fingers found a pillow and held on. It felt as though she was a raft in a storm, and he the rocking waves. She had been wound so tight that every tiny movement against her felt as though the pleasure was splitting her apart again.

"Like this?" he asked. "Tell me, Emily."

"Like that," she managed. "There. Keep going."

"Mm." He made a satisfied noise, as though he had not been content until he received her instruction. And when he returned to her, it was with increased vigour. Her world turned to white, ripped apart at the seams, and her body rocked as he finally pushed her over the edge. Her climax washed over her. Waves and waves of it, the storm picking her up and tossing her across the seas until finally—finally—she reached the shore and came up for air.

Oliver climbed up her body, his hand resting lightly on her stomach, his nose pressing against her jaw. She turned, blindly seeking his mouth, and he offered it to her. He kissed her slowly, unhurriedly, though she could feel the urgency in the erection lying against her leg. She knew she wasn't beautiful, knew objectively she was plain, and she had made her peace with that. Until now, she had never thought she felt a need to be anything more. But Oliver made her feel as though she could be—as though he truly believed her to be.

And so, in this moment with him, she was.

A little of the ice around her heart cracked.

"Thank you," she said, drawing back.

He kissed her nose. "As always, you are very welcome. Especially if"—he rolled them so she lay across his body—"you might be inclined to please us both in return."

"If I said no?"

He grinned, unrepentant. "I would beg. You've heard me often enough already today, but I would be amenable to more."

"You don't think it's unbecoming for a man to beg for a woman in this way?" she asked seriously.

"Unbecoming? Darling, it's one of the most arousing things to happen to me." His hand slid up and down her side. "The only thing that would be unbecoming would be to break your trust."

She kissed him then, as deeply as she could manage, and slid down onto his erection. He cupped her breast, and the feel of him, everywhere, was so good she felt as though she might cry.

Suddenly, she wanted more—more, more, more. She was greedy for it, needy for it, desperate for it. For him. Every single last bit of him that he gave her. She wanted it all.

He made a sound in the back of his throat, and she caught his lip between her teeth, biting it hard. A new wave of pleasure washed through her. Her climax had made her sensitive, but not so much that she couldn't fathom bringing herself to another peak.

His eyes bored into her, holding her captive. "I won't forget this until the day I die."

"You're too young to make such outlandish claims."

His hand gripped her hip, not guiding but merely holding. "I'm not too young to know what I want."

She dug her nails into his skin, holding on so tightly she thought she might draw blood. She wrapped a hand around his neck, needing to feel in control again. Everything was slipping, too bright and too fast, too wonderful for her to fight.

"Can I hold you here?" she asked, careful not to lean any of her weight on that hand.

His eyes were dark, and he brought his free hand to her wrist, encouraging her to apply more pressure. "I trust you."

Such liberties. She could not have imagined taking them before—not with anyone else. Until now, she had not known such desires existed, had never suspected that such things took place in the bedchamber.

She squeezed her fingers, just a little. His breath rasped, and she felt it. Right there, she felt his life as clearly as she felt her own, and she *held it.* The magnitude of that thought overwhelmed her, brought to the edge in such a rush of slick desire that he gasped. He thrust up into her, his hips rolling in a surge of pleasure that scattered her thoughts. There was nothing in her world but him.

"Don't stop," she gasped.

His face was tight with strain, alive with desire. He was every perfect creation mankind had to offer, and just for now, for this one last precious moment, he was *hers.* He had offered; she had taken.

Her heart clenched at the thought of the inevitable parting that would follow, and that was the moment her body chose to release its tension. She shuddered, eyes rolling back in her head, and Oliver kept going, kept obeying her demands until his own climax overtook him, and jerked free, withdrawing and finishing messily across his stomach.

Sweat misted them both. As he panted, she flopped beside him and slid her fingers down the long column of his throat—the one she had held and squeezed and felt his life beat through just moments ago—to his chest and the ragged pounding of his heart. It matched hers.

"I never thought I would do this again," she murmured.

He cocked a brow. "Do what? Lie with a man?" His gaze sharpened. "Or lie with me?"

She laughed, the admission slipping from her more easily than she would have guessed. "Both. Either."

"Do you regret it?"

She paused, looking at him carefully. They were tangled together—not embracing, but close. "No," she said eventually. "Not yet."

"I hope you continue not to, then," he said, and rolled off the bed to find a cloth to clean her up with. Emily lay back, her hands across her chest as she stared at the ceiling and allowed her body to settle into this feeling of having been so thoroughly pleasured.

Along with the pleasant buzzing through her limbs, however, and the rush of boneless satisfaction that had filled her, she was aware of a slight ache in her heart. As good as this had been, it would be—by her own decree—their last time. Probably her last time ever. Now she had experienced what it could be like with a man who submitted, could she ever return to intimacy that required a man compelling *her* into submission?

Yet how empty the years seemed to her now without that intimacy.

When Oliver returned with the promised cloth, he leaned over to kiss her again. She allowed it, wanting to thank him for everything he had shown her even as she knew that every time she let him, it would be worse when they parted.

"Emily," he said against her mouth. "Emily, I can't bear it any longer."

"Can't bear what?" Her brows drew together, and she sat up, examining him. There were marks on his skin—*her* marks—and she should not have felt such a rush of exhilaration at the sight. "Did I hurt you?"

He shook his head, but there was a new expression in his eyes now. All his teasing had fallen away, revealing something that looked just as raw as her heart felt. "No," he said, and sucked in a breath. "I know you said I should expect nothing from you, and I admitted that I'd have no chance of convincing you otherwise, but I can't bear this. I can't. Let me care for you and Isabella—we can find her a good home, I promise. Another husband. I have connections—my sister is a duchess. You are the daughter of a gentleman; we are not so very disparate if you consider it. I can provide for you so you'll never have to go hungry again, and perhaps your sister will take some time forgiving us, but she *will*, and—"

"What are you saying?" Emily asked, her lips numb, the last of the post-coital bliss tightening and sinking until it resembled a lead weight inside her.

He gave a desperate, crooked sort of smile. "You know what I'm saying, darling. I'm asking you to marry me."

Chapter Twenty-Three

Emily gaped at him in horror. Of all the things he could have done and said on this, their last night together, he had to say the worst thing possible.

Asking her to marry him when he knew she could not. *Would* not.

At her expression, he came to sit at the edge of the bed. "I know you're scared," he said, "but there's no reason to be. I'm not Marlbury, and although no one can protect against death indefinitely, you are not your mother, or your father. As for Isabella—we can take her with us. I have connections that—"

"Enough." She didn't recognise her voice, or the cold, almost cruel edge to it. "All this to trick me into marriage?"

"Trick you? If I had tricked you, I would have a marriage certificate in my pocket, or we would be making our way back to Gretna Green." He ran a tortured hand through his hair. "I've finally found something I want, Em. And I think you might want it too, if you would only let yourself want something for once in your damn life."

She *had* allowed herself to want something—she had allowed herself to want this, and he had thrown it back in her face. "I told you my reasons for remaining unmarried," she said, her calm disintegrating. Anger was safer than grief. "I told you repeatedly I would not marry you—and you promised never to ask me. You *promised.*"

"Would marrying me be so terrible? I'm not the finest gentleman in the land, but I can help you. Surely it would be better than the life you've been living."

There was this awful cracking feeling in her chest, a hollow ache that she knew would not go away no matter how hard she tried. "I'm not some pity project, Oliver. You don't get to swoop in like one of Arthur's knights of the round table. I'm not a princess in a tower."

"I wouldn't be saving you," he said, face suddenly alive with frustration. "You'd be saving me! And I'd be helping you. That's what marriage is—or what it can be."

Despite her best attempts, she imagined what her future with Oliver could look like. A house in the country—modest, but well-proportioned. Larger than the one she had grown up in. Stables with several horses and a carriage. Servants. Seasons in London. New dresses and shoes and absurdly rich and titled relations.

Security.

And Oliver. She would wake beside him every morning. Write his letters for him. Watch him strive to become better in ways she now knew he would.

It was all so very tempting.

But they had known each other a handful of days—not long enough to know if they had a foundation for marriage. Perhaps his motivations had changed, but he had left for the country with the intention of finding a wife to spite his brother. If she were that wife, her relationship with his family would be strained, probably for the rest of time.

A mere week ago, he had intended to marry her sister.

Isabella.

How could Emily ever marry the man her sister had hoped to marry? This was one thing—a short, fateful affair that would end when he took her home. But marriage?

She couldn't.

"Isabella," she managed.

Oliver rolled to his feet, finding his breeches and awkwardly tugging them back on. "That again?" There was disgust in his voice. "How many times must I bring up her selfishness for you to believe it? She never loved me, and while she may love you, let me tell you now, she would not sacrifice herself for you if the positions were reversed." His eyes were hard now, no sign of gold or green in their brown depths. "You are denying yourself for a sister who does not respect you enough to do the same."

"And what would you know about my relationship with my sister?"

"I know enough." He snapped his jaw together. "You know she never once mentioned bringing you with us when we married. Every time we spoke of the future, she mentioned her visions for herself. I assumed we would bring you, given your situation, but she did not once ask me."

Emily stared at him, stunned. It felt as though he had reached a hand inside her chest, taken hold of her lungs, and squeezed. The pressure was so intense, she couldn't move.

Nothing suggested he was lying—even now he groaned and strode across the room, dragging his hand through his hair in such visible frustration, she almost pitied him. Almost. The ache in her heart was too great for much else.

"She will have wanted me to accompany you," she said, her lips numb, tasting the words as she said them and praying she could find truth there. Surely she could find truth there. Isabella loved her. Yes, she could be young and headstrong and impetuous—as were all girls her age—but she *loved* her.

"Perhaps," Oliver said. "But listen to me. If I told her that leaving you behind was my condition for marrying you, I have no doubt in my mind that she would have agreed." He came back to kneel before her the way he had done more than once, taking her hand in his and smoothing his thumb over her knuckles. Almost a week of no work, and they were slowly beginning to heal. "Do not," he said quietly, "sacrifice your happiness for her sake."

"My happiness?" Emily choked on a laugh, but there was no humour in the sound. "How can you be so sure that we will make each other happy? Real life is not as idyllic as you imagine. You think you want me now, but what of tomorrow? What of next week when you encounter a prettier girl? You are only three-and-twenty, and—"

"Do not assume I am incapable of knowing my own mind. Do you think me so fickle?"

"Yes," she said, ripping her hand from his and also standing. Where were her clothes? "I think you are eager for acceptance and a place in the world, and you think that I can provide that, but it is out of the question." She snatched her chemise from the floor. "I can't stay."

"Where will you go?" He stared at her, something bleak in his eyes.

"To Dalston."

"Now? In the dark?"

"Yes, in the dark. I was a fool to agree to stay."

He picked up his shirt with one arm and painstakingly wiggled into it. "Fine. Then allow me to escort you."

"No."

"I won't come inside," he said impatiently. "I'll see you to the front door and leave you there, never seeing you again if you wish." His words were bitter, and she wondered if he had intended them to be. "But I cannot in good conscience let you make the journey alone."

"I am perfectly capable of handling things alone," she said, wrestling with her dress. Her hands shook, and she forced them to steady. This would not break her. If he had not asked for marriage, they could have parted amicably. Now there would be this frustration standing in the way.

Her head pounded. Tiredness, that was all. Once she returned home and found Isabella safe, she could repair any damage her absence had caused, and everything would go back to how it had been.

Isabella would forgive her in time. They would be happy.

"Let me do this one last thing for you," he said.

"I should never have come here." Her voice broke, and she pretended it didn't. "Why did you have to go and ruin everything?"

He gave her a soft, sad smile. "I think you know why." Finally dressed, if approximately, he came to stand before her, looking every inch the gentleman and nothing like the man she had ravished just minutes earlier. "Wait for me in the taproom," he said. "I'll hire us a carriage."

Then he was gone, and she was at liberty to sit helplessly on the bed, press her hands against her face, and give way to tears.

Oliver could not have proposed *more* badly. There was no way he could have made a worse go of it.

Not that he didn't think marrying her was an excellent idea, but he could have chosen a better occasion for announcing it to her. Any other time would have been better than the tender, vulnerable, naked moment directly in the aftermath of strictly unwed debauchery.

He scowled as he stomped through the inn, informing the hassled innkeeper that they would not be staying and that he required a carriage with immediate effect. Then he scowled some more when he stepped outside to find it was raining once again. The snow had all but turned to slush. Soon, it would flood. There was already mud everywhere.

And, of course, it was dark. Already.

They were only perhaps an hour from Dalston, and from there, he would have nowhere to go.

Only an hour left with her.

He rather doubted he would get much of a goodbye.

Confound it, what had he been *thinking*?

He'd been so afraid of losing her, he had broken his word and guaranteed her loss far sooner than he would have otherwise. The question, the solution to her problems, had fallen out of his mouth without any assistance from his brain, and he had ruined everything.

He might as well just be honest with himself and call it love. Nothing else could make such a fool of him.

His mood only deteriorated further when he re-entered the taproom, having bargained for the use of a carriage with almost all his remaining money, to find Emily's face blotchy and her eyes red-rimmed.

She avoided his gaze.

Wonderful.

"I'm sorry," he said in a low voice, taking her elbow as he guided her through the room, which was now increasingly filled with rougher-looking locals. When she flinched and stepped away from him, he dropped his hand. "I never wanted to upset you."

"Then why—" She cleared her throat and found her composure again. "You should never have asked."

"No," he agreed. "I shouldn't. But that doesn't mean we can't part as friends, Em. Whatever else I may feel, I don't want to lose my friendship with you."

In the middle of the courtyard, a rickety carriage waited for them, a drenched ostler holding the reins and an equally drenched coachman glowering at them in the light of the oil lamp. Emily hesitated in the inn's doorway, and Oliver removed his coat, sliding it clumsily over her shoulders. His bad arm ached, and he wished he were anywhere but here. All his euphoria had deserted him.

Still, he put his hand against her back and guided her to the carriage. Up close, it was even more dilapidated than he had thought—certainly a relic from the last century. He shivered as he handed her in and shut the door. Inside, it was even darker, and he debated lighting the internal lamp swinging from its hook by the door, but eventually decided against it.

"You cannot give me your coat," she said, shucking it off and tossing it at him. "I won't take your charity."

He huffed an incredulous breath. "Is that why you think I proposed?"

"I'm not ashamed of the life I lead."

"I never once suggested you ought to be," he said, feeling as though he had sunk into a fever dream. Just an hour ago, he had been inside her, and it had been bliss. "But what comes next? Are you going to stay in that old house for the rest of your life as it slowly rots around you?"

Her sharp intake of breath was enough to tell him his words had landed, and he instantly regretted them.

"I happen to like that house," she said.

He closed his eyes. "Of course you do."

The swaying motion of the carriage threatened to disrupt his stomach, and he had flashbacks to the last time they had been in the vicinity of a carriage—and one a deal sight better than this. *Then*, the weather had been equally bad, and he knew that he had not been inebriated.

He did not have the same faith in the coachman.

Darkness continued to fall.

The silence stretched between them.

"What will you do once you've dropped me off at home?" she asked. "It's late."

"I still have my watch and ring." He shrugged. "That should get me a room for the night, then I expect I will have to take the stagecoach down to my brother. If the worst happens, I should be able to travel post."

She closed her eyes; he saw little in the dim light, but he saw that. "You shouldn't have come with me."

"If I had procured a decent carriage in daylight, I might not have done." Especially given he had offered for her, and she had refused him. This proximity and coldness was akin to torture. "But, unfortunately, that was not on the cards for today, and I would prefer to be here in case something happens."

"Nothing's going to happen."

As she said that, the carriage turned a particularly sharp corner, and the springs creaked ominously as they leaned to the right. Emily reached for his knee, and he gripped her as tightly as he dared, holding his breath as the carriage righted itself.

She let out a long, shaky breath, and when he squeezed her fingers, she didn't pull her hand free.

"Just in case," he repeated.

And this time, she said nothing to counteract his claims.

Chapter Twenty-Four

The darkness of winter did not conceal the bitter reality of the house Emily lived in. As they approached, the dilapidated carriage swaying alarmingly, the golden lamp on the front illuminated the barren front garden and the gate, which had largely fallen off its hinges. Beyond, the house loomed, half its windowsills rotten, and the other half boarded. Emily had done that herself after a particularly bad storm the previous winter had blown the glass in.

Weeds strangled the path to the door, half dead, poking from the slush like gravestones.

Quiet despair settled on her heart at the sight. Her father's home, fallen into disrepair. The remainder of her life to be spent here with no reprieve.

Opposite her, Oliver looked at the house without speaking, no doubt thinking many of the things she was. She had rejected him for this; it could not fail to be a blow to his ego. Or worse, a blow to his heart. No matter how transient his affections may be, she had no doubt he felt them for her.

Time would heal them, but for now, she expected he felt the sting as painfully as she did.

He swung his gaze to her. "So this is goodbye."

This was so much worse than she had imagined it would be. His fingers still curled around hers, and she freed them without effort; he released her at once. His eyes were shadowed in the dim light, but she saw the inner corners of his mouth press into a thin line, and she felt his pain deep in her chest, as though she were a tree and he wielded an axe, and he had just sent her tumbling down.

"Don't think ill of me," she said. "If you can."

His mouth softened, just a fraction. "I could never think ill of you."

"I'm sure you could contrive to. But thank you for saying it." She wished she could lean in and press her lips to his, one last time, but that would be foolish. So, instead, she folded her hands on her lap. The moment stretched between them. All the things she wanted to say crowded her throat; she could say none of them.

"Goodbye, then," she said as the gruff, maybe-drunk coachman swung open the door. Rain splattered inside, and she climbed out into dreadful, miserable weather. The rust on the gate bit into her hands as she swung it open, and she cast one final glance back at the carriage. The door still hung open as Oliver watched her from inside the carriage.

A cold wind tucked under her collar, and she put her head down as she hurried to the front door, pushing at the handle to open it. Locked.

Of course it was locked; Emily should have thought about this, but she had not thought to take a key with her. The only thing she had taken was the pistol, but that would be no help now.

She rapped on the door, peering through the nearest window to see if she could find a light. Nothing. Only cobwebs and blackness. After a few more moments of silence, she made her way along the path to the back of the house, familiarity leading the way even in the dark. The back door led into the kitchens, and even here, the windows were blank.

For the first time, panic crept into her throat.

If Isabella were here, she would at least have a single candle lit. They usually spent their time in the kitchen, but it was entirely plausible that Isabella had instead gone upstairs. But the upper floor lay as dark as the lower. And there were no footsteps approaching at the sound of her knocking. No sound stirring at all. It was as though the house had been abandoned.

Her damp cloak pulled around her, Emily pounded harder, hitting the wood until her hands ached. Still, there was nothing.

Where could Isabella be? Of course, it was plausible that she had left the house to go to the tavern or somewhere for entertainment. When was the dance at the *Rose & Crown* that she had mentioned? Emily rubbed her forehead, trying to think. There was no money for that; if Isabella *had* gone, where had she found the funds?

Had she gone to stay with a friend? If so, Emily couldn't imagine whom it could be; Isabella was generally loved by everyone, but very few people had enough surplus over winter to feed another mouth.

"Isabella!" she called. "It's Emily. Open the door."

No reply.

She turned, about to hurry to the front door and try again, when a figure loomed from the gloom. A scream built in her throat; she sucked in air to release it.

"It's me," Oliver said urgently, his hand finding hers. His skin was so warm. "What's wrong?"

Rain drowned them both. He had abandoned the relative safety of the carriage for this. "I'm not sure," she said. "The door's locked and Isabella isn't letting me in."

He glanced at the house. "She doesn't seem to be here."

"Then where could she be?" Emily demanded, her panic getting the better of her. "You don't understand—we have *nothing*. Even if we had family somewhere for her to visit, she could not have afforded to travel there."

"There could be a wholly reasonable explanation."

There could be, but that creeping feeling of dread was crawling up her spine again, the feeling that something was terribly wrong.

There had been enough food for the week, if Isabella had been careful—she wouldn't have starved. But could she have fallen ill? Without Emily, there was no one to look after her.

"Do you want to come back to the *Rose & Crown* with me?" Oliver asked.

She shook her head. "I want to find a way inside. If she isn't there—surely she'd have left a note for in case I came back." Unless she had assumed Emily would not be coming back at all.

"All right." He reached out to tap a window she had boarded. "May I?"

"Break it?"

"It strikes me as being rather easier than attempting to kick down a door."

"I thought you were leaving?"

He huffed a derisive breath, his hair plastered to his scalp. "I can leave after we discover where Isabella is."

"Thank you."

He said nothing, just gripped the boards nailed across the window and yanked them free. Emily had evidently done a poor job fixing them down, as they came away almost immediately.

"Let me," she said once the empty window was revealed. With Oliver's bad arm, she didn't want him climbing inside and potentially hurting himself. Besides, she knew the layout of the house far better. Before he could protest, she climbed inside and landed on the hard stone floor. Inside was almost as cold as the air outside—had Isabella not been laying the fires?

Perhaps she *was* lying ill upstairs somewhere.

No, she couldn't think like that.

This was the pantry. Using her hands, she felt her way out and down the corridor into the main kitchen. There, she navigated the large table she had sat at so many times, and reached the back door. Once, this had been where the servants had received the deliveries, but there were no deliveries to be had any longer, so she had bolted it shut years ago. They rarely opened it.

She gripped the large bolt and tugged. Rust briefly held it in place, and she despaired of getting it open, especially with the wood swelling in the rain, but eventually she yanked it open.

Oliver hurried inside and shut the door again, slamming it against the howl of the wind. By the sound of it, the weather was working itself up to be a veritable storm.

"Wait there," she said, moving to the fireplace where the tinderbox resided. From there, she found a candle and lit it, struggling for a moment with her cold, wet fingers.

Finally, light bloomed, and she looked around at the empty kitchen. She hadn't expected anyone to be here in the dark, yet her heart somehow sank at the distinct lack of human life.

"Is there another candle?" Oliver asked. "We should search the house."

She didn't question his *we.* Until she found Isabella, she would take all the help she could get. "I think so," she said. "Hold on . . ." She found a stub, the tallow greasy against her fingers, and lit it with the first. Then she handed the first candle to Oliver. "You check downstairs and I'll go up. We don't use most of the downstairs rooms, but check them anyway, just in case. I'll meet you back here if I don't find anything."

He nodded, expression grim, and left the room. She hurried for the closer servants' stairs. At this time of night, Isabella shouldn't be asleep, but she couldn't suppress the small nub of hope that she might be, and all this would be over.

Upstairs felt just as dark and dank as downstairs. The wooden floor underneath the carpet creaked as she walked past. "Isabella?" she called, making her way to the bedroom they shared. "Isabella, where are you?"

The door hung slightly ajar, and Emily's heart squeezed in her chest as she pushed it fully open with a squeak of the hinges.

A rush of cool, still air greeted her. Silence. As she'd expected, the room was empty, the covers thrown back on the bed, and a pillow dislodged and sitting at an angle. Judging from the staleness of the air, no one had been here for several days.

So Isabella *had* left, after all.

Emily closed her eyes, pressing a hand to her stomach. She had to *think*.

Isabella could be somewhere in the village. If she was, that likely meant everyone knew of her disappearance, which would be another hurdle to face.

If she wasn't . . .

Where could she have gone? There was nowhere Emily could think of.

One thing at a time.

Before she came to any conclusions, she searched through the trunk that contained Isabella's dresses. Almost all were gone, along with her chemises and stockings and shoes. Her brush, too, was missing, as well as what few cosmetic items Isabella possessed. Their mother's pearl necklace—one of the few things they hadn't sold—also gone.

So Isabella had packed before she left. And presumably, she didn't intend to come back.

Emily pressed her fingers against her forehead. "Bella, you fool," she muttered. "Where have you gone?"

"Emily!" Oliver's voice, urgent, from the base of the stairs. "She left you a note."

A note. Her knees went weak with relief. "Oh thank heavens," she said, hurrying so fast that her candle flame flickered.

Oliver waited at the base of the stairs, a sheet of paper in one hand, the candle illuminating the bleak expression on his face with the other. "I'm sorry, Emily," was all he said as he handed her the note.

By the looks of Isabella's handwriting, the note had been scribbled in a rush, and there was a blot of ink at the bottom of the page.

Emily, the note ran. *By the time you receive this, you are no doubt married to the gentleman I had intended to catch for myself. Do not think me ignorant of your scheming. No matter; I have found a greater prize, and one you failed to win. Are you not proud of me? You ought to be, considering the lengths you went to in order to steal Mr Beaumont.*

When we next meet, you will have to curtsy and refer to me as 'my lady' for I will outrank you.

Isabella

"My lady," Emily whispered, brushing the page as though she could summon her sister from it. "Oliver . . . Does she mean what I think she does?"

Oliver stared at the note, his mouth in a hard line, the candlelight gleaming in his eyes. "It's possible another lord travelled to the area."

"Possible, but likely? This week? Lord Marlbury is the only lord I have ever met in all my years living here. Which means—it has to mean—"

"She has run off with Lord Marlbury," he said grimly.

Chapter Twenty-Five

Marlbury.

Of course it damn well was. Oliver had been the one to draw Marlbury's attention to Isabella; after seducing Emily, Marlbury probably thought it would be amusing to seduce Isabella, too. Both sisters. A set.

He pinched his nose, trying to think through this mess.

"But how," Emily said blankly. "Isabella didn't even *know* Marlbury. I did everything I could to keep them separate."

"That doesn't matter," Oliver said. "I told him about my intentions towards Isabella—as they had been at the time."

"So what, he sought her out?"

"If he discovered I left with you, it's a possibility."

"For what reason?"

"Boredom? Spite? His father sent him to rusticate in the country because of his debts and bad behaviour in London. He'd become an embarrassment to his father—no doubt he was entertained by the prospect of causing havoc here, too."

Emily merely stared at him. He should be thankful he wasn't blaming him for this, but he wished she would. Marlbury was his friend, and he felt responsible. If he had never come to this part of the country, none of this would have happened.

"I expect they'll be at Bidlington Hall, if that's the case," Oliver said. "We can go there now and bring her back." And he would have the pleasure of confronting Marlbury, preferably with his fists. His sister, Annabelle, had married a lord with many a boxing ring under his belt, and Oliver had picked up a thing or two. He had never been especially physically minded, but he would enjoy this.

"If they are at Bidlington Hall," Emily said, inhaling deeply as though to find her equilibrium, "then all the servants will know."

"Servants always know these things."

"And if the servants know, the village will, too." She swung her gaze back to Oliver. "But I won't force Isabella to marry him, Oliver. I won't."

"I doubt you'll be able to, even if you wanted to." He plucked the letter from her hands and put it aside. Then he took her hand with his. "Right now, we must focus on retrieving Isabella. Do you want to join me in visiting Bidlington Hall?"

Her eyes were wet as she stared at him. "Join you?"

"Well, it is my carriage. Unless you intend to walk in the rain?" At her astonished blink, he clucked his tongue. "Did you think I would leave you here and now? Someone has to punch Marlbury in the face, and I'm sorry, darling, but I can't let it be you—though I admit that you have prior claim."

"Oliver . . ." She reached for the banister, holding herself upright. "What if she isn't there?"

"Then I will help you find her."

"Isabella is not—you do not need to do that," she said weakly.

"Need is such a strange word. If my conscience prompts me to, does that make it a need?" What was a need, entirely aside from his conscience, was to ease the worry from her face. "If there's anything I can do to help, I will. Besides"—at the thought of her confronting Marlbury alone, something dark and furious rose in his chest—"I would much rather you were not left to go alone." At her slight frown, he suppressed the dark anger. "Do you have blankets? The night is cold."

She opened her mouth, as though she had prepared to say something else—to argue again, probably—but his question disarmed her, and she merely nodded. "Upstairs. Wait here."

He did as he was told, glancing around the ruined house. Once, it must have been fine; there was no ballroom, but he had passed a spacious drawing room and a grand dining room. Certainly a gentleman's abode.

It might still be saved; he hoped, for Emily's sake, it would be, but he didn't know how she would contrive to save it. As it stood, she barely had the funds to live in it and not starve.

The problem felt like his to solve, but she'd spurned his—impulsive, stupid—offer of help. Finding Isabella, forcing his former friend to face justice, was the only thing left he *could* do.

"Here," she said, hurrying back towards him and thrusting musty-smelling blankets in his good arm. Immediately, he proceeded to shake one out, draping it over her shoulders.

"Oliver," she started.

"I won't have you catching a chill all for the sake of your foolish sister." At the thought of the note, his gut burned with anger again. "She did this out of spite, you know."

"But how did she know I'd gone with you?" Emily asked weakly. "I never showed her the note. She was asleep when I left. When I disappeared, why did she assume I intended to steal you from her?"

"There are two options," Oliver said. "Either she saw you and me together when you thought she was asleep, or you disappeared and she went to Bidlington Hall and asked for me—only to find I was also gone. Marlbury will have seen to the rest, or perhaps he merely took advantage of her natural suspicions. She's mistaken about one thing, though." His voice was colder than he had intended, matching the spray of rainwater as he unbolted the door. "I was never hers to steal."

Wind rocked the carriage as it made its laborious way to the house on the hill. Bidlington Hall. Emily had only ever been there a few times before, sneaking to the servants' entrance where Lord Marlbury had been waiting for her.

"Are you all right?" Oliver leant forward, his good elbow braced against his knee. She could see so little of him, save for shapes, but somehow she knew him so well that she already knew what those shapes made up. Without seeing, she knew his eyes would hold concern and his oft-playful mouth would be tight with worry.

"Yes," she said.

He huffed a breath that told her he knew she was lying. But all he said was, "We're nearly there. I should go in first and enquire after him."

"No." Emily shook her head, feeling as though her breath was too tight. "I need to be the one to do this."

"Emily." He hesitated. "If the servants come to know you've been travelling with me—"

"There's no point in trying to preserve my reputation." She tightened her fingers around her cloak until her knuckles ached. "I respect and admire you for the attempt, but I have no interest in my reputation when my sister's is at stake. Do you really presume no one will know where I've been? Or that I'm with an unmarried man? Rumours fly, especially if Isabella was so bitter as to run away with the man I warned her against."

"You warned her against him?"

"Yes. And now she thinks she has won some great victory over me because *she* will be the one to marry him." Emily sighed, peering out of the dark window. "I suppose she thinks she is a better marriage prospect than I."

"She would be wrong," Oliver said shortly.

"You didn't think so initially. And she *is* prettier than me. Even you can't deny it."

"To a stranger, perhaps," he said, "but not to me."

She shook her head, deciding not to argue the point. That didn't matter now. None of it mattered except getting Isabella back.

The coach rolled up the driveway to the house, most of its lights extinguished. An unpromising sign, but evening had now advanced into night, the darkness absolute. Perhaps they had retired.

If they had retired to bed—

No, she wouldn't think of it.

"I'll ask if he's at home," Oliver said. "If he is, I'll come and fetch you. No point us both getting wet, and I would rather the servants didn't know you were with me unless absolutely necessary."

Even now, knowing everything he did about her past and with Isabella's shame hanging over her, he tried to preserve her reputation. Emily tried not to love him for it, and failed.

"Hurry," she said.

Oliver opened the door, letting in a brief flurry of rain before he slammed it behind him. She looked up at the imposing house beyond, familiarity hitting her in a nostalgic wave. This was the first time she had been here in seven years. She let her gaze trail across the magnificent facade, cloaked in rain and darkness. What a spectacularly beautiful house, and what rottenness it held inside.

Once, she had come here with her heart in her mouth and anticipation in her chest, believing that she would one day be mistress.

So much for that.

Seventeen, it seemed, was the age for foolishness—hers and Isabella's. But she had been young and ignorant. No one had warned her away from Marlbury. Isabella had the benefit of her experience, and she had still made the same choices.

Oliver turned away from the door after speaking to the butler.

No, worse choices. If Marlbury had asked her to run away with him, she would have refused. Isabella, apparently, had jumped at the chance.

Oliver strode back towards her, his face shadowed. Over the course of their time together, it was as though she had seen him grow from a boy into a man, the transition happening before her very eyes. And now it was complete; he had left boyishness behind him, at least for the present.

She found she missed it.

She found she adored the man he had become.

"He's gone," she said, shocked by the cracked desperation of her voice.

"Three days ago, according to the butler," Oliver said, pounding the roof once to let the coachman know they were ready to set off. "And his father is due to arrive to the house tomorrow. He sent a letter ahead informing Marlbury of his imminent arrival, and the same day, Marlbury left." At her blank look, he added, "You may believe his father will disapprove of his actions, and so he is attempting to evade the consequences."

"But if he took Isabella with him—did he?" she asked, looking into his face.

"The butler confirmed he took a young lady with him, and I can only assume it was Isabella, yes."

"Then why?"

"Either she volunteered to go with him, or he offered to take her."

"But why," Emily said, her lips numb. "Surely—why would he go to all the trouble of taking her if he meant nothing by the association?" She sent him a pleading glance, although she already knew the answer, deep down. "Do you think he could be intending a runaway marriage?"

Oliver hesitated. "I think it unlikely," he said at last.

"Then why take her at all? I don't understand. Surely he must know he would attract censure for such a thing."

"In London?" Oliver sighed, and she felt the full impact of her naivety. In London, of course there would be no one who would really notice or care. Isabella was a nobody. Society only cared when one of their own was affected; otherwise, they were more than happy to turn a blind eye.

Marlbury was the son of an earl. There were plenty of things such a man could do and get away with.

The thought made her sick to the stomach.

"We don't know anything for certain," Oliver said. "Tomorrow morning, we'll set off after him."

"Not tonight?"

"Not in this weather, I'm afraid." He grimaced. "I don't have the funds."

And neither did Emily. She fought the urge to drop her head into her hands. "So what now?"

"Now I'll take you home and discover what direction he went in." Oliver met her gaze. "I'm sorry, Emily. This mess is at least partially my fault."

"No." She shook her head. "Let's lay the blame at the appropriate door. Marlbury is most to blame here. And Isabella." Once, Emily would not have believed her sister capable of such things, but she would have been wrong.

"Then we'll have to make sure he suffers for what he's done." Oliver's knee brushed hers. "Will you let me in later tonight if I come to the back door?"

She knew what he was asking. If he could stay the night with her.

She could not bear to spend it alone.

"I'll leave it unlocked," she said.

"I won't let you down," he promised, and heaven help her, but she believed him.

Chapter Twenty-Six

The house was cold and quiet without Isabella or Oliver. Emily lit a candle, hating the tallow stench, and made her way upstairs. Once there, she lingered in the bedroom she had shared with her sister. The bed lay unmade, a nightgown discarded on the floor.

Emily closed her eyes. She gritted her teeth. And then, candle safely on the nightstand, she removed her soaking clothes, hanging them where they might drip, though not dry. Once in her nightgown, blankets thrown over her shoulders, she lit the fire with the remainder of the coal, coaxing the flame into life. Grit from the floor dug into her knees, and she laced her hands together, saying a prayer for the first time since her father's death.

That had been when she'd given up on God. On Sundays—most of them—she still went to church for appearance's sake, sitting at the back with Isabella and wishing that she could find the joy from faith that others did.

If he was the Holy Father, he was an absent one.

But now, on her knees before a flame as feeble as her hope, Emily clung to the last thing she had left. If there was a chance that God listened to prayers, she had to try. There was no dignity when there was desperation.

And she had more desperation than she knew what to do with. It poisoned her every breath.

"Please," she begged, her fingers clasped before her, the cold creeping down the gap between her collar and the bare skin of her back. "I know you probably hate me, but let me save her."

The flame flickered. It flared, its light seeming brilliant in the gloom, and Emily allowed herself to believe her prayer had been answered. Signs were easy to come by if one looked hard enough; one could pick apart the world in order to find the answers they were looking for in the wreckage. Ordinarily, she was not one to cling to such blind belief, but now she needed something to cling to.

As the coal dust caught and the embers glowed red with trapped heat, the chill in Emily's bones slowly fled, replaced by exhaustion. She rose, the blankets around her shoulders feeling impossibly heavy, and made her way to the bed she had once shared with her sister. Now, the dip where Isabella's body lay was cold.

So many times, they had giggled together. Small happinesses that had been born of love, not of luxury; they'd had cold toes pressed against each other's shins, and threadbare clothes that needed constant repairs. They went to bed hungry and spent those dim, hazy, in-between moments together dreaming of a different life.

Emily rested her head on her pillow. Tomorrow, she would return to being strong. But for now, she let herself feel.

Sleep took her the moment she closed her eyes.

Oliver paid the coachman and ducked into the still-bright lamplight of the *Rose & Crown*, the ale-soaked air immediately familiar. In the two weeks he'd been in this corner of the country, he'd come here often, although this time, he wasn't here to forget. He strode to the comely girl polishing glasses. Her gaze took him in and sharpened, no doubt recognising him.

He gave her his most winning smile. "I don't suppose you happen to know which direction Lord Marlbury went when he left Dalston?"

"What's in it for me, little lord?" Her voice was throaty and determined, her gaze already on the coin in his hand. One of the precious few left to him, but he would leave behind debts for Henry to berate him over if that was what it took.

"I just need to know if he was going in the London direction."

She took the coin and bit it. Satisfied, she put it in her apron pocket. "If anyone's seen the lord's coming and goings, it's John by the door. You'd be best off asking him. I can't tell you what he saw or hasn't saw."

Oliver tipped his hat at her, making her giggle, and wound through the smoke to where the doorman stood, arms crossed over a barrel chest. He was grizzled, close to his sixtieth year if Oliver had to guess, and his eyes were a pale blue as they met Oliver's.

"Have you seen Lord Marlbury's coach about three days ago?" Oliver asked, not waiting for the usual pleasantries. Emily waited for him at her hollow shell of a house, and he didn't intend to be long.

"Aye, that he did."

"In which direction?"

A laugh rumbled through him, and he hawked, spitting on the cobbles by his feet. "Headed south, of course," he said. "Towards London, in my mind, like the devil was on his tail. Gave you the regular slip."

"That he did," Oliver agreed. "Thank you for your time."

John nodded, scraping a hand along white stubble. "I hope you catch him."

"Yes," Oliver said. "I hope so, too."

The back door was unbolted as promised. His questing hands found a candle and flint, and after some tries, he succeeded in lighting it. The house groaned and protested around him as he made his way through it, following the smell of smoke until he reached the room Emily occupied. A fire sat in the grate, a blackened guard standing protectively before it.

And in the bed, Emily lay asleep under a pile of blankets, her face in flickering shadow.

Placing his candle on the table beside the stump of hers, he stripped and joined her in the bed, flinging the blankets over them both. As she rolled against his body, she shuddered, half waking from sleep, eyelids fluttering.

"Oliver?"

"I'm here." He kissed her forehead. "I'm sorry. All my clothes were wet."

"You're cold." She made a sound like a moan, then she pressed herself more firmly against him. "Where did you go?"

"Checking for certain that he went to London—or as sure as I can be—and procuring us seats on tomorrow's stagecoach. I'm afraid I don't have the funds to better get us there."

To his surprise, she turned her face up to his, her lips soft and lax with sleep, and kissed him on the mouth. "Thank you."

"It's the least I could do."

"I despise false modesty." She rested her head against his bare chest, and he held her close, one hand in her loose hair. "You did not need to help, but you did. And I will not forget that. When this is over—" She pressed a hand against his heart. "Whatever you wish from me then, you may have."

He almost asked if she meant marriage—and he thought she might. In gratitude, she would marry him, if he wished it.

And he did, he had not changed his mind about that, but he didn't want a pity wedding. A bride who married him out of gratitude and nothing more.

If they were ever to marry, it would be because she wanted him for a husband, independent of the things he had done for her.

He couldn't be sure that would ever happen. There had been real fear in her eyes when he'd proposed and she'd imagined a life with him. She'd told him love was poison, and he didn't know how a mere week with him would convince her any different.

At least she believed—hopefully—that Isabella had never loved him. That was a start, a single impediment removed.

"Sleep," he said, stroking her hair. "Don't think about that now."

To his relief and gratification, she did as he instructed, her body softening and her breaths turning languid and deep, warm against his skin.

He tried to imagine his life without her, and could not.

Everything he said to her was true—he would go into the maws of hell, if that was what it required, and he would drag Isabella back out. He would restore Emily her sister and her life, and from there, she could decide what she wanted. And he could dream, in that hopeless way he found himself indulging in more often this week than he ever had before, that she would decide she wanted him.

If not, he would find a way of walking away.

As she slept, she let out a sigh.

In the darkness, with no witnesses but the frayed edges of his own tattered heart, he gave voice to the words that had been burning inside him for so long. "I love you," he whispered. "I love you, and I think it might kill me."

Unknowing, she slumbered on.

Chapter Twenty-Seven

Emily woke with her head on Oliver's chest, his arm looped around her waist. The sensation was so unfamiliar, she took a moment to fully process it. Here she was, in her childhood bed, a naked man holding her. His breath lightly brushed her hair, and his chest rose and fell.

Grubby pre-dawn light streaked in through the threadbare curtains, illuminating his face just enough that when she raised her head, she could make out the faint, faded freckles across his cheeks and his luxurious half-moon lashes. In sleep, he was fully at peace, relaxed and at ease. If only he could stay this way. When he woke, her troubles would greet him, chasing away his smile.

First she had hurt him, and now she relied on him for his help.

How terribly, bitterly ironic.

She slid her fingers along his chin, brushing the steadily growing stubble there. The roughness sent heat through her, though she had no time to indulge in that. Part of her wished she could—wished she could put the grief and anger and fear in her body to rest just long enough to take him.

His eyes opened. Soft hazel, pupils pinpricked to reveal the rings of green at their full brightness. His lips moved against the palm of her hand, his hand firming at her waist. "Good morning, darling," he said, voice low and hoarse with sleep. "Did you sleep well?"

She had. Remarkably well with him there.

"This was the first time I've woken with a man in my bed." She pressed a kiss to his shoulder. "I only wish the circumstances were better."

Oliver slid his hand into his hair, and with an impressive show of abdominal strength, sat both of them up. He kissed her. "They could still be," he said against her mouth. "Not this morning. But perhaps next week, or the week after. All is not lost."

For several long, glorious seconds, she lost herself to the feel of his mouth on hers. By the movement of his body, he was more than ready for more, but she forced herself away, catching his face in her hands.

"I can't. Not here." She glanced at the pillow, where Isabella's head so often lay. "Not where she usually sleeps."

His face softened in understanding, and he pressed one final, chaste kiss to her lips before sliding out of the bed. The covers fell from him, and she had the perfect view to see the full extent of his nudity. And, incidentally, the full extent of his arousal.

"It'll pass," he said with a wry smile directed over his shoulder. "I often awaken like this, even without a beautiful woman in my bed."

Her cheeks heated, though she ought to have known better. "You are a flirt."

"I," he said solemnly, finding a case and opening it for a fresh shirt, "am yours, body and soul, Emily." He tugged it over his head, wincing as it caught his arm, then grinned. "And I am also a flirt. Flatter me and tell me I'm good at it."

"Why should I?"

"To satisfy my ego? Or perhaps because I have never once meant the flattery I've given a woman as much as the flattery I offer you. I say nothing lightly, you know. I think you are as damn near perfect as any woman I've encountered." Then, as though he had not delivered this with all the ease of informing her it might rain, he fastened his breeches and shrugged on his waistcoat. "We'll breakfast at the *Rose & Crown.* I have enough left for that, at least."

Emily frowned at the case containing his things. "You retrieved that from Lord Marlbury's house?"

"Well, I have no intention of coming back, and I confess, it's pleasing to be wearing something clean and fresh for once." He examined his waistcoat, which was particularly fine and looked out of place in her dingy room. "Pack your Sunday best for meeting my brother. Appearances matter to him a great deal, and although he will agree to help us, I have a vested interest in ensuring he approves of you."

Because he intended to marry her after all? She had offered to—and part of her even wanted to—but the thought terrified her.

"I doubt a pretty dress"—though she didn't have one of those—"would make him approve of me."

"Nonsense. He will like you a great deal."

"Don't lie to me merely to placate me, Oliver."

"You and he are rather similar," he said ruefully. "He took it upon himself to manage our father as much as he could and made the best of a situation I, certainly, could not have touched. And, from the outside, he seems somewhat . . ." He hesitated, fingers skating lightly across her cheekbone. "Cold."

Amusement, as bitter as it was warm, tinged her smile. "Like me?"

"Once you get to know him, you will discover he is secretly kind, and very dutiful. He cares a great deal about us all. I believe that is why he's been so harsh with me." He sat on the edge of the bed, looking uncommonly serious. "He'll help us, Em. For my sake if not for yours, but I think he will for your sake, too."

"How can you be so certain?" she asked, searching his eyes.

"Because I will ensure it. If there is one thing you can trust me on, it is that I will make this happen, one way or the other. Whether I must sacrifice my inheritance or commit myself to working on his estate for the rest of my life. Whatever it takes." He squeezed her hand, then kissed her fingers. "I'll admit my life thus far has not amounted to much, but it will amount to this. Trust me."

And Emily did. She could not have had any choice; with his earnest assurance and the determination in his eyes, she could not have done anything but surrender her doubt and place herself fully in his hands.

She could not have done anything but love him.

The journey to Licolnshire took four days. Emily spent a great deal of it silent, staring out of the window, and Oliver endured every bump and pothole the English roads had to offer. All the while, he thought about how he might persuade Henry to help. Louisa, he had no worries over—but he had stolen Henry's carriage and sworn he would marry the first girl he saw.

That resolution had been the cause of this mess.

Every night he and Emily spent together was another form of bliss and torture—a hint of what he could have if only she chose him.

Finally, on the fourth muddy, exhausting day of travel, they reached the inn at the village closest to Henry's estate. Oliver helped Emily out, and he collected their luggage from the roof. Emily had taken very little with them; he suspected because she had little to take.

"The house is about five miles that way," he said, nodding down the winding country road. "I'll see if we can hire a horse. Or perhaps a cart."

"I don't mind the walk."

"You aren't tired?"

"I'm very tired," she said, with a wry smile. "But a horse is an unnecessary cost when we have legs. And at least it's flat."

Considering he would have had to pawn something else to afford said unnecessary cost, Oliver resigned himself to the inevitable and picked up his case. "True. Compared to Cumbria, at least. Come on, the sooner we start, the sooner we'll get there." He shot her a glance. "I think it might rain."

"So much for looking presentable." She smoothed the skirt of her dress, which might once have been a very passable gown. "Even Henry won't blame me for the rain."

They walked in silence, or near to it. Oliver's arm ached from carrying his case, and his other arm ached within his sling. But that was nothing compared to his fear that Henry would react against Emily before even getting to know her, dismissing her as another of Oliver's whims rather than the lady he would have chosen to spend the rest of his life with.

Henry could judge him all he liked, but not Emily. Never Emily.

"Are you nervous?" she asked as they rounded the corner and Henry's house came into view. A large property made from golden sandstone, with twin pillars decorating the front by the door and two wings extending in an L behind. "To see your brother again?"

"Mm, a little. He'll be angry with me, and understandably so. I behaved badly the last time we parted. But I'm not ashamed of the reason I have come back, or of—" He almost slipped and said *loving you.* That would never do. "Or of you."

The sea breeze, heavy now with the scent of brine, whipped at Emily's hair, tossing it across her face. She was as lovely now as she had ever been, even travel-stained, and he hoped Henry would see past the patch on her skirt and the worn, faded lines of the muslin, and see the vibrancy of the woman that lay underneath.

She reached out a hand to his and squeezed once. He entwined his fingers with hers, bringing them to his mouth. Then, shoulders squared, he dropped her hand and strode to the door, and knocked.

Chapter Twenty-Eight

Emily held her breath as a footman opened the door, his expression barely cracking when he saw Oliver. His gaze travelled to her, and she did her best to remain utterly impassive. The corner of his mouth twitched, though whether in disapproval or amusement, she couldn't tell.

"Mr Beaumont," he said.

"I've come to see Lord Eynsham, Warren," Oliver said. "Can you take us to him?"

Once again, the footman glanced at her, then back. "And your companion, sir?"

"This is Miss Brunton," Oliver said, taking her arm possessively. "And she comes with me."

"Of course, sir." The footman gestured inside. "Right this way."

Emily steeled herself as she stepped inside the house—though it was more of a mansion. Even her childhood memories couldn't conjure something quite this grand. Marble hallways, statues mounted on plinths around the circumference of the large entrance hall. A beautiful mural across one wall. Grand windows overlooking the distant sea.

Oliver was right: these people certainly had the means to help her, if only they had the will. If she could have contrived without appealing to them, cap in hand, she would have done, but she would sacrifice even her pride to protect her sister.

As they walked through a series of large rooms, Emily noticed the lack of portraits. She had expected a family with such an impressive lineage to display their heritage in the most ostentatious way possible, but not Lord and Lady Eynsham.

Interesting.

"Oliver?" A dark-haired lady in sprigged muslin, a sheaf of dried flowers in her hands, entered the library from the other door and frowned. "It *is* you. What an unexpected surprise. Thank you, Warren, I can take it from here."

The footman inclined his head and returned the way they had come. The lady advanced across the room towards them. She was perhaps ten years older than Emily, and although she was remarkably pretty, there was a certain cynicism in her hazel eyes.

"So," she said, giving Emily an assessing glance, "am I to presume you did, in fact, marry the first girl you saw?"

Oliver's back stiffened, but red rose to his cheeks. "Not quite, Louisa."

"So this lady is not your wife?"

"No," Oliver said.

Louisa—Lady Eynsham—looked fully at Emily. "If he has made you promises, let me know and I will ensure he keeps them."

Oliver groaned. "If I were to do such a thing, would I really bring her *here*?"

"I confess I'd expected you to bring a wife here." She leaned in and kissed his cheek. "It's good to see you, Oliver, *so long* as you have not compromised this poor girl."

"Her name is Miss Brunton." Oliver, Emily noted, made no mention of having not compromised her. A fair thing to do, given the opposite was true. "Emily, this is my sister-in-law, Lady Eynsham."

Lady Eynsham smiled at her, and Emily knew, suddenly, that this woman would be an ally here. "A pleasure to meet you, Miss Brunton. Please forgive my welcome."

"I know it's somewhat presumptuous of me to arrive in this way," Emily began, but Oliver shook his head.

"I was the one to bring her here," he said. "We've come to speak with Henry."

"But the business Mr Beaumont wishes to speak to Lord Eynsham about is mine," Emily said. "My sister has . . ." She hesitated, but they had come asking for help; she could conceal nothing. "My sister has run away with a known rake, and I need help finding her. Mr Beaumont has been so good as to champion my cause."

At *Mr Beaumont*, Oliver blinked, glancing at her with sudden amusement. Lady Eynsham, almost certainly, also caught the look, but Emily didn't have the energy to worry about that.

She was an unmarried woman arriving unchaperoned with an unmarried man. There were certain conclusions that could be drawn from that—and really, were they wrong?

"In that case, may I suggest you take this time to freshen up?" Lady Eynsham said. "You have been travelling, and did you walk here?" She glanced at the mud along the hem of Emily's skirt.

Emily flushed, hating that wealth—or lack thereof—could make her feel like this. "I have no further clothes to change into, my lady."

"Call me Louisa," Lady Eynsham said cheerfully. "We don't stand on ceremony here, and if you're a friend of Oliver's, you're a friend of ours. As for clothes—I am *certain* I will have something that suits your complexion far better than mine. Are you hungry? I'll send for a tray to be sent upstairs."

"Louisa," Oliver said. "Our request is of some urgency."

"Not so urgent that you can't make yourselves presentable," Louisa said. "And eat something. You look half dead, the both of you." She gave Oliver a stern glance, and to Emily's surprised, he ducked his head.

"If you insist."

"I will not allow you to neglect Miss Brunton's needs. Now, my dear, please do come with me. Allow me to rectify the incivility of my welcome."

Emily was too tired—and yes, hungry—to argue. "Thank you, my lady."

"I recommend you do the same," Lady Eynsham said pointedly. "You look just as dusty and disreputable, Oliver."

"Yes, yes," he said impatiently. "I'll meet you down here shortly?"

Lady Eynsham clucked her tongue in obvious amusement. "You may be sure I will deliver her back to you safe and sound."

Emily spared Oliver one last glance as she was ushered from the room.

Everything happened so quickly after that. Louisa escorted Emily through the great house to a guest room, and once they arrived, she rang for some dresses and food to be sent up.

"I have excellent taste, generally speaking," she said, sinking gracefully into the chaise longue by the fireplace, "but sometimes I fall in love with a gown that doesn't suit me and I buy it because I have the means to do so. Inevitably, the gowns never suit me, and I rarely wear them. Your complexion, I think, would suit them better."

"You are very kind," Emily said stiffly.

"Don't get on your high horse," Louisa said, smiling slightly. "There's no shame in receiving help once in a while when it's necessary. Tell me something, Miss Brunton. Does he love you?"

Emily blinked. She felt a little faint—from the walk and the lack of food, probably. Her thoughts buzzed about her head like bluebottles, throwing themselves against the walls of her mind.

"Oliver," Louisa said when Emily didn't speak. "I presume he does, or he wouldn't have brought you here all this way." She rose from where she'd been reclined, picking a white towel from where it lay beside a pretty copper bowl of water. "Here," she said, holding it out to Emily. "You are under no obligation to wear one of my dresses, but you should wash your face."

Emily accepted the towel reluctantly. "It must have been a shock seeing me after he left in such a way. Stealing a carriage, too. He's very remorseful about that."

"He can convince me of his remorse—or otherwise." At the stern note in the other woman's voice, Emily glanced up, but Louisa smiled, softening the sentiment. "If he came back of his own volition, then I believe he is remorseful. And for you to defend him shows there is hope for him yet."

"You're not angry that I'm here?"

"Well, has he abducted you?"

Emily could not help her snort at the thought. "No."

"Are you here against your will? Do you feel as though he has taken advantage of your situation, whatever it may be, for his own purposes?"

"If anything," she said, holding the towel tightly in both hands, "it is I who have taken advantage of him."

Louisa's eyes gleamed with interest. "Ah, now that story seems worthy of telling."

In as few words as possible, Emily outlined the situation, explaining Oliver's intention to marry Isabella, how he encountered her instead, and how when they'd returned home, it was to find Isabella gone with Marlbury, a known rake.

As she spoke, she washed her face, surprised to find that such a simple act made her feel so much more human.

A knock at the door interrupted her as she reached the end of her tale, and Louisa waved the maid to the bed, where she lay out a whole host of dresses that Emily would not consider wearing. Pale green ones, soft pinks that Emily would not for a thousand years have thought to wear with her red hair, and one a soft dove grey. All simple morning dresses, yet all exquisitely made.

"Let us set aside the topic of your sister for a moment," Louisa said. "And, if you please, you may decide which dress you would like to wear for the remainder of the day. I think you would suit them all, and heaven knows I would not suit them. They will languish sadly at the back of my wardrobe until someone takes them off my hands."

While Emily knew this was an exaggeration, she appreciated the other woman's kindness. Just like Mrs Chambers, she had accepted Emily's situation and need for assistance without batting an eye. The least Emily could do was be grateful, even if she despised such things were necessary.

"May I try on the green?" she asked.

"Certainly." Louisa waved to her maid, but Emily had already half shrugged out of her muddy dress without assistance. It had been too long since she'd had help dressing.

"I'll wash this for you, ma'am," the maid said, picking Emily's dress from the floor and folding it neatly over one arm.

"Oh, you don't have to—"

"It's no problem, ma'am."

Louisa returned to the chaise longue as Emily dressed, the maid combing out her hair and pinning it back. At the feeling of it, Emily closed her eyes—she had not realised how much she'd missed this.

It was only when the maid retreated, taking Emily's dirty dress and the discarded ones with her, that Louisa spoke again.

"I have a great fondness for Oliver. As far as I'm concerned, he *is* my brother. But he has also spent most of his life fleeing every possible responsibility and living out his father's legacy. So to see him here championing your problems and standing up for something . . . That is why I asked if he loved you. I can see you care for him."

Emily flushed a little. "It would be impossible for anyone to remain indifferent, I think."

"Obligation can be a powerful motivator."

"I don't mean obligation. I am *grateful* for many things, but that is not why I—" Her face grew warmer. "Why I think very highly of him," she finished.

Louisa's eyes shone with understanding. "Ah. So that's how it is."

"Excuse me?"

"You love him."

"I—" Was there any point in denying it? She didn't know if she did or not; the sensation felt very different from the infatuation she had felt for Marlbury. Less all-consuming, but richer in its nature. "I don't know," she admitted finally. "Perhaps I do."

"And yet you are not engaged?" Louisa helped Emily into the dress and working on the tiny buttons at the back. "Has he neglected to ask you?"

Emily closed her eyes. "Things are not that simple."

"If he loves you and you love him, what reason do you have for not marrying? Are you concerned about his family's acceptance of you?"

"That's not the reason," Emily said awkwardly.

"Well, let no fears of that cross your mind. I am a staunch defender of the right to choose one's partner in life, and if you choose each other, then I will ensure no one stands in your way."

Confessing that Emily had vowed never to marry at all, especially when she all but admitted she had fallen in love, felt ludicrous. Little-girl silly, as though she were a child ignorant of the way of the world, professing that she intended to ride a flying horse one day. So, instead, she said, "We have known each other little more than a week."

"Ah. So you are worried about his constancy?"

"Either one party is inconstant, in which case the other must suffer, or they are devoted to the point of insanity, and should something happen to one, the other must lose their faculties and their will to live." Emily shook her head and paced away from the mirror. "How can either possibility be worth the prospect of temporary happiness?"

Louisa's hands dropped to her sides as she watched Emily, such an expression of sympathy on her face that it nearly broke Emily's heart. "I see. Yes, that does seem particularly bleak. I'll admit. But what if there was a third option?"

Emily pressed a hand to her forehead, trying to shelter her eyes, which felt like watering. "What would that be?"

"I have seen it myself." Louisa came to sit on the bed, one hand wrapped around the ornate bedpost. "Moderation."

"Love doesn't know moderation."

"Good love doesn't obliterate its subjects. Here." She patted the bed beside her. "Did you know I fell in love with Henry twice?"

Emily sank onto the bed, grateful for the excuse to sit before her knees gave out. "Oliver told me very little about you and Henry."

"I thought we were ill-fated at first. We first fell in love when I was a girl and he a young man. He broke my heart and fled the country, and I was forced into marriage with another. Eight years later, after my husband died and Henry returned from war, we reunited and I fell in love with him again. Losing him the first time was a terrible blow, but I survived it. If I'd chosen, I could have remained angry and bitter, believing that love was ruinous, and I would have missed out on this life." She smiled softly, and it was as though her entire face was illuminated from within. "We can never predict the future, and there is very little that is within our control, but if we are fortunate enough to fall in love with someone who loves us in return, and if there is nothing stopping us being together—then we should not let our lives be ruled by fear. If I lost Henry again, it would hurt, but I would survive. He is very dear to me, and I love him completely, but he is not my entire world. I have my painting, things that I love aside from him, and they would sustain me in the event of his passing." She turned to face Emily, that small smile still on her face. "You could do worse than falling in love with a man who would take you halfway across the country in order to humble himself before the relatives he most looks up to."

She could. She could do a lot worse.

If they were to marry, she would have a home that didn't fall apart around her ears. She would have freedom, stability, security.

If Emily could just trust that loving Oliver would not ruin her—or perhaps instead come to terms with the fact that whatever she chose, she loved him now. If she lost him through her own stubbornness, it would break her own heart. There was no saving herself.

"What is standing in your way?" Louisa asked gently.

Isabella was the only remaining obstacle.

Isabella, who had run away with the very same man who had broken Emily's heart, and who had bragged about it in a letter, thinking she had claimed a victory Emily had not.

Some of it may be attributed to ignorance and naivety and hurt, but Emily had been making excuses for Isabella's behaviour for too long.

It had to stop.

If she could bring herself to marry Oliver and conquer her own fear of love, then why should she throw it away for Isabella's sake when Isabella had done so little for her?

"I can't marry him until I get Isabella back," Emily said.

Louisa clapped her hands. "Then let us plan how that might come about."

Chapter Twenty-Nine

Oliver squared his shoulders before entering Henry's study. Any solution they came to about Isabella would have to be done with Emily present, but he needed to face his brother alone first.

They had some matters to lay to rest.

Jarringly, considering how different he felt from the man who had left this space not quite a month ago, the room looked identical to the way it had when he had last entered. Henry sat behind the desk, a pair of wire-framed spectacles on his nose, and open books before him. The bookcases were just as meticulously sorted as always, and although the room could not be strictly called tidy, there was order amongst the chaos.

How fitting.

At Oliver's arrival, Henry removed his glasses and leant back in his chair, the expression in his stern blue eyes speculative.

"Oliver," he said.

"Henry." Oliver took the seat before the desk. "Thank you for receiving me."

"You know I will never turn you away." Henry's gaze fell to the loose arm of his coat, and the bulge under his clothes where his sling lay. "Are you badly hurt?"

"A broken arm. Not too bad, so long as I keep it still."

"It's been seen to, I presume?"

"Had a physician take a look. He says there's nothing to do now but wait for it to heal."

Henry nodded, laying down his pen and steepling his fingers. "The carriage? I presume it did not survive as well as you appear to have done."

Oliver did not have to wonder how his brother knew about the carriage; if it had still been functional, he would have driven up to the door in it. "It did not."

"What happened?"

"The weather was poor, and I crashed."

"Why were you driving in those conditions?"

"For once," Oliver said, with self-deprecating wryness, "I was trying to save a woman's reputation, not ruin it."

"This being the lady you arrived with?"

"The very same."

"Did you bring her here so I might bless the union?"

Oliver almost smiled. "Why, would you have agreed to the match?"

"That depends entirely on who she is and your intentions in marrying her."

All amusement fled from Oliver. The last time he had left this room, he might have done so determined to access his inheritance at all costs, but that could not be further from the truth with Emily.

"Let me be clear," he said. "If I marry Miss Brunton—and that is an if entirely at her discretion—then it will have nothing to do with you or your approval. I will have chosen her as the partner of my life, and her circumstances do not make her any less appropriate a wife."

"I see."

"If we had intended marriage, I would not have dragged her all the way down here in this fashion. The reason we came has nothing to do with us or our relationship. Well," he amended, seeing the injustice there, "nothing to do with her. The fault for her situation lies with me, and I hope you can help me put it right."

"Is that so?"

"But before I tell you, I must make one thing plain." The steel ring in his voice surprised even him. "What I tell you now does not leave this room. And when you see her next, you will not disrespect her in any way."

After a long moment, Henry tipped back his head and gave a low bark of laughter. "By God," he said. "You love her."

Oliver scowled. "What of it?"

"I take it she knows of your feelings?"

"Some," Oliver said cautiously. "I offered her my hand in marriage. Perhaps my timing could have been better"—he knew damn well his timing could have been better—"but I don't think she wishes to marry me at present, and I will not force her to out of gratitude. And I will also not bring her into my family's home only to have her be disrespected by my own family members."

Henry held up a placating hand. "I have no intention of treating her with anything but respect, Oliver."

"Good." Oliver drew in a breath, then he explained everything that had occurred to get them to this point, including his cursory courting of Isabella and his mistake in taking Emily instead. The whole sorry tale, culminating in their trek across the country. "I could think of nothing else to do," he finished. "I am to blame for the whole sorry affair, and this was the only way I could think of to put it right."

At a sound outside the closed door, Oliver glanced up, and Louisa barged in, Emily following on her heels. Clean, wearing a green morning dress that made her hair gleam as though caught in a sunset, she briefly took his breath away.

"I see Oliver has already told you the pertinent points," she said as she approached the desk.

Emily came to stand beside him, instinctively moving to the side with his unimpeded arm; he used it to draw her protectively into his side.

He hadn't lied when he'd said he thought Henry and Emily would come to like each other in time, but he also knew that they could both be prickly when they were first meeting a stranger, or when they felt as though they were being judged.

"Are you all right?" he murmured to her. "Louisa can have a heavy hand when it comes to managing."

"I heard that," Louisa said, raising a brow at him. "Don't mock your elders."

"She agreed to help us," Emily whispered, her hand sliding into his. He swiped his thumb across her knuckles.

Henry looked at his wife with mingled exasperation and affection. "You already pledged my help?"

"No." She touched his shoulder lightly. "I pledged *my* help. You may do as you please."

He reached up to take her hand, holding it in his. Then he looked straight at Oliver. "You believe he's gone to London?"

"He's escaping Lord Rotherham, who recently went north," Oliver said, and Henry nodded in understanding. "My guess is he went to his lodgings on St James Street."

Louisa sighed, shaking her head. "Young men are so very predictable, and so very stupid."

"Easy enough to find him," Oliver said. "The problem will be what to do with Isabella once we do."

"Bring her back to Bolton House," Louisa said at once. "We have been meaning to go to London in the next few weeks; we can bring our plans forward easily enough."

"The problem arises with after," Oliver said. "He may try to besmirch Isabella's name, and it's likely Dalston knows at least a little of what she's been up to. Going home would be . . . difficult."

"You mean," Louisa said with a smile, "she needs family members she can retire with until any possible scandal has died down a little?"

"Ideally, there would *be* no scandal," Oliver said. "But yes."

Henry tapped his fingers against the edge of the desk. "I know Rotherham. Not well, but a little. I could speak with him. He is not the sort of man who would let a situation like this go unpunished."

"My family name holds no weight except in the small part of the country I come from," Emily said, looking directly at Henry. She didn't flinch away from his returning look. "There is no one to stand in our defence."

"Wrong," Oliver said. "There is us."

"He's correct," Henry said, and something in Oliver's gut eased at the confirmation of his theory. Henry would help. They would have the full force of the Eynsham name and wealth behind their cause. "It would not matter if you were a princess or a pauper; the case remains the same. Lord Marlbury took advantage of a vulnerable girl and ruined her, with full knowledge of his actions and no interest in repentance. Thus, action must be taken. As we are in possession of the details, we should be the ones to do so, and if we can do so with the least injury to the girl's reputation, so much the better."

"We can find someone to take her in," Louisa said. "For a year or two, at least."

Emily pressed a hand against her chest. "I know this is a lot to ask, and I understand if it's not possible."

"Nonsense," Lousia said. "Do you think your sister is the first girl to be foolish? No, and she will not be the last. Once she grows out of it, as I'm sure she will, she will be of a mind to find a husband in a more . . . typical manner."

"Will she?" Emily asked, and Oliver could hear the slight tremor in her voice. "I mean, will she find a husband if she is not—if she is not virtuous?"

Oliver resisted the urge to say Emily had found someone—him—who would take her no matter what her past might be.

"Of course she will," Louisa assured her. "One way or the other."

Oliver squeezed Emily's hand, and she glanced at him, a slight smile springing to her lips.

"It's settled, then," Louisa said. "Tomorrow, we will set out for London, and once you've retrieved this sister, you can bring her back to us. Henry will meet with Lord Rotherham, and we will smooth everything over. There will be no scandal—or at least, none containing a name." She rang the bell. "Time for dinner, I think. And a good night's sleep. Things will seem better in the morning." For the first time, she glanced at Oliver's arm. "You seem to be bearing the wounds of battle, Oliver."

"My own foolishness, I assure you."

Louisa smiled, a little sadly. "Alas, the worst wounds always are."

Chapter Thirty

The journey to London took them three long days, but finally, on the eve of the third day, they entered the outskirts. Oliver watched as Emily peered out of the windows at their surroundings, the passing carts and donkeys and street vendors continuing to hawk their wares even into the night. Streetlamps, lit by the watchmen, illuminated the streets.

He tried to imagine what it might look like to an outsider who had never seen the capital before. To him, this time of night, it seemed remarkably quiet, but to her, it was probably bustling. Her face betrayed very little, however.

"Somewhere in here is Isabella," she said quietly.

"Almost certainly in his lodgings." Oliver injected as much optimism into his voice as possible. "There's nowhere else he'd have taken her. Of course, St James's isn't the best place for a lady, but once we get her out, no one will be any the wiser."

"If she ever enters London again, Marlbury will do his best to discredit her." Emily brought her feet up onto the seat, hugging her legs. The movement of the carriage rocked her side to side. "She'll never be free of him."

"That's if Marlbury is around to say anything at all."

Emily frowned, glancing at Oliver. "Are you planning on killing him?"

"God no," he said, trying not to laugh at her. "That's not the sort of justice I'm in the habit of doling out, darling. But his father has, by all accounts, been openly debating sending him to the continent for an extended period."

"Why?"

"Because he has been causing too much of a ruckus here. From what I understand, he's got a few maids with child, and they've had to be sent to the country to recuperate. If Marlbury had his way, he would have abandoned the girls, but because they're part of his father's household, his father forced him to fork out for them." Oliver shrugged, embarrassed that he had overlooked this behaviour. There had been rumours, of course, but Marlbury had portrayed the girls as grasping, eager for a taste of his wealth, thinking they could somehow charm him into marriage, and Oliver had believed him.

He hadn't wanted to investigate further. Letting the issue lie had been easier, and now Oliver was ashamed of his complicity.

That ended now.

"If he's on the continent, that won't change anything," Emily said. "Or teach him to behave properly."

"Perhaps not. But it *will* get him out of England, which you must admit is ideal for our situation. I doubt he'll even know when Isabella enters London again as a debutante, and there's very little he can do to ruin her reputation from afar."

Emily leant back against the seat. "You must be wondering why I'm going to all this trouble for such a girl."

"She's your sister," Oliver said, recalling the same words Emily had given to him what felt like long ago. "And you love her."

"I know she wouldn't go out of her way for me," Emily said, and Oliver could only thank his lucky stars that she had at least come to realise this. "But that's not really the point. I refuse to base my behaviour on hers. If she's in trouble, I will help, because she's my sister and that's who I am."

"Then you must know that I'll support you," Oliver said.

"Even if you don't agree with me?"

"Helping her is one thing. Sacrificing your own happiness for her sake is entirely another."

Her cheek curved as one corner of her mouth tilted up. "I have no intention of doing that, Oliver."

Hope erupted in his chest, and he forced it away again. Once this was over, he would then think about his future. Until then, he would focus on Marlbury and rescuing Isabella.

"It might be safer for your reputation to stay in the carriage while I go inside and confront him," he said as they approached St James's Street.

"If you think I'm going to remain inside while you have all the satisfaction of rescuing my sister, you are mistaken." Emily withdrew the pistol from within her cloak. "Besides, I came prepared."

Oliver almost laughed. That was his Emily, and he adored her more than he could say. "One should never confront a rake without a gun."

"That was my theory, too. It went excellently the first time."

This time, he really did laugh. "Ought I be thankful you didn't shoot?"

"Extremely."

"This is a poor moment to tell you this for the first time, but I love you."

His eyes seemed to gleam as she looked at him. Then she smiled, a little. "I know."

"I fear I've been less than subtle," he said ruefully. "But neither of us know how the night will go, and I wanted you to know now."

The carriage came to a stop outside Marlbury's lodgings: a nondescript house set in a street of similarly nondescript houses. Each large house was split into a couple of apartments; the perfect bachelor houses for young men who aspired to avoid all responsibilities.

Oliver, too, had apartments in St James's.

"This is it," he said, looking at Emily. "Last chance."

She met his gaze steadily. "I'm coming with you."

He hadn't expected anything else. As the coachman opened the door, he extended a hand and helped Emily down. Then he rang the doorbell.

Emily had expected something more openly salubrious from a street that was inappropriate for women to enter, but it appeared just the same as many other streets. Houses and shops and taverns—although she suspected these were gentlemen's clubs. Nothing like the taprooms she was accustomed to.

Beside her, Oliver was still and quiet. He was not an especially large man, but he had an air of menace today that made her feel surprisingly safe. Marlbury's actions had been a betrayal, and she had seen shame in Oliver's eyes more than once.

When they had first met, she had tarred him with Marlbury's brush. A man's friends were a reflection of himself—and in some ways it was true. Marlbury was a reflection of Oliver's worst traits: his propensity to avoid all responsibility; his selfishness; his arrogance.

Yet he had grown past that, demonstrating to her without doubt that he had left those traits behind him. No longer would he accept poor behaviour without question or examination.

No longer would he turn a blind eye to cruelty or injustice.

The fact he was here beside her now proved that. Yes, he was doing this for her, but she thought he was also doing it for himself. And that was far more important.

Oliver rang again. Emily steeled herself, her fingers tight around the handle of the pistol. If it were a smaller pistol designed for a woman, she might have fit it into her reticule, but this was too large for her to do anything but conceal it as best she could.

As satisfying as it would be to confront Marlbury with it, she was determined to use it only as a last resort.

Footsteps sounded and when the door swung open, a servant stood behind it. Emily blinked, but Oliver seemed entirely unsurprised to see him.

"Hello, Smiths," he said. "I've come to see Lord Marlbury."

"I'm afraid his lordship isn't receiving visitors right now," Smiths said, but before he could shut the door in their faces, Oliver stuck his foot inside.

"He'll see me." Without waiting for a response or permission, he barged inside. Emily followed on his heels, determined not to be left behind. "Marlbury!" Oliver yelled, his voice too loud for this time of night. "I know you're here."

There was movement in the doorway, then Marlbury emerged, a glass in his hand and his cravat undone. He wore a crimson robe over his shirt, and by the flush on his cheeks, he was more than a little drunk.

For a moment, Emily remembered all the things he had done to woo and hurt her. She had seen him at a distance, of course, since the day when he told her he could never feel anything for someone like her, but never this close.

Bile filled her throat at the sight of his dark hair and arrogant mouth. Once, she had thought him unbearably handsome, and now she found his smarminess repulsive. He walked through the world as though he expected to be applauded for existing, and he looked at women as though he expected them to fall to their knees before him.

How could she ever have fallen for such conceit?

At the sight of them both, his dark eyes narrowed. "Beaumont. And is that Emily Brunton?" He gave an unsteady, delighted laugh. "I ought to have known you would come here together. You know, Beaumont, your throwing that girl over in favour of her sister was cold of you. I applaud the gesture, although it did mean I was subject to her whining."

Rage punched Emily in the chest; she hadn't known she was capable of such anger until that moment. Her teeth clacked together audibly. "Where is she?" she demanded.

"Where is who? Be specific."

"Marlbury," Oliver said, his jaw clenched. "It's over. Give her up."

Marlbury sneered. "I really thought you would be more sporting, old chap."

"Where *is* she?" Emily repeated. Her heart pounded in her chest, and although the fire had long since slumped into embers in the hearth, her palms dampened with sweat. Ignoring Marlbury's self-satisfied smirk, she pushed past him. "Isabella!" she called. "It's me, Emily. I've come to take you away from here."

To her everlasting relief, when she reached the stairs, she found Isabella's pale face looking back at her. She wore a white lawn nightgown that was draped around her in a positively scandalous fashion.

Emily's stomach dropped.

She hadn't really believed Marlbury would have taken Isabella all the way down here without also taking her to bed, but to see such blatant proof—neither Emily nor Isabella owned such garments—made her feel as though she had swallowed ice.

"Let her go without a fight, and this doesn't have to be hard," Oliver was saying to Marlbury.

"She has no wish to go with you," Marlbury said, that sneer still in his voice. "She thinks you abandoned her, Beaumont, and I can't say she was wrong. I never thought you'd be the type to choose the ugly sister, but I misjudged you."

"Enough."

Emily held out her hand to Isabella. No matter what Isabella had done, all she could feel at the sight of her sister's pale, resentful face was pity. This was a cruel fate for someone so young, and she probably hadn't realised quite how dire things had become.

"Listen to me, Bella," she said. "I know he has promised you marriage, but he won't ever go through with it. He lied to you so you would be quiet and compliant, and I know he was convincing. Believe me." She took a single step up the stairs, and when Isabella didn't flee, another. "But if you stay here with him, you won't have a future."

Isabella's scared eyes flicked from Emily's face to one side. Marlbury leaned in over Emily's shoulder, his breath stinking of brandy. "Do you recall how convincing I am, Emily? It's been such a long time; I thought for sure you had forgotten me."

The next second, his head was wrenched back, and Oliver stood between them, his face alive with fury. "Don't touch her!"

"Lord Marlbury," Emily said, gathering herself, her fingers aching on the pistol handle. "Tell my sister, if you please, what you truly intend with her."

Marlbury grinned lazily up at Isabella, not seeming to mind that Oliver stood primed to hit him. He must be further gone than Emily had imagined, the brandy dulling his reactions. "I have lots of things planned for us, love," he called up the stairs. "Come down now and tell them that you would rather stay with me."

"No man who intends to marry a lady would bring her to St James's Street," Emily said.

Isabella ventured a little further down the stairs, her nightgown clinging to thighs. "Victor," she said, a plaintive note in her voice. "Stop playing around and tell them the truth."

"The truth is that he will not marry anyone like us," Emily said, shrugging out of her cloak and hurrying up the stairs. "I know it must be hard to accept, dearest, but you must. I won't allow him to ruin everything."

But Isabella was now staring wide-eyed down at Emily's hand. "What is *that*?" she demanded tremulously.

"A pistol," Marlbury said with apparent indifference. "She means to take you from me by force, love. Are you going to let her?"

"Don't call my sister *love*!" Emily snapped. "You don't care the slightest bit for her or you wouldn't have ruined her."

Isabella shook her head, blonde hair swinging around her head. "You don't understand. He wants me."

"That's right," Marlbury called, swaying a little. "Tell them."

Oliver grabbed Marlbury's loose cravat with his good hand. "Shut up," he hissed.

"Lust is not a reason for a gentleman like Lord Marlbury to choose marriage." Emily brushed the hair back from Isabella's face tenderly. "You foolish girl. I know you wanted your revenge on me, but this was not the way to take it."

"Bring her downstairs, Emily," Oliver said, shoving Marlbury back to clear a space at the bottom of the stairs. "Let's leave before things get ugly."

Marlbury smiled, and it was as though a stone dropped into the very pit of Emily's stomach. Unnamed dread, a sense of the pained inevitable. "Oh," he said, raising his glass as though to toast them all, "things are already about to get ugly."

Then he smashed the glass against the side of Oliver's head.

Chapter Thirty-One

Pain exploded across Oliver's head. In a distant way, he knew shards of glass had sliced into his skin. His head rang, and his vision blurred. Someone screamed—Isabella.

A *bang.*

Shaking the dizziness away, Oliver moved, grabbing Marlbury with his good arm and hurling him at the ground. A vase crashed against the floor.

Blood dripped down the side of Oliver's face.

To his right, he could see a hole through the wallpaper where Emily's shot had hit.

Good thing it hadn't hit Marlbury; she might have wanted her revenge, but she didn't want to be a killer, and heaven knew he didn't want that for her, either.

Marlbury groaned, sprawled across the floor on broken glass. Oliver hoped it cut him. His head throbbed, and there was blood sliding into his eye.

"Oliver!" Emily was by his side, her hands cupping his face and trying to wipe away the blood. He thought she might have been crying, but he couldn't quite see.

"I'm all right," he said, his voice surprisingly calm. "Get Isabella. We're leaving."

Emily pointed the pistol at where Marlbury was now sitting up, his palms as bloody as Oliver's temple. There was no more ammunition in the pistol, but if there had been, he was certain she would have fired.

"Steady, sweetheart," Oliver said. At the endearment, she glanced at him. "If you kill him, I'll be forced to flee to Europe with you, and then you'll *have* to marry me."

A tiny smile flitted across her face. "Is that what it will take for you to ask me again?"

"No. You only need to tell me you love me, and I will get on one knee. But not here, darling, please. I must have my dignity." He kissed her forehead, hoping he got no blood on her. "Fetch Isabella now, and take her to the carriage."

Marlbury groaned, his eyes unfocused. "What the devil—"

"Quiet," Oliver snapped.

Isabella descended to the bottom of the stairs, white-knuckled fingers holding the cloak in place. "Emily," she said, her voice faint. "You tried to shoot him."

"Don't worry, dearest. I missed." Emily once again put her arm around Isabella and ushered her from the room. This time, either because of the pistol Emily still held or because it had finally become evident that Marlbury had no honourable intentions, Isabella put up no resistance.

Oliver turned back to Marlbury as his former friend hauled himself to his feet. "It's over," he said. "Just let her go."

"You've changed." Marlbury's face twisted. "What does it matter who I entertain myself with?"

"If you've paid a whore, that's one thing, but this is entirely different. She's a lady. Respectable—or was."

"Is that what you thought when you took off with the sister?" Marlbury's lip curled. "I got there first, you know."

Oliver moved before he knew what he had done. His fist connected with a satisfying thud against Marlbury's jaw, and he shook out his hand as Marlbury staggered back. Rage boiled in his chest—not that Emily had lain with another man before, but that the man in question had seduced her so callously.

He might have been able to forgive many things, but he could not forgive Marlbury hurting the woman he loved.

"That was for her," Oliver hissed. He swung again, planting his fist in Marlbury's side. Marlbury choked, doubling over, and Oliver kicked him to the ground. "And that was for me."

Marlbury coughed and spat. "All this over a girl?"

"All this because you never learnt basic respect, and I never thought to teach it to you."

"Respect?" Marlbury choked a laugh tinged with insanity. "We are the same, you and I. You know it and I know it. I wouldn't have even chased the girl if you hadn't wanted her first."

They might have been more similar once, but Oliver barely recognised the man he had been. And there was one crucial difference. "No," he said. "I intended to marry her. You intended to use and discard her, just the same way you used and discarded Emily." Disgusted with Marlbury and the conversation, he turned to leave, wiping the blood on his cheek with the back of his hand.

"So you'll marry the shrew?" Marlbury slurred, staggering to his feet. "Is that it?"

Oliver turned and bowed, channelling Henry's icy disdain. "If she deigns to have me, I will be the most fortunate of men," he said, and grinned. "Oh, and one more thing. Your father will be hearing of this. Pack your bags, Marlbury; I doubt he'll have you remain in London much longer. I wouldn't even be surprised if he disinherited you. And good riddance."

Isabella huddled in a corner of the carriage, Emily's cloak around her shoulders. Oliver dabbed at his cheek with a handkerchief, wiping away the worst of the blood. He was fortunate the glass hadn't gone into his eye, but the injury didn't seem to bother him overmuch.

Emily kept replacing the scene in her head, the way Marlbury had raised the glass and brought it down on Oliver's face. The way her finger had squeezed the trigger without even meaning to; the jump of the gun in her hands.

Oliver, promising he would ask her to marry him so long as she told him she loved him. Asking her not to kill Marlbury, as though he had thought it was a possibility.

And Isabella. For a moment, Emily had thought Isabella would choose Marlbury over her. Over her *family*. Even knowing that Marlbury was a good-for-nothing rake, Emily had thought Isabella would choose to stay with him.

Oliver hissed a breath as he dabbed at his cut. "I'm all right," he said before she could even ask. "It'll heal into a very fetching scar."

Emily didn't have the energy to reply in kind. All her words had dried into nothing. There was just a hard ball of emotion in her chest, wrapped up so tightly she hardly knew what it was.

Finally, Isabella sniffled and looked at Emily. "Are you happy now?" she demanded in a whisper. "Now you have stolen both my chances of happiness from me?"

The ball of emotion splintered, releasing pity and anger in equal measure. "Is that what you think happened? That Marlbury was a chance of happiness?"

"I *was* happy with him. Besides, I saw you." Isabella raised an accusatory hand and pointed it at Oliver. "I saw you get into his carriage. How can you argue that you weren't trying to steal my chance of happiness?"

"Because I thought he was trying to arrange an assignation with you," Emily snapped. "And I wanted to confront him somewhere private. With this." She held up the pistol.

"Now that I can confirm," Oliver said. "She threatened me with it once we reached Gretna Green."

"I felt so dreadful when I realised Mr Beaumont intended marriage—after my experience with Lord Marlbury, I came to expect the worst." She softened her voice. "I am sorry you were hurt. And about . . ."

Isabella hugged the cloak tighter around herself. "I don't want to talk about it."

They would have to at some point, but now wasn't the time. Isabella would need time to lick her metaphorical wounds; even if she didn't love Marlbury, she had still believed he would marry her, and that disappointment would be hard to overcome.

Eynsham House, by the time they arrived, was alive with lights and bustling servants. Emily wrapped an arm around Isabella's shoulders as she hurried inside, trying to shield her from any prying eyes.

Louisa was there to greet them in the vast hallway, the picture of reliability and calm. Emily felt the last of her jangled nerves ease at the sight. They had done it. Isabella was safe; Marlbury would suffer at least a little for the consequences of his actions, and she had Oliver.

He loved her. He still wanted to marry her even after all this.

Some part of her would always be afraid, she imagined. Both of losing him and of losing herself, but when she had seen Marlbury raise his hand against Oliver, she had known with sickening clarity that she would suffer just as much if she lost him now, when there was nothing but emotion between them, than she would if she was his wife.

If all they would ever have were a few years, she would rather spend them together and brave the rest of her life without him than start now, mourning his loss without any of the joy being with him would bring.

"This is my sister," Emily said. "Miss Isabella."

Louisa smiled kindly at her. "I'm Lady Eynsham, Mr Beaumont's sister-in-law. Welcome to my home." She glanced at Oliver and tutted. "You do always seem to be in the wars, Oliver. Are you much hurt?"

"Just a scratch," Oliver said cheerfully. Considering all they had been through, he seemed in remarkably good spirits. "Where's Henry?"

"Out, but if you wait for him in the library, I'll make sure Branson sends him to you."

"Excellent." Oliver touched Emily's hand. "I'll find you when I'm done," he said, his eyes holding a promise that set her heart on fire. Then he strode away, taking the stairs two at a time.

"Come with me," Louisa said, beckoning Emily and Isabella upstairs. "I have a room made up for each of you. Miss Isabella, today has probably been a shock. I recommend you eat up and sleep."

"I will—" Isabella pressed her lips together, but her eyes brimmed with tears. "All my gowns are with Lord Marlbury."

"Then we will have to find you some new ones," Louisa said, her pace almost a stride. "That shouldn't be too much of a trial, I think. We are in London, after all."

"Then what?" Isabella asked in a small voice.

"My husband has some relations in the country; you may live with them for a year or so until this nonsense has died down and you've got some sense in your head." Louisa paused by a door, glancing over her shoulder at Isabella. "And then, if you can prove that you have enough common sense to warrant it, I will sponsor a Season or two in London so you might have an opportunity to find a real husband."

Chapter Thirty-Two

Henry did not arrive home for almost another hour. After changing and cleaning the cut on his cheek, Oliver sat in the library and plotted how he might approach the subject with his brother.

If he was to marry Emily, he would need to request Henry's help as he'd said he would do all that time ago. But the prospect of confessing that he had always struggled with the most basic of intellectual abilities—reading and writing—felt pathetic.

But he'd had enough of hiding.

Despite his resolution, when Henry strode in, Oliver's nerves had been wound so tight that he turned around and blurted, "I'm going to marry her."

Henry paused in the middle of the room, shock wiping the tiredness from his face. "Is that so?"

"Presuming she'll have me, but I think she will."

"I don't doubt it. Congratulations." After a moment, Henry sat, gesturing for Oliver to join him. "I presume you will therefore be asking for your inheritance."

"That's not the reason I'm offering for her."

"I never said it was," Henry said mildly. "I have no objection to your marriage, or the lady herself. I like her, Oliver. More to the point, she is not a lady one marries for the sake of one's inheritance." He held up a hand as Oliver half rose from his chair. "By which I mean she is far too clever to be taken in by baseless flattery. She has even had the wisdom to refuse you once, which shows strength of character and good sense."

"Of course it does," Oliver muttered.

"If this is what she wants, then I give you my blessing, and I will get in touch with my lawyers. Louisa, too."

"Thank you." Oliver took a deep breath. Time for his second announcement, the far more nerve-wracking of the two. "I have another request."

"Oh?" Henry rang for some brandy—an unusual occurrence. There had been a time when Henry had refused to drink a drop, all for the sake of never turning out like their father. Now, he had eased somewhat.

On occasion.

"About the inheritance. The property." Oliver took a breath. "I would like to learn how to run an estate. In a practical sense. You see, I know there are books on the subject, but I have never found . . ." He cleared his throat, shame like a stone in his neck. "I have always struggled with reading. Letters, words. They just don't make sense to me the way they ought. I have tried—as a boy, my tutors all despaired of ever getting me to learn. And I didn't—or at least, I can, very slowly, if I put my mind to it. But it has never come easily to me, and frankly put, I don't like doing it."

There was a sternness in Henry's eyes. "This has been the case since you were a boy?"

"Well," Oliver admitted, "I never did pay much attention to my lessons before I went to school, so I don't think I realised quite the extent of my situation, but it became apparent once there." He swallowed, rubbing his hands together as though for warmth, although the room was perfectly warm. His skin prickled. "It was easier playing the fool. But I've had enough of that. I would like to do things properly—and provide Emily with a home she can be proud of. She'll help me," he hastened to add. "She knows of my affliction, and I know she'd help with letters and the like. And if I need to, I'm sure she would read me books on estate management, but—"

Henry held up a hand, and Oliver stopped his rambling. "Do you truly believe I would refuse to help you?"

"I know it's shameful."

"You're my brother. Why would I turn you away when you ask me for help? If I'd known—" He frowned, and Oliver finally realised it wasn't judgement he saw in his brother; it was regret. "You ought to have told me. However, I know why you didn't. I have been . . . exacting." When the butler brought the brandy in, Henry poured two glasses and handed one to Oliver. "I suppose that's my fault."

"So you'll help?"

"Oliver," Henry said, and held up his glass in a toast. "I thought you would never ask."

Emily sat in the bedchamber she'd been assigned, anxiously awaiting the sound of his footsteps outside the door. She brushed her fingers along the lace of her nightgown—the one that had been left out, and was quite as daring as the one Isabella had been wearing. Such garments felt unfamiliar against her skin, and so did her reflection in the mirror, but for once there was no self-consciousness marring her anticipation.

Oliver would like what he saw, she knew. He loved her—not because of her looks, but for *her.*

Everything else didn't matter.

She chose this.

The door opened and although she had been expecting it—waiting impatiently for it—she still jumped at the sudden motion. He had changed, his crisp white shirt, flamboyant waistcoat, and intricately tied cravat made him look like a gentleman of fashion, despite the bandage on his face. Far more reminiscent of the man she had first met at gunpoint than the man he had grown to be.

Yet when she looked in his eyes, she saw a familiar smile. Yes, this was still her Oliver.

"You'll wear the carpet down if you're not careful, darling," he said with those warm eyes laughing at her, and held out his hands. "Have you been waiting for me long?"

"Only this past half hour." She joined him, putting her hands in his, no longer ashamed of the roughness of her skin. He kissed her healing knuckles tenderly.

"Then I'm sorry for keeping you." The smile died from his eyes as he looked back at her, serious in a way that made her heart flutter. "My darling, I have a question for you, and—"

"Marry me." The words burst from her lips in a way that would have made her embarrassed if it weren't for the wonder dawning across his face. She adored everything about him—the humour that danced so often in his eyes; the way he disguised his selflessness as whimsy; the kindness that never failed to spark when there was something he could do for someone. She adored the freckles across his nose and the wickedness of his smile when he was teasing her—and how she loved the way he teased her.

For seven years, she had been existing, and he had taught her how to live again.

His smile was perfectly crooked. "You look even more beautiful when you're asking me to marry you."

"Is that a yes?"

"Emily." He slid his good arm around her waist, pulling her to him. "I love you more than I ever knew a man could love a woman. If you asked me to, I would throw off the bonds of family and live in that dreadful, creaking house of yours. So yes, I will marry you. I would walk to the ends of the earth for you."

This happiness was too big a thing; she feared she might drop it and it would shatter. But if she did drop it, Oliver would catch it for her. She trusted him utterly.

"I love you," he said again, kissing the very tip of her nose. "I confess this was not exactly how I had envisaged this conversation going, but the end result is the same."

"You'll marry me?"

"As soon as you like." He kissed her. "Tomorrow."

"That might be impossible."

"It might," he conceded with a brief grin. "Then when? Next week?"

"We could have the banns read."

"Three weeks?" He stared at her in mock horror. "You expect me to wait three weeks?"

"It might be sensible. After all, I could then change my mind." At his immediate glower, she leaned up to kiss him. "If we wait three Sundays," she murmured, "then we would have known each other over a month, which feels a far more reasonable courting period."

"Ah." Humour sparked in his eyes. "So it's wooing you want?"

"Does not every woman?"

"Darling, I pretended to be your husband for a week. Was that not sufficient?"

That had been surprisingly wonderful, if she were honest, and she wanted more of Oliver playing the role of young, flirtatious, overly protective husband.

That was, she supposed, why she was marrying him.

"Three weeks," she insisted. "Announce the engagement. Bring me flowers, you cad."

"Little Emily," he teased. "A secret romantic."

"If I am to marry, I may as well do the thing properly."

"I can think of something else you could do properly," he murmured, his good hand finding her hip.

"Oh?" She pretended at innocence. "I suppose I ought to go bridal shopping. Do you think Louisa would go with me?"

He huffed in mock irritation. "Don't bring up my brother's wife when I'm trying to seduce you."

"Oh, is *that* what you were doing?" She rose on her tiptoes and kissed him, muffling his complaints against her mouth until he gave in, kissing her back with such enthusiasm, she wondered how they had ever got through the past day *without* kissing like this.

Then he broke away. "There's something else I want to say."

Emily looked into his face, startled by the lack of concern such an announcement provoked in her. "Why?" she teased. "Have you changed your mind already?"

He hooked a finger into his collar. "I realise it's somewhat late for me to have developed a conscience, but if you would now rather wait until we're married to—"

"Oliver. I was not a maiden even before you. What chastity do you think you're preserving?" She took his good hand in both of hers. "Stay with me tonight. Please."

"As my lady wishes," he murmured, eyes crinkling as he smiled. "But that is exceedingly scandalous, Miss Brunton."

"Tell you what, Mr Beaumont." She kissed his knuckles. "I'll marry you to make up for it."

Chapter Thirty-Three

If she had wanted, Oliver would have waited until marriage—or after—to be with her again. She dictated the pace of their physical relationship; that was the way it would always be.

But he couldn't deny his relief that she wanted him as much as he craved her. Helped, he had to admit, by the spectacularly delicate nightgown she was wearing.

"Your gown is delightful," he murmured into her ear. "Would you mind terribly if I took it off?"

She paused, and he wondered if, as punishment for asking when she had not offered, she would withhold permission. Part of him craved the idea of her riding him, nightdress still intact, forcing him to use his imagination instead. The memory of her using him for her own pleasure made his cock strain against his trousers.

But another part of him needed to see her. A primal, wordless urge to make her his—and, more importantly, to offer himself wholly to her so she could make him hers. For that, they would both have to be without clothes. Naked, together.

Perhaps she saw that need in his eyes, or perhaps she felt the same way, because she smiled a little.

"Be my guest." Stepping back, she turned so he might access the ribbons criss-crossing her back.

This was a nightgown designed to be unwrapped. One unmarried ladies did not habitually wear. If Louisa had provided it—

He shut the thought away. The less he thought about Louisa at a time like this, the better.

His mouth went dry as he tugged at the silken ribbons, loosening the nightgown at the back. Soft, freckled skin emerged, and he trailed his fingers down her spine before sliding the material free of her shoulders.

She stepped free and turned, letting him see every inch of her. He nearly groaned; no matter how often he had her, it would never be enough. Need consumed him—she consumed him. Every imperfectly perfect inch of her body. Her small breasts, nipples pink against her skin, already pearled in the evening air. The smooth lines down to her waist, ribs just visible under her skin, and the jut of her hips. Slender—everything about her felt compact, and he adored that although she might have been near his height, her body still felt small compared to his.

And the thatch of hair between her legs. He ached to touch her.

But he didn't. Instead, he drank her in, waiting for her to come to him.

"Emily," he said, his voice a trifle hoarse. "I love you."

Her chin tipped up, and her eyes met his, and in them, he saw something he hadn't often seen before—wonder.

"I know," she said.

"Does that scare you?"

A soft smile lit her face. "Not as much as it did." She slid a hand across her stomach, and the juxtaposition of her overworked, rough skin against the pale softness of her stomach made him throb. By God, she was perfect. Perhaps not by usual standards, but for him.

"Can I touch you?" he asked—near begged.

A smile caught her lips, and she shook her head.

"Not yet. Let me undress you."

It took effort, but he held still as her hands roamed over his shoulders, gentle with his injured arm and exploratory elsewhere. This, he understood, was a claiming of her own. They had come up against Marlbury, and now she needed to ensure that he, Oliver, was still hers. Marriage was one thing, but there was honesty in vulnerability.

He could not hide his arousal, nor the strength of his need for her. Just as she could not hide the flush that painted her cheeks, or the vividness of her eyes in the candlelight. In this, they were wholly united.

She undressed him with her customary brisk efficiency, though her hands lingered somewhat when she finally encountered bare skin. And when she carefully drew his trousers down over his erection, she made a tiny hum of approval in the back of her throat that made his cock jerk in response.

"Emily," he said.

She looked up from where she knelt before him, and his heart almost stopped. "Yes?"

"I think I might have died and gone to heaven."

She smiled then, so beautiful he couldn't take it, and gently kissed the tip of his erection, licking her lips at the moisture he left there. One hand glided up his thigh to his stomach, and the other wrapped around him.

His legs were sure to give out. The last time she had done this, she had tied him—however ineffectually—to a bedpost, both so he had support and no way of touching her.

Now, she trusted him to ask permission before touching, and relied upon the structural integrity of his knees. A fool's error. When she took him entirely in her mouth, he prayed to God above that he could hold out. With his one good hand, he reached for something to support him. There was nothing, and so he dragged that hand through his hair. The torment of her tongue overwhelmed everything.

She licked him slowly, as though savouring him, and sent her other hand between her legs. He cursed under his breath. His thigh muscles trembled as they endeavoured to keep him upright. Blood pounded in his head, and pressure tightened at the base of his spine. He ought to look away, but all he could see was her hand delving between the dark hair.

The subsequent rush of heat almost made him spill, and he jerked free of her. Saliva slid down her chin, and he reached down to wipe it away. Touching her had become an obsession, and he had to have his hand on her. If only his other still worked—he flexed his fingers in the sling, gritting his teeth at the sudden throb from his arm. No, that would not be an option. But one hand alone was not enough.

She looked up at him, chin tilted to expose the long, elegant line of her throat. Emotion threatened to overwhelm him.

"Sit there." She pointed at the edge of the bed, and with a groan of relief, he sat. His erection throbbed hungrily, still perilously close to the edge.

"Now what?"

"Now," she said with deliberate slowness, "you watch."

"Watch what?"

She positioned herself before the fire, lying on the carpet with her knees bent and legs wide, showing him very clearly what lay between. His jaw clenched.

"Emily," he rasped.

"I like the way you watch me." A smile flashed across her face, and he had to sit on his hand to prevent himself from reaching for her. Or worse, stroking himself to completion when it was obvious she wanted more from him than his instant gratification. If this was what she demanded, then he would offer it.

If he could.

"Is this an exercise in education or restraint?" he asked, unable to stop himself from staring hungrily at her as she touched herself, fingers sliding through the slickness that awaited them.

"It is an exercise in my pleasure," she said. "Next time, perhaps you can do this to me."

"Why not this time?" Even he heard the desperate whine in his voice.

"Because I want to learn my pleasure so I can better guide you. And how else ought I do it?" She drew a small circle across herself, and her entire body tensed. He watched the way her muscles rippled and breath caught, and if this was supposed to be letting him down further from the edge, then she was very mistaken in her intentions. "Would you prefer me to do it in a private room on my own, or would you rather watch?"

"I would much rather watch."

"Well, then." She sent a single finger inside herself, and her hips canted slightly. Now it was his turn for his breath to catch. "I see we are in agreement."

Oliver watched as, with painful slowness, she brought herself closer to the brink, teasing herself with small, delicate movements. He read the flush in her cheeks, the quiver in her legs, the tensing of her stomach muscles, and knew she was close, even if she never quite let herself fall over the edge. It was torture of the most delicious kind, and he paid attention to every detail. He ached for her, so desperate that he would have handed over everything he might ever own just for a taste of her. Logic held no court here; all he knew was desire.

All he knew was Emily.

When she finally allowed pleasure to take her, she cried out, back arching as she shuddered and her fingers jerked across herself, lost in the intensity of the sensation. Oliver throbbed, overwhelmingly tempted to touch himself to ease the pressure—it bordered on pain. But with some effort, he restrained himself, and when Emily finally looked up again, it was to see him exactly where she had left him.

At her smile, he knew he had done right with this, at least. She trusted him, and he would never do anything to make her question that trust.

"I have never been so enthralled in all my life," he told her as she came to straddle his thighs, both hands going around his neck. "But I warn you, that has done nothing to dim my enthusiasm for you. Rather the opposite, in fact." At the brush of her thigh against him, he jerked, and she chuckled.

"I see."

"Go slowly if you want me to last, darling."

"I'll be the judge of how quickly I go." She slid closer, positioning herself above his erection, and guided herself down on him.

Hot. Wet. So slick, he felt her arousal coating him; he slipped inside with barely any resistance. At the feel of her inner muscles contracting, he grunted, bringing his arm around her hips and dragging them more firmly against his, careful to avoid his sling. With him seated fully inside her, she dominated his senses; with every breath, he took more of her in.

"Oliver." She brushed at his hair, which had grown just long enough to flop across his forehead. Her eyes were big and starry, and he felt like he could see entire galaxies in them.

"Emily." She shifted against him, and he groaned, trying to focus on anything but the idea of spilling. "In the future, I will do a better job of lasting."

"Mm." She bent her head and lightly bit the curve of his shoulder, just hard enough for the flash of pain to transform into pleasure. He throbbed inside her. "I rather like that you are incapable of holding back."

"Oh no. I have held back, believe me."

She trailed her lips across him, still remaining remarkably still—which was a good thing, because for all his talk of restraint, he knew it would take very little for him to tip over that edge.

In his daydreams, he had made love to her for hours upon languid hours, lavishing attention on her until finally she begged him to stop. Reality had not been so flattering to his ego—yet the feel of her made it plain that she was highly aroused. Evidently she had not been lying; she enjoyed his eagerness as much as he had enjoyed her performance.

"I love you," she whispered, and finally began to move. She rolled her hips slowly, just enough that sensation burned hot and heavy through him, yet not enough for him to immediately reach the point of no return. She built him up gradually, seconds turning into minutes, the minutes stretching golden like sunlight. He kissed every part of her he could reach; cupped her breasts and told her, over and over again, how perfect she was for him. How much he adored her.

At last, however, as her breath fractured, it became impossible to hold back. He did his best, trying to give her as much time as he could, but his release could not be denied.

"I'm close." He didn't have the words for anything more poetic, though they hardly did justice to everything she had done to him. "Where should I—"

"Inside me." She kissed him again, smothering any doubts he might have had. If Emily ever decided something, she did not do it on a whim. And he was too far gone to argue, too far gone to do anything except hold her tight as his release came upon him.

She rode him until he squirmed underneath her, and then a little more until he pulled her free and turned her, laughing, onto the bed.

"Marry me," he said as he collapsed beside her.

"You know I will. I asked you first."

"Stay with me."

Her eyes turned soft and limpid. "This is my room."

"Love me."

"I already do," she said, and pulled him into her arms.

Chapter Thirty-Four

Emily didn't have the chance to speak with Isabella until after breakfast, during which Isabella's appearance—dictated, no doubt, by Louisa—was characterised by sulky silence.

"Come, Oliver," Louisa said, picking up her letters and sweeping from the table. "We have lots of preparations to make."

Emily stayed where she was, sipping at her tea and trying to pretend as though Oliver had not slipped from her bedroom earlier that morning.

Isabella glowered at her plate, her eyes red-rimmed.

Emily should have known this wouldn't be an easy conversation, but sometimes the most necessary ones were the least pleasant. She had the benefit of being in a gown far finer than she was accustomed to, engaged to the youngest son of an earl, and hosted by a marchioness.

There were worse things in life.

"Are you going to marry him?" Isabella asked at last.

Emily nodded, putting her teacup back on its saucer. "I am."

"And you love him?" This question was phrased somewhat belligerently, but Emily merely nodded again.

"Yes."

"Do you not think you ought to have let me marry him instead?" Isabella demanded, suddenly passionate. "He promised *me* he would marry me."

"He did," Emily said, "and believe me, that was my original intention. And I am sorry for any distress it may have caused you. But, you see, Oliver never fell in love with you, and I don't believe you loved him either."

"That isn't the *point*." Isabella turned tearful blue eyes on her sister. "He was mine first."

"That's not how people work, Bella. You don't own them or their choices. He shouldn't have flirted with you and suggested you might marry for the sake of his inheritance, and you should not have encouraged him to, though I can understand why you did."

"I don't want to go back to the life we had before! Am I supposed to just accept my position? We were born as gentlemen's daughters, and yet we lived in drudgery. How is any of that *fair*?" Isabella looked glassy-eyed at the table. "You seemed content with it, but how could I be?"

"Content?" A bitter laugh left Emily's lips. "What would you know about how I felt, Bella? Did you ever ask me if this was the life I wanted? If I missed the days of having servants and not having to crawl about on the floor lighting fires? Tell me what you did to help with the household chores, hmm?"

A line appeared between Isabella's brows. "I don't understand."

"Yes you do. You would just rather not understand, because understanding means taking accountability for your actions. I made excuses for you for years because you were so young when our parents died, but no longer. What about when Father died? You were fifteen then, only two years younger than I was when Mother died and I had to take on everything." Emily pressed a hand to her chest. For years, she had kept all these feelings trapped inside, and it felt good to finally let them out. "Did you truly think that you *deserved* a better life because you are prettier than me?"

Isabella's sullen expression told Emily everything she needed to know.

"Well, then," she said, inhaling deeply. "I suppose this is a lesson for you. People are not entitled to things just because they happen to have something. Oliver was never entitled to my love—I offered it to him because he proved himself worthy of it. And you were never entitled to his hand in marriage just because you are pretty, though I agree he treated you badly. But that is no reason to run away with Lord Marlbury when I warned you of what he was like."

"What he was like seven years ago to *you*." Isabella's jaw jutted out stubbornly, and Emily realised that Isabella had assumed that because she was prettier, she would have a greater hold over Marlbury.

Such conceit, and it was partly Emily's fault. Isabella had grown up being about the prettiest girl for twenty miles, but she didn't have the understanding of the world that such beauty required; she didn't know that it just made her prey for less noble minds.

With no prospects or dowry, she had no appeal as a wife, but she had plenty of appeal as a disposable dalliance.

Emily sighed, rubbing the centre of her forehead. "I suppose it's too much to assume you insisted on waiting until you were wed."

More silence.

"He said he would take care of me." Isabella's voice broke. "Why is it every man who promises me anything lies?"

"Oh, Bella." When Isabella put her hands over her face, Emily rose and crossed to the other side of the table, wrapping her arms around her sister. "Foolish, foolish girl," she murmured. "How did you come to meet him so he took you with him?"

"I saw you and Oliver together and I assumed you had married and gone back to Lord Marlbury's house, so I went to confront you. But instead I found . . ." Her voice trailed off, and Emily understood. Instead, she had found Lord Marlbury with his shallow charm, no doubt prepared to be outraged that Oliver would throw over such a pretty girl in favour of *Emily*.

The rest was history.

"He said he would marry me to make up for Oliver not, only it was more complicated than merely going to a church, especially because I was under the age of majority. As the son of an earl, he couldn't risk a runaway marriage, so we would have to await your return home to get your permission."

"No doubt he would have loved to see the look on my face," she said grimly.

"It made *sense*, Em." Isabella shot to her feet, wiggling free of Emily's arms. "And he made me feel as though I was the first woman to ever make him . . ."

"I know," Emily said softly. "And it's easy to believe him when you want to."

"He talked about his time with you, and he told me he regretted leading you on when he had no intentions where you were involved—because of course things were different when he was so young." Her face flushed with the strength of her feelings. "You would have believed him too."

"That's all very well, but why did you go to London?"

"He received a letter and said he had urgent business in London, and if I came with him, he would marry me there, with or without your permission." Isabella wiped under her eyes plaintively. "I had already been staying with him for a day or two at the house—I thought that if you knew I had no chance other than to marry him, you would *have* to give your permission."

Of course. Because Isabella had known that if Emily could have refused the match, she would have done. And it hadn't occurred to her even once to doubt Lord Marlbury's name.

Emily slumped back into the chair. So much of this could have been avoided if Isabella had not been so determined to marry above herself.

"And so you followed him to London where you had no friends and no protection," Emily said. A pang of pity made its way into her heart. "Oh, Bella."

Her face crumpled. "I don't understand. Why didn't he want me?"

"He *did*, Bella. But he doesn't want a wife at present—and if he did, he would want neither either of us could offer. We have neither a dowry, position, connections . . . Gentlemen like Marlbury marry for little else. We could not have advanced his position in any respect, and so we were not worthy. It took me a long time to come to terms with that, and I'm sorry if it hurts you. It hurt me too. The world can be a cruel place." And once, Emily had only ever seen its cruelty. Now, however, she felt a small smile cross her face. "But it is not *only* cruel. There is goodness to find, too. You should put less emphasis on your physical charms, dearest. You *are* beautiful, but it cannot be your only character trait."

Isabella looked down at her shoes. "When you and Oliver marry, will you invite me to live with you?"

"We will be in the country," Emily warned. "And it will be a quiet life. Is that what you want?"

"I would rather live with you than strangers. Besides." Isabella shrugged as though it was nothing. "I missed you."

Emily felt a new warmth in her chest. Isabella might have plenty to learn, and lots to *un*learn, but they were still sisters.

"When we're settled in, of course you can come to live with us." She enfolded Isabella in her arms. "I'm still angry with you," she whispered against Isabella's hair, "but I love you. No matter what you do, even if I don't particularly like you sometimes, I will always love you. That's what sisters do."

There was a tremor in Isabella's voice as she said, "Why didn't you come back?"

"I tried, I promise, but with the snow and the wrecked carriage, we couldn't." She hugged Isabella closer, feeling as though they had stepped back in time to after their mother died, when all Emily knew how to do was hold on. "I'm sorry, dearest. I never intended to leave you. Can you forgive me?"

Isabella sniffed. "Can you forgive me for running away with Lord Marlbury?"

"Oh, darling." Emily kissed Isabella's tearstained cheek. "I already have."

By the time Oliver rejoined Emily, she was alone in the drawing room, having sent Isabella upstairs to wash her face. He came to sit quietly by her, waiting for her to begin.

She rested her head against his shoulder. "Where did you go?"

"If we are to marry, we must have a marriage licence." He patted his pocket. "With it, we may marry whenever you'd like, banns or no banns—although I agree we should do things properly." He slanted a small smile at her. "There's an announcement to be published in the newspaper tomorrow, if you would like to cut it out and paste it to the wall of your bower."

"I don't have a bower."

"I expected you could, in our new home." He took her hand, sliding his fingers between hers. "If you wanted."

She wasn't sure if she did want. "I don't think I sound like the sort of lady who has a bower."

"What sort of lady are you, then?"

"The sort that has a quiet country gentleman for a husband, and who gets her dresses muddy as she spends time in the garden. I would like chickens—"

"Petition for one to be called Doris," he said immediately.

"—And strictly *no* pigs."

He grinned. "And here I thought you and Clarabella might have bonded."

"I do *not* bond with vicious swine who chase me across farmyards." She squeezed his hand. "Does that sound acceptable?"

"A life with you sounds better than anything I could imagine." He hesitated. "I told Henry about my . . . difficulties yesterday. And I expressed my hope he would teach me how to run an estate."

Pride swelled in her chest. "What did he say?"

"Something about how I should have told him years ago, and that of course he will teach me." He looked at their linked fingers rather than her face. "If you like—if you are amenable, that is—I would like you to be there too. So we can learn together." He frowned a little, his eyes uncharacteristically serious. "It's not your responsibility, but—"

"Oliver," she said, so proud she could hardly think straight. "Of course I will help you in any way I can. Your life is my life."

"I'm afraid I may need you to write all my correspondence."

"Then it is fortunate that my handwriting is excellent." She smiled at his nervousness. "I am not a stranger to hard work, remember? And you will learn well."

"I hope so. If I can learn in a more practical way. It may, of course, require us living with Henry and Louisa for a time after we're married. Ideally, I would have done this all beforehand, but . . ." He let the words trail away. She didn't need him to finish the sentence. That had been a different time, when he had been fleeing instead of chasing.

They had both let fear dictate their lives.

No more.

"We should also discuss your house in Dalston," he said, glancing down at her head. Her stomach gave a little flop of nerves. That house had been the bane of her existence for seven years, requiring repairs she could neither afford nor undergo, and slowly falling apart around her ears.

And yet she loved it.

"If we are ever to visit Mr and Mrs Chambers," he said carefully, "we will need a place to stay. It strikes me as convenient to establish the home as a small place of residence in the north—perhaps we could arrange something with Louisa and Henry so they might contribute somewhat to its upkeep in exchange for having use of it. After all, Cumbria is a rather splendid part of the country, and—" His words cut off when Emily flung herself in his arms and kissed him full on the mouth.

"I love you," she declared, "and if I could, I would marry you all over again."

He smiled, looking absurdly pleased with himself. "If I had known that was all it required to win you over, I would have made far more rash promises from the very beginning. As for marrying me"—his smile turned soft—"once will do. So long as you promise to stay by my side for the rest of my days. I will be quite lost without you now, you know."

For once, perhaps the first time, fear did not squeeze her heart. All she felt was contentment. This was the future she had never known she wanted, and it tasted sweeter than the richest honey. "I won't make promises I can't keep," she said, and when he frowned, she leant forward and kissed him. "But I will stay with you for the remainder of my days."

He kissed her back. "Well," he said. "That will have to do."

Epilogue

Two weeks later

"The most important part of any marriage is listening to your husband," Louisa said as she fastened the pearl necklace around Emily's neck. She had offered diamonds, but Emily had wanted nothing more than her mother's pearls. "And then, if his judgement should be faulty, doing as you please anyway."

Isabella snorted from where she sat on the bed. Emily touched the pearls, then looked up at her reflection. Two months ago, her life had been the same as it always had, and she had been the same as she always would be, and she had—well, she had been resigned to the prospect. Now, she looked as though she were a woman of fashion, in a silvery silken gown that accentuated her slender curves with well-placed ruffles. Louisa had taken her to buy all her bridal clothes, and Emily was very sure Oliver would be pleased with the result.

They had not, as it transpired, been able to wait the full three weeks. But they *had* been courting for a month now, and every day that passed convinced her that she had made the right decision.

"Is that what you do with your husband?" Isabella asked from her position in the bed, her head slightly cocked to one side. In the two weeks they had been living in Louisa and Henry's house, Isabella had slowly been returning to the girl Emily remembered.

Not perfect, and still eager to avoid anything approaching hard work, but at least remorseful. When Emily had asked if she wanted to be included in her wedding day, she had declared that if Emily had the temerity to fall in love without consulting Isabella, the least she could do was allow her to take part in the wedding.

All Oliver had said to this was, "She's your sister, darling. Do as you must."

Louisa propped a hand on her hip as she looked at Emily's reflection over her shoulder. "I am fortunate in my choice of husband," she said absently, "and he has been so influenced by me that he is infrequently wrong."

"But he *is* wrong," Isabella persisted.

Emily touched her curls, which Louisa's maid had painstakingly tamed. "Just because you're afraid of him, dearest, doesn't mean you must prove his fallibility."

"He's human, and thus is wrong, on occasion," Louisa said, and passed Emily a silver bangle to wear on her arm. "Here, my dear. It suits you far better than it ever suited me; my complexion calls for gold. There. You look beautiful."

Emily met Isabella's gaze in the mirror, and her sister smiled, though it didn't reach her eyes. "She's right, Em. Oliver is going to fall even more madly in love with you."

"He never fell in love with me for my looks," Emily said, sliding her gloves over her fingers.

Louisa picked up a glass of champagne. "As it should be, but the man is besotted now. You will take his breath away." She pressed the champagne into Emily's hands. "For courage and warmth."

Emily recalled the way Oliver had handed her his drink at the inn the very first time they had met, and she had been so irritated with him for being right. "And celebration," she said, raising the glass into the air in a toast. "For my wedding day."

Oliver waited at the head of the church, the pews largely empty. This was a small affair; he was not important enough in the eyes of the *ton* to warrant any more interest, and he much preferred it that way. This was between Emily and him and the people they cared about—no one else.

His brother-in-law Jacob stood beside him as best man, and his sisters were in the pews. The moment they had heard he was marrying, they had descended en masse, fussing over him, delighted with Emily—how, indeed, could anyone not be—and generally making themselves a nuisance.

Jacob caught Oliver's gaze and winked. "Nervous?"

"Not in the slightest." And it was true. There were plenty of things he was nervous about—running the estate was one, and how he would manage children was another—but not marrying Emily. That was the only decision in his life of which he could be wholly certain.

Dr Grant, the vicar, cleared his throat at the head of the church, and seconds later the doors opened. In stepped his future bride in a gown that made her look like sunset over the sea—red curls above a silvery, glimmering dress. His breath stopped as Henry, stern and serious as always, especially at such an event, walked her slowly down the aisle.

His mother sobbed openly in the pews, and his sister Annabelle dabbed a handkerchief gently against her eyes. Isabella followed in Emily's wake, her eyes downcast.

Oliver took all this in at a glance, but his gaze returned to Emily, who met his gaze and smiled.

The rest of the worry fell from his shoulders. No matter what happened in the future, they would have each other, and that was all they needed.

"Hello," he whispered as she drew closer, taking her hands in his.

"Hello," she whispered back, her smile stretching even wider behind her veil. "Too late to change your mind now."

"Never."

"All rise," Dr Grant said, and the ceremony began.

After the requisite wedding breakfast, during which everyone crowded around Emily and congratulated her, they took a carriage south to the property Louisa had bestowed on Oliver. The journey took several hours, and as the sun was setting, they finally arrived at a stone house on undulating land framed by trees.

"A mere cottage," Oliver said as the horse drew up outside the front door.

In Emily's opinion, this was more than a cottage—it was a modest house, to be sure, and nothing approaching the enormous mansion that Henry and Louisa lived in.

"It's perfect," she said, and meant it. While she would have done her best with a large property, this felt far more manageable, and better suited to what would be a relatively modest lifestyle. Yet there was quite a bit of land attached to the house, and it was that which Henry would be teaching Oliver to run. Their lessons had begun, and Emily had made notes as Henry spoke, referencing books and demonstrating his meaning through samples of his own accounts.

After their brief sojourn, they would be back to London to continue this education, but Oliver had been keen to show her the land—their land—and in truth she was just as keen.

When they lived there properly, there would be servants—at least a butler, a valet, a lady's maid, a housemaid, a cook and a kitchen maid, as well as a groom and stable boy, but for now they had come alone, just a coachman to care for the horses and the stables, and a local woman who would come in to help with the cooking.

Emily had insisted. A last tribute to the life she had lived, and a chance for the kind of privacy they would never have again. She wanted to explore the land with him, hand in hand, windswept and quite possibly rained upon. She wanted to make love in every room of the house without fear of being walked in on.

They entered the small hallway. From it, there was a living room, a parlour, a dining room, and a room she thought could be a music room. Isabella had always been the more musically inclined—when she came to live there, she could have some say as to how the rooms were decorated and laid out. But the space was well laid out, and when she looked around, Emily felt at home.

The way she had when she'd been a child.

"There's space for a vegetable patch in the garden," Oliver said, leading her to the fireplace in the drawing room. There were logs to one side, and he knelt, placing them into the fireplace. As she watched, he added kindling with the confidence of a man who had done this before.

"Did you . . . practise lighting fires?" she asked in disbelief.

He grinned at her. "I asked a kitchen maid to show me. That way, this isn't your responsibility all the time. And, what's more, I even asked her how to boil a kettle, so I can be at least some help with breakfast."

"Oliver." Her throat felt full; her eyes certainly were. She felt the hot tears streak down her face. "You didn't have to do that."

"No," he said, blowing on the sparks to ease them into flame. "You didn't. But you see, darling, I wanted to." He glanced up, and when he saw her tears, he clicked his tongue. "All this because I wanted you to be happy? For shame." With some difficulty, he levered himself to his feet and wrapped his slightly sooty good hand around her waist, drawing her against him. "I love you," he murmured against her hair. "Dance with me?"

There was no music, but that didn't matter. This was a scene from her childhood, replaying in her head as she swayed a waltz with Oliver across their drawing room, the curtains pulled tight to fend off the night.

For years, she had viewed these memories as tainted—it was hard to view them as romantic when she had seen how utterly such a love had destroyed them. But now she understood, at least a little.

Love had not destroyed her father; his own weakness had. He had not had the will to keep going, and thus he had allowed himself to fade away, choosing oblivion over his family. That was not the fault of his love but of his poor character.

"If I die," she began, and Oliver sighed gustily.

"On the day we married, Em? Really?"

"If I die, Oliver," she repeated, leaning back so she could see his eyes. Behind them, the fire popped as it grew in strength. "I want you to promise you will keep on living."

"All right." He said the words easily, and she scowled.

"You *are* allowed to grieve me, though."

"Darling, if you die I will be inconsolable, for a while." He nuzzled the underside of her nose, then bit her lobe lightly. Heat flooded her. "I shall miss you every day of my life. And some part of me will always love you. But," he added before she could protest, "I will not fade away into obscurity. I have a purpose now, you know. Aside from making you happy. That will sustain me, I'm sure."

"Is this the life you wanted?"

"With you?" He smiled down at her. "Always."

"Even quiet and in the country?"

"You have quite reconciled me to the country, so long as there is an absence of pigs. Made even better by a certain someone in my arms."

"Arm," she said, and smiled. "Oliver?"

"If you are about to talk about your imminent demise one more time—"

"I love you."

"Oh." He spun her slowly, that one hand making its way to the very lowest dip of her spine. Positively scandalous in public, and positively teasing in private. There was a wicked light in his eyes. "I love you, too. Now what say you to defiling this rug right here?"

"I think," she said, biting his lip with enough fervour that he moaned, "that is an excellent start to the rest of our life."

He drew her down to the ground, raising her skirts to her hips. "I could not agree more."

THE END

Acknowledgements

This book was one of the hardest I've written, for a whole host of reasons. Thank you, dear reader, for waiting so patiently while I fumbled in the dark, trying to find the heart of this book. I like to think, eventually, I succeeded. The series is now over, and it's time for me to look for the next!

None of this would have been possible without my two writing besties, Charlotte and Kelsey. Without getting mushy, you have both stood by me and helped me so endlessly over the years, and I am so incredibly grateful for your friendship, wisdom, brainstorming, and writing feedback. It has been with such patience that you've listened to my chaotic rants, my various ideas for this book, and one of the roughest first drafts I have ever sent you. Thank you for loving this book even when I didn't, and showing me the light when I really didn't know where to go. It's because of you that Oliver in particular is who he is, and I really could not have done it without you. Like, literally. Thank you so much. I will never stop appreciating you and trying to give back any way I can.

To the girls of Velvet Steel, who have brainstormed with me, commiserated with me, supported my many chaotic breakdowns and crazy deadlines when it has come to this book, and who stand as a rock in this wild writing world: I love you all so much, and it is my privilege to know you. Thanks for making me laugh on my worst days, and thank you for all supporting me endlessly even when I don't think I can do this (*especially* when I don't think I can do this).

A massive shout out to Jenni Howell and D. L. Taylor for sprinting with me so much this year, and providing much-needed encouragement and also throwing endless ideas at me for me during my breakdown era (most of this year). It's been a stressful one, but sprinting and hitting my deadlines alongside you has been a rare privilege.

Historical Hoydens, my HR-writing gal-group—you are all fabulous. I always feel supported when I moan (let's be honest, it's always grumping) about various things, or generally just freaking out about "but what if I can't do this!". Knowing we're all in the same boat has been endlessly reassuring.

Finally, my husband, my rock, and my biggest cheerleader. Thank you for believing in me so steadfastly even when I don't believe in myself. You may not be some of my more depraved fictional boyfriend fantasies, but you never stop teaching me what real love can be. Thank you for bringing me coffee and water and yummy treats, and sorry I've been ignoring you so much to write instead. I probably won't stop.

And to you, readers, if you've got this far through (a miracle): thank you a thousand times over. I must be feeling mushy as I write this, but it's such a wonder and a joy to write books and have people read them (and sometimes even like them!). I'm beyond grateful for everyone who reads a single word I've written, whether you've been with me from the start or have just picked up this book.

Here's to many more.

Also by Terri Mackenzie

Finders Keepers

In Search of a Hero

To Marry the Devil

The Picture of Desire

His Ample Desire

To Have and to Hold

To Steal a Bride

Later in Life

The Spinster's Seduction

Printed in Dunstable, United Kingdom

77947693R00180